FLYING AWAY

Flying Away

A NOVEL

Richard Ward

RolyPoly Press

For Helen

When shall the stars be blown about the sky,
Like the sparks blown out of a smithy, and die?
Surely thine hour has come, thy great wind blows,
Far off, most secret, and inviolate Rose?

W.B.Yeats

I

A bright summer afternoon looking down on a poolside party, the gay attendees informally attired in fine cotton twill, the American men wearing gray or navy flannel shorts and dark calf-length stockings along with brilliant white starched shirts, their English counterparts more circumspect in dress, white cotton pants, white shoes, white shirts, a few in summer blazers, navy blue with polished brass buttons. The women wear casual dresses, mostly white, again the Americans bolder in style, daringly décolleté, the English gentlemen subjected to the mild censoriousness of their women for staring rather too forthrightly, not terribly serious any of it, the English ladies teasing the American girls for their scandalous lack of decorum bordering on wantonness. Easy laughter all around. There are children, ranging from toddlers to adolescents, and they are largely ignored by their parents, content and trusting of the Chinese servants who mind them, which they do with much nervous scolding and harrying attention, especially when feeling the occasional monitoring gaze of their masters like cold tongs on their necks. The children are feeling happy and a bit wild, as they usually are on these occasions when the grownups are laughing and talking animatedly, drinks in hand, the youngest running from their keepers in screaming hilarity, while those a bit older spend more time in the shallow end of the pool as the Chinese hover over them anxiously. The few adolescents are more reserved, staying together in a privileged group that has no truck with any contingent, self-conscious and vastly superior in the way of their age, sharing secrets, giggling and laughing in general derision. There is the usual fascination and subterfuge concerning their own ripening sexual fruit. Money is of no interest, as ordinary a part of their lives as the air they breathe. They know their fathers work hard but not quite what it is they do and in any case it is boring. There is awareness they will someday have to deal with responsibilities, as parents and teachers with their wearying lectures constantly remind them. And of course there is alcohol, as natural as money and sex. All the grownups drink and it is understood that they will do the same and indeed some do already.

The adults talk anxiously of the belligerence of Japan, the rise of the Nazis, but mostly the conversation is light, the latest match at the Cricket Club in Central or at the East Point polo ground, the races at Happy Valley, the newest issue of Vanity Fair, films they would never hope to see until returning home, Noel Coward's new operetta, Max Baer's ascendancy to the heavyweight throne. The year is 1935. Stepping back one sees from the Peak the panorama of the great harbor below, Hong Kong, less active than usual as it's Sunday, the hulking ships, like toys, moored silently, their coal-fires banked, a few junks navigating the calm blue water to Kowloon, the normally bustling dry docks resting, the great swath of white Victorian buildings a thick, calcitic crust lining the shore, the soft emerald mitigations of rustling trees farther inland patched densely between the self-assured structures of empire concealing small parks where English families take their picnics. It is true that the world is troubled but here there is a special certitude of place and destiny. No one questions their superiority, steeped in tradition, annealed in struggle and conquest, standard-bearers of technology and industry, guided by irreproachable Christian values. There is a sense of continuity as well. The Americans, a bit outré, not quite ready for the mantle of rule, but undeniably capable, energetic and clearly a colossus in the making, will go higher and farther than anyone, an estimation obvious to all but the stodgy, snobbish and mean-spirited, but also, it is generally agreed, with none of the class, grace and gravitas of Britannia. Thus the good-natured acceptance of their eager cousins. They will someday run the world, it is true, but are not to be taken terribly seriously. For their part the Americans take the condescension in stride. It is clear to them too, this imperial destiny, and theirs is the easy affability of certitude. The British, they will admit privately, are rather comically effete, a race whose blood already runs thin, and while slightly intimidated by the dank, monarchical formality, the Americans can feel their robust animal superiority, their Rough Rider grit and jism, the formality be damned. Let them snigger down their jolly mustaches, the century belongs to us.

The afternoon is growing uncomfortably warm and though the adults sweat in their attire, they are content to have the children as surrogate spirits in their bathing suits free and cool. The drinks will hold them and perhaps later they will swim. In the heat more of the children move to the water, the adolescents still holding out on their deck chairs, watching the splashing play, the shrieks and piping voices rising over the company like a canopy of crystal sound. The teenagers, four of them, watch the younger children in amusement. It was not so long ago they played with similar abandon and the spirit is infectious. They observe in silence and then there is a stirring. Abruptly a freckled, carrot-topped muscular boy in his tight blue Wilkies bathing suit rises from his chair, trots to the edge of the pool and dives in the middle-depth, sending an arc of water onto the deck heedlessly splashing some of the adults' shoes. He swims underwater for ten seconds or so, surfacing under the diving board at the deep end to mild reproach and general attention. With this single impulsive act he has announced the vitality and unfettered essence of his peers, which elicits a mixture of admiration, amusement, jealousy, irritation and even awe from the company, not unlike the feelings the Americans evoke from the English. In a matter of moments all but one of the teenagers are in the pool, laughing and shouting in their vibrant way, at turns audacious and self-conscious, childlike and sexual, their primal exuberance stripping the adults of their self-importance. The boys pull themselves out of the pool, the water dripping from their perfect, glistening bodies, so intoxicating is the sight of their Apollonian forms emerging from the sparkling water into the brilliant sun, trot to the diving board leaving their wet footprints on the cement, and with everyone watching they execute precise and graceful dives, emerging to bravos, well-dones and subdued applause. This is repeated several times, the two boys inevitably in silent competition, a little higher, closer to the board, cleaving the water in determined perpendicularity, classic swan dives and jack-knives, the adults watching closely, more critically, murmuring between dives and silent as each is executed. The last of the teenagers, a blond girl of about fourteen in a white bathing suit, watches from her deck chair with an expression of subtle amusement and hauteur, a palpable energy emanating from her studied casualness of form, and several of the adults are looking in her direction, suppressing the urge to summon her to the competition. One of her peers however, a large, slightly overweight girl in a blue bathing suit standing shoulder-deep in the water, yells aggressively and gleefully for her to join the boys in their diving and instantly the call is echoed by the adults, as if this were a drama recapitulated routinely yet increasingly heightened, the tension correspondingly more exquisite, the outcome, while never in doubt, anticipated with barely restrained glee, a child's enthusiasm for a favorite tale one hundred times told. Playing her part as the lofty danseuse, a pool-side Pavlova rising reluctantly from her green canvas chair to grace the hoi-polloi with one glimpse of transcendence, a hint of smile playing at the corners of her mouth in response to the cheers and urgings of the onlookers, but overall affecting the boredom and hint of disdain that is her signature even at this early age, she walks matter-of-factly through the plebs, her clear hazel eyes fixed on the board six feet above the calm greenish water, focused on what she is about to do but also somewhere else, as if she were contemplating the presence of a more entertaining company, or some long lost Xanadu. Her stride is naturally graceful, with the strength and firm muscularity of the athlete. There is almost something boyish about her, but judging by the look of the males this hint of androgyny only adds to an obvious appeal. They and the women stare admiringly at the tanned well-formed body and its self-possession, the easy nature of its proportions. A quiet descends as she reaches the board, raises a foot to the first step and pauses momentarily, seeing the mysterious mainland bulking in the distance, her expression serious, ignoring the rising chorus of encouragement, suppressing the momentary giddiness that assails her whenever mounting the board, anticipating the weight-lessness at the apogee of her dive high above the harbor (sometimes thinking of Icarus) of which she will catch a glimpse before focusing at the glimmer of light at the bottom of the pool towards which she orients her entry into the aquamarine water. On the board now, poised at the familiar spot marking the three steps to the edge where she will spring into the air, focus of the rapt upturned gaze of the gathering, a pause, the characteristic shaking of the right hand, her body straight and seemingly inches taller, a calm restorative breath, her eyes leveled at the horizon. The first step is slow, almost languid, as if walking through water, but with no sense of effort or tension, followed by the second step at twice the speed, a sudden escalation of coiled intensity forecasting the swift explosive unwinding power of the last step and propulsive spring and unerring touchdown on the balls of her sure callused feet at the board's edge, bending it lower to the water than anyone can believe, lower even than the heavier boys, and then with the onlookers surrendered to the admiration and envy that such a display commands from one so young, so perfect, the kinetic power of the takeoff is transformed into a magnificent golden Leda soaring above them in suspended apotheosis, arms outstretched, the graceful parabola, the expression reposeful and conquering, an image encased in an amber pocket of memory and she, winged arms encompassing the pool, the now visible blue harbor, the entire world, omnipotent and immortal in this moment of supremacy, the graceful plummet straight down, always much closer to the board than anyone expects given the soaring compass of her flight and, touching the bottom of the pool, she is laughing triumphantly inside, once again the goddess she knows herself to be, once again coming up to break the surface of the water and hear the rippling applause, to know she has taken wing, to feel the difference in her boldness and grace from all the others.

***

The fire of the sun lay over the ocean, still as molten lead. The beach grass stirred. The house timbers expanded in the coming heat. Standing in the small bar next to the kitchen she sensed all the elements of her home, the foundation, firm, like Atlas with the world on his shoulders, two-by-fours, plumbed, leveled, the fat nails holding them together, siding, bracing wood, cedar shingles with their many coats of pink paint, the last the summer before. A small army of painters had descended with their drop cloths, ladders and endless buckets of pink and white paint—a collection of busy, jovial, tobacco-smoking tradesmen who smiled and flirted with her. It was a good time. She felt as the house was painted that she was being covered with a fresh coat of some restorative substance herself by a platoon of confederates who sensed her disquiet and joined together in giving her succor. There were a couple she would have bestowed favors upon, summer-boys with curly hair and honey skin perched insouciantly atop their spindly ladders, joking, singing and whistling in that glorious way of all young men.

But then only two months later came Carol, the hurricane of '54. The irony was bitter. Her name, her storm, her fury, had undone what had been done. The house was severely damaged. The fresh paint that had covered her soul like healing waters blasted, chipped and eroded by sand, wind, water. A third of the house had been ripped away. In spite of being told to evacuate the night before they had waited until morning when the wind raged off the ocean like the very breath of Shiva and the waves pounded fifty yards from the house, dull, churning mountains of water advancing by the second. Then she, Phil, Emma and the boys had packed the two cars in the gray howling dawn, the noise so great they couldn't hear except by screaming into each other's ears. The last thing they did before leaving was try to close one of the garage doors, the force of the wind overpowering their efforts. In a tableau etched in her memory, she, Phil, Emma and even Eddie (with Mark in the car, eyes wide in fear and wonder) together strained behind the huge door. Defeated, they piled into the cars and drove off the beach, inland. An hour later the ocean overwhelmed the dunes, devastating everything in its path. Next door the Goldens' house, larger than theirs, had been swept away. The water roared through the downstairs of their own house through the garage and out the front. Had they been able to close the door, giving the ocean one more thing to push against, the house may have gone.

Thus, yielding, the house was saved. Carol rinsed a glass with tap water and poured some vodka straight into it, drank it down, grimaced, poured another and looked out the screened window over the sink at the empty beach where last year stood the Goldens' house. Some rubble, beach grass, sandpipers' nests, a big, new, hopeful dune pushed up by bulldozers, a snaking red snow fence running down the middle of it to catch the drifting sand was all that remained. Another hurricane would wash the whole thing away. A facelift. Stanley Golden was a cosmetic surgeon with a practice in Upper Saddle River. He and his young son sometimes tossed a medicine ball back and forth on the beach. Stanley Golden stood firm when the ball smacked into his ample stomach. But now his ample house was gone. Carol and Phil Heizer had looked on with condescending amusement at father and son throwing the heavy ball at each other. A year ago on an afternoon in late July, the painters gone and the house empty of their sexual, nurturing energy, as she stood drinking Bloody Marys bleakly staring at the ocean chopped and flattened by a hard southeast wind, she watched the doctor and his son walk onto the beach and launch a white long-tailed kite into the sky. Carol thought he looked wonderful, his stout tanned body and steel-gray curly hair and wire-rimmed glasses, solid as Gibraltar, gripping the string, holding the kite down as it flew out over the ocean hundreds of feet in the whipping blue sky. She couldn't imagine Phil ever flying a kite with his sons. More than a little drunk, exhilarated by the wind, sky and soaring kite, Carol put on her windbreaker and straw hat and negotiated the steps from the porch to the beach and with a swirling head ran past father and son, flinging her hat in the air with a whoop, the wind carrying it fifty yards down the beach and when it hit the sand it skipped and hopped thirty more. She whooped again and raced after it and threw it again and again until the doctor and his son were out of sight and then she lay on the sand breathless and heartpounding, staring into the sky.

It was Paul who taught her how to make Bloody Marys, the same summer she'd first got seriously drunk on her parents' vodka. Later she would develop an equal affection for rye. Gin, of course, would always do, but it was vodka that was the sentimental favorite. As Paul was the "older man" in her life (two years her senior and stunningly sophisticated at seventeen) and vodka his spirit of preference, Carol naturally followed suit. Paul's family lived a bit higher on the hill than her own, all part of the company compound. Their fathers worked to-gether in South China marketing the company product, which was oil. Her father, Robert Sanborn, Harvard class of '15, was district manager of the South China provinces of Fukien, Kwantung, Kwangsi and Kweichow. Among the famous but discreet drinkers of the compound, Robert Sanborn was equally famous for his quiet conviviality. Paul's parents, Lawrence and Vivian Eggleston, were also great bons vivants. When the men were home, returned from the remunerative and dusty duties of empire, much programmed gaiety ensued, with regular cock-tail parties (all formally attired) attended assiduously by Chinese servants with their kowtowing irony that Paul and Carol reenacted privately with mocking hilarity. Alcohol flowed with casual profligacy and forgotten, half-filled drinks easily spirited away for children to develop their own habits and tastes. At an earlier age the very young Paul and Carol, prefiguring a more serious involvement, met giggling under linen-draped tables sipping illicit cocktails surrounded by unsuspecting and slightly befogged elders. Crates of alcohol it seemed almost daily were brought up by the tram on the afternoon run, more alcohol than could ever possibly be accounted for, and it was easy enough to take a bottle of something when no one was looking, the sort of thing that began to happen with increasing regularity the autumn of Carol's fifteenth year. The day after she'd gotten herself solidly smashed in her parents' living room Paul demonstrated the sophisticated way to deal with hangovers, the way his parents did it, the hair-of-the-dog sort of thing, by mixing Carol his own version of a Bloody Mary (insisting she have one though she had little hangover to speak of despite having drunk nearly a half-bottle of vodka) which consisted of vodka, gin, vermouth, tomato juice, Tabasco sauce, bitters, salt, pepper and a slice of lime. This hair-of-the-dog resulted in Carol getting smashed a second time in as many days as several more Bloody Marys followed the first. She and Paul stumbled giggling downstairs to his room to "play cards" and even managed to do one hand of rummy but they'd made another discovery recently in addition to their growing fondness for alcohol...

Carol finished her second drink and poured another. Her leg ached from the piece of glass she'd stepped on, from a glass broken a month ago in the middle of the night standing at the bar naked with the car dealer waiting in bed, knocking it off the counter in the dark, thinking to clean it up in the morning, pouring a new drink, stepping wide to avoid the pieces that lay in the dark like something evil and feeling the maverick sliver lodge in her heel with what seemed like purpose, the pain shooting up her leg, radiating to her fingertips. She'd felt no sharp point sticking from her heel the next morning, thinking to dig it out with a pin and tweezers, but in the midst of everything else it was forgotten until the next evening when the sliver announced itself with a low throbbing. The events of the night before were vague and Emma had swept the shards. But this sliver of glass pierced the fog and took on a significance. This was glass, not wood, and would inexorably work its way in, not out. This was a deadly thing slicing through tissue, muscle, vein, artery, something that might enter her circulation and flow into her heart. A piece of glass stuck in the red, pumping muscle.

She heard Emma walking up the stairs. Emma, with her little pig eyes and black sweating skin. Servants were the same all over the world. Emma wasn't any different than the Chinese in Hong Kong with their counterfeit deference, their absurd bowing and scraping, but there they were, living with you, privy to the secrets and all the dirty laundry. Emma, from South Carolina. Emma, with her magnolia, red-dirt sweetness and southern Negro superstitions—fascinating voodoo, that stuff. But these glimpses of Emma's root-nature were mostly obscured by her stilted formality—stereotyped behavior that drove Carol to the point of despair.

As Carol stood by the sink, a turbulence, eighteen hundred miles away, passed over the Leeward Islands, a small nexus of Caribbean and Atlantic cobblestones connecting two great continents, desolate outposts of forgotten empires, pirates, slaves, sunken vessels and dreams, battered by nightmare hurricanes, haunted places with names like Willikies, Beggar's point, Horse Shoe Reef. Six months ago in the Bahamas on the island of New Providence she'd had a glimpse of something. Stepping off the plane onto the tarmac, blinking in the dazzling sun, Carol was filled with a vague sense of dread and longing, and a curious comfort. Her steps from the plane to the terminal were sure, the island ground familiar under her feet.

She fled Emma's presence and tiptoed down the stairs—not to alert the boys—and retrieved the morning's edition—delivered seven days a week punctually at seven-fifteen a.m. All the news that's fit to print. The world dipped as she bent to pick up the paper. Then back up the stairs quietly, holding the banister, weaving a bit. Carol stopped three-quarters of the way up and on an impulse opened the paper to the obituary section, a bit unsteady, focusing her eye on the print, moving her sandaled left foot over the sandy step. Below, two boys, one five, the other eight, towheaded, in blue bathing suits with white piping, stood in the doorway of their bedroom shyly observing her. She didn't see them. A headline and smiling face, bejeweled and festive, proclaimed the death of Carmen Miranda at forty-one.

"Carmen Miranda is dead at forty-one!"

The boys looked up at their mother standing on the steps talking to herself—the drawn, weary face, the scar beneath the cheekbone covered with makeup, the distant, distracted expression. Carol stared at the picture of the gaily-smiling entertainer until the features danced and became grotesque and meaningless.

"Surely, The New York Times has an editorial on the death of Carmen Miranda."

Weaving on the stairs, forgetting herself, talking, while the two faces in the doorway stared at her.

"Oh, Carmen, Carmen, Carmen, where are you, Carmen?"

Fumbling with the august newspaper and finally arriving at the editorial page, her eyes focused with some difficulty on the last lines of a sonnet by a certain Trudy Drucker and she read them aloud:

> The present cannot bind me, but,
> The past,
> Implacable and huge, will hold me
> Fast

Carol repeated the lines and trudged up the stairs, the sand grating beneath her sandals. *Implacable and huge the past—the present cannot bind me.* But what past is it that holds so fast? The desolate ruins of coastal battlements, the scurrying chameleons, the heat pressing down like flatirons, the chalky uselessness of the landscape, the pellucid glittering water, the vaulted leap of pale sky, the utter disembodied astralness of New Providence made her feel like a revenant. This was her most recent past. Curious to think of what she might have been. African slave? A trader's alcoholic adulterous wife? Creole concubine? A limpet? A lizard? A lionfish? English schoolgirl drowned in the Tongue of the Ocean trapped in scuttled ship off Cistern Point? These last go-arounds certainly had a consistent theme, death by drowning, death by drinking, a whelming of the spirit, awash in too many spirits, rudderless flotsam—must have been some great (ha! how Eddie had made her laugh in the breezy New

Providence cabana as she lay listlessly on her bed while he staggered around the living room in mock dipsomania pleading with Mark for a drink, "Please, I haven't had a drink since childhood!" but uncomfortable too, sensing his displaced anxiety about her own drinking in an unconscious burlesque. Even Mark, barely five, had fallen all-too-easily into the spirit of the thing.) shattering downfall to make her like this, too traumatic to remember. The enlightened ones could remember their past lives. Something had wrecked her so soundly that she had spent a century or so floundering in the drink—*the present cannot bind me, but the past, implacable and huge, will hold me fast.*

Emma was in the kitchen clearing the breakfast table and most certainly marking Carol's progress and making her own shrewd calculations. Damn her fat black face and little pig eyes anyway! There was a stillness in the kitchen as Carol made her way across the living room to the deck. Bloody hot. The newspaper stuck to her sweaty fingers. Ten-thirty Saturday morning. Phil arriving soon from the city. Heat. Tired waves. People on beach. Small fishing trawlers plying back and forth. Utter quiet. Heavyweight of newspaper. Metal table. Open umbrella. Sit down. Now here was an item. Yesterday at eight-fifteen a.m. thousands in silent prayer—tenth anniversary—80,000 dead. And another. Hurricane Connie 400 miles east of San Juan, 115 mph winds, storm moving at 12 to 14 mph. Should be here in a week or so. How quiet it is now, so bloody hot.

A recurring dream of drowning had assailed her in New Providence. Perhaps it was the heat, like now, that provoked it. Even under the umbrella the heat was overbearing. In the mornings in New Providence she'd remove the top of her bathing suit and lie on the deck, knowing the man in the adjacent cabana could see her. Harold Rosenberg, sports writer for *The Chicago Sun-Times*, an interesting, embittered, oversized man twelve years older than she who'd been in Spain during the civil war as a correspondent and had drunk with Hemingway, whom he described as having great charm and *cojones*, and who obviously was enjoying the time of his life. He admired Hemingway with a fervor, and Carol, who despised the overpuffed *fanfarrón*, appalled that he had won the Nobel Prize, had maintained a pointed silence whenever the topic arose. Well, he could write short stories. Bloody Macomber. Take the Mannlicher and blow out his brains. The bloody bitch blowing out the bloody brains. The Man-Licker. She could lick any man in the house. *A Farewell to Arms*. Should have been called *A Farewell to Legs*. Silly, stunted book. Phil, like all American males, she supposed, liked Hemingway. He was a necessary invention, a myth, created by the collective as much as by himself. Squeezed from the bloated condition like some glistening self-aggrandizing splinter. Men —what children. What was it the white hunter (his name— Wilson, Spaulding, MacGregor—some sporting goods name) observed about American males, that they stayed adolescent until middle age and then suddenly—*carawong!*—they were dead like the poor bloody lion?

Carol sat in the canvas sling of the faded blue director's chair, the sweat seeping through her shorts, sliding between her breasts. She may have driven poor Rosenberg crazy in New Providence. She was half-tempted to take her top off now. The fucking constraints of this world. At least the Goldens were gone. She wouldn't have to suffer their censorious clucking.

Carol could imagine them clucking away like self-righteous pea-fowl. The Goldens were gone. The beach was an emptier and wilder place, a frightening place. Without the Goldens the sand-pipers had taken over. And the tourists. Didn't they know there was a fifty-dollar fine for walking on the dunes, these boorish aliens with their transistor radios, garish beachwear and suntan lotion? These were the new Americans, loud and liquid. They parked their fat convertibles on the side of the road and piled out over the dunes, reeking of provincialism and dialect: Canarsie, Flatbush, Astoria, dive-bombed by the furious pipers, trudging across the blistering sand festooned with paraphernalia from Korvettes, whole families of latter-day Balboas excitedly dis-covering the placid watery blue for themselves, their shrieking skinny-armed children hurling stones at the birds that plunged kamikaze-like at their eyes—their radios—the new, mobile man and his music, loud, fast rock 'n roll, tuned to the holy stations. Their audacity amazed and horrified her. This was Whitman's man, transistorized, chromed, triumphant, conquerors of the Shinnecock and Montauk, of the Nazis—and now, with their atomic power and barbecues, defenders of the American way of life, lovers of baseball, boxing and Eisenhower, haters of Com-munists, Negroes and Jews.

A sudden hot wind lifted the pages of the newspaper as if the world had sighed. Carol was just now allowing herself to remember the evening before. The image of her striking Eddie, four, five, six times, pushed forward in vivid Technicolor. This was probably why she had got so drunk already. Slumping for-ward, Carol closed her eyes and shook her head in negation. I am damned, forever damned, she thought. Poor Eddie. All he wanted was to go home, little guy, trapped in Alexi's bizarre gypsy trailer with his drunken mother so intent on becoming drunker and waiting for Alexi, hot Alexi, the sub man, the torpedo man. Why had she even taken him? He was anxious and wanted to go home. She became enraged and struck him again and again. Why, mommy? Why? Why indeed, little bastard, she would kill him! Why couldn't he just shut up? And Eddie, quietly excited to have come to Alexi's, not Alexi's trailer but his restaurant in front that had such a carnival feeling with the lights and colorful signs that told about the sandwiches with the funny names, the sizzling energy of the place, the smoke and good smells and the sizzling energy of Alexi himself with his big smile, sweaty, hairy chest, rasping voice and cigarette and always free cold Cokes for the boys, fishing around in the icy water, retrieving the dripping bottles with a flourish and opening them on the side of the red chest: kchtt! Alexi was fast and talked fast and made Eddie shy but he liked the strange place and Alexi even though there was something a little frightening about it all, something about the way mommy acted or the way Alexi treated mommy...

Then mommy in the mean way she got wouldn't let him play miniature golf after his hamburger and Coke (Alexi had a nine-hole miniature golf course next to his restaurant, under a skein of colored lights and humid night-breeze, with loop-di-loops, a windmill, water hazards and a big clown mouth you shot through) and made him stay in the trailer with her while she waited for Alexi. He didn't want to watch television, there was nothing for him to do at Alexi's trailer, why couldn't he play miniature golf? Why, mommy? And each time he asked, Why?

she would get angrier but he couldn't stop asking Why? because he was frightened and confused and felt there was no reason for her to be so angry and mean and he really wanted to know, Why? and so he couldn't stop asking and the more he asked the angrier she became until at last she was hitting him hard burning slaps, a towering Amazon who moved him back across the room into the little place where Alexi's bed was, the colors spinning around and he couldn't go anywhere else, all the time asking Why? in the middle of his crying and mommy getting angrier and slapping him more.

Finally she exited the trailer with the screen door banging and sat on the steps to smoke a cigarette while Eddie sat wretched on Alexi's bed. They stayed like this, separated by the aluminum shell of the trailer, for about twenty minutes, Carol smoking her cigarette and watching the miniature golfers, Eddie on Alexi's bed oscillating between inconsolable misery and quavering self-possession. At length she took Eddie and left the scene. Alexi came later to her house.

Carol watched a red ant move over the newspaper ("Bermuda Shorts, *The* Uniform for College") and across the white metal expanse of the circular table to the rounded edge where it began a hurried circumnavigation. It went around and around three or four times at the same determined pace before it seemed to realize the dead-endedness of its explorations. Obviously it was trying to get home, somewhere below in the sand. How did an ant's wanderings get it to this point, a table-top on a second-floor deck and now going around in circles? What led it here? What was it looking for? The ant seemed aware of the futility of its course and it began a scrambling cross-hatch of travels that conveyed a methodology, a deliberate, systematic effort to find a way off the table and home. Its purpose and energy astonished Carol. She blew the ant from the table onto the deck where it continued off.

Aware of something, Carol turned and saw Eddie looking at her through the big living room window. He stood unsmiling with his baseball glove on, holding a white tennis ball in his right hand, his slim body clad in the usual blue bathing suit with the white piping. Last night Eddie had been beaten down and here he was this morning with his bathing suit, ball and glove. Nothing stopped for her or because of her. The season pressed down with its usual liquid weight, the beach grass swayed with the torpid breeze, the great Prussian-blue beast lapped at the shore, always the same.

Suddenly there was a disorienting flurry of events. The phone rang, a gust of wind blew a part of the newspaper off the table and Emma came through the dining room door onto the deck carrying a cup of instant coffee. Eddie had disappeared.

"Ah brought you some coffee."

The wind picked up and blew more pages off the table. They skittered under the railing onto the sand below, at the base of the dune. The phone rang like a plague. Who could be calling? There didn't seem to be any point in answering. Maybe Phil wasn't coming. It seemed an impossible distance to the phone, as if it were ringing from another realm, one that had already slipped away. All these tiresome connections to a dying world! She rose wearily and unsteadily from the table and walked along the deck to the outside door of her bedroom, leaving Emma standing with the coffee. On the deck of the house directly to the west, separated by a stretch of sand, beachgrass and board-walk, yet so close Carol sometimes felt like a high-rent tene-ment dweller (a house even larger than theirs, unscathed by the previous summer's hurricane), stood Theodore Evans, holding a glass of something, apparently trying to communicate with Carol as she laid her hand on the doorknob to her bedroom. The Evanses were great drinkers, comfortably Protestant, middle-brow, Republican. His wife, Marge, was a fall-down drunk, clobbered by two p.m. each afternoon, a source of embarrass-ment and renewed tragedy to her family, her hoarse Virginia drawl slurred by alcohol, frail body gone to ruin, a cigarette in one hand and a drink in the other, leaning on the deck railing inviting any and all to come on over for a cocktail, waving her cigarette in amiable, absent half-circles.

Carol had no time for Theodore Evans who, in any case, seemed to be talking to himself and she yanked open the door, quickening her pace to get to the phone, suddenly panicked at the thought of missing the call. Reaching the night stand next to Phil's side of the bed, upon which sat the ringing phone, Carol paused and looked at the black insistent object and was per-plexed. What was the point? No one could reach her, and yet if it was Phil, damnable, pigheaded Phil, who, despite his deficien-cies and lack of understanding, nevertheless had the strength of his demands. She would answer the phone because it probably was Phil and because he insisted. Phil with his determination to keep her in the world. These were the responsibilities. And if he didn't understand her then he would use his force to see that she complied, though in the depth of him there was fear.

Carol sat on the bed and picked up the phone. Phil was on the other end. The connection was bad but the artifice of his tone was clear—resolve, a modicum of good cheer, a measure of sternness.

"Hi, darling. How are you?"

"Just darling, my Philippic. And your precious self?"

"Hot as hell. It's already eighty degrees and it's only eleven o'clock. I called last night. Where were you?"

"Oh, I took Eddie to Alexi's for dinner and some miniature golf. Of course, he had his usual hamburger and Coke, and he played his usual golf by his usual self." (The image of him sitting forlornly in Alexi's trailer). "You know our boy. Or you usually do. Mark stayed home with Emma. It was kind of late."

"And how's our friend Alexi?"

"Oh, very friendly, as usual."

"I'll bet he was. You've been drinking already, haven't you?"

"Silly Philly, what would ever possess me to do that? My God, we've no faith in our old Carol, have we? My God, Phil, did you know that Carmen Miranda died? Where are you, old Philippino? Why don't you come take care of your old Caroleeno?"

"That's what I'm calling about, Carol. I won't be coming. Things are very busy at the studio—way behind. We had a big electrical problem yesterday. We almost had a goddamned fire— wires, ladders, electricians all over the place. In fact, I'm at the studio now—we're getting ready to shoot. Are the boys okay? What are they doing?"

"Ah, the boys, my sweet boys. Eddie's—fine, off somewhere with his ball and glove, making catches for the Giants or something. Mark's in his room being his cherubic self. We may cross the cherubicon this afternoon."

"You what?"

"I said we may go into town this afternoon."

"Listen, Carol, I want you not to drink any more today, do you hear?"

"Oh, Phil, Jesus God! Are you my anointed keeper? For God's sake I've had hardly anything—no, no, that's all right, I'm not going to have anything more to drink—not today, not tomorrow, not ever. You're absolutely right, Phil, no more drinking—no more goddamned drinking. Oh, Phil, you're such a sneaky man, always busy, going somewhere, working, working, no time for your little ol' Carol. You don't love me, Phil, that's it, isn't it? You don't love me. You're a bad boy yourself, Philly-Willy, and you know it."

"Come on, Carol, I don't have time for this nonsense. I need to know if you're okay and if the boys are okay. Is Emma there?"

"Yassuh, she here."

"Why don't you take the boys for a long walk on the beach today? Get out of the house, put on your bathing suit, go for a swim—do something besides sitting around on your ass drinking. Do you hear me?"

"Oh my, listen to the roaring lion! The loutish Leo! Lippity, lippity! Leo the Lippity—"

"Look here, goddammit—"

"Oh, go to hell, loopity-lippity!"

Carol hung up the phone. She'd angered Phil, which was a simple thing to do, and she felt guilty for it. Too simple. And Phil was doing his manly job, though he was so inadequate. But who the hell wouldn't be inadequate in the face of her? Only Paul, perhaps. He knew her well enough, even with his dreary Catholicism. Paul knew her well enough:

Carol dear,

Hundreds of letters arrived on board yesterday evening...mail dated September and October...of the hundreds about twelve were for me...of these twelve none were from you...I do not complain...I have received five from you to date which is pretty good...I do not complain...that averages one a month which is only a fair average...but one letter from you keeps me happy for a month anyway so I do not complain. I know that you are very busy making ends meet and that you probably think of me more often than you have time to write. I hope before I get home, about Pop's birthday, that you will have made ends meet and will have time to sit down and write a letter such as has never been written before...the letter incomparable...the letter par excellence...though I heartily suspect that before this has been accomplished you will see me drooping at your doorway after that exhausting climb up your damn stairs. So you see I do not complain. I am merely despondent.

Now dear Sanborn grip more firmly this letter...be careful that it does not slip from your nerveless fingers and flutter to the floor. I have been received into the Catholic Church. From this day until the time that my body crumples into dust I am a living, breathing, practicing Catholic...and wipe that silly grin off your face. I am somewhat hazy as to just how it got started...just what spark kindled into flame my earnest desire to know just what the hell this life was all about. But I have found out to my complete satisfaction. The teachings of the Catholic Church as handed down from A.D. One are truly sublime.

Besides the personal daily instructions from the ship's chaplain I have read the subject exhaustively...it is my firm belief that opposition to the Church is founded on ignorance of the true meanings and motives behind the doctrines, traditions, and dogmas. I am not the victim of some glib-tongued padre. My eyes were wide open and they widened even farther as I progressed in my reading and instruction. The Catholic Church was the ONLY Church for fifteen centuries...obviously any other Church is either an off-shoot of the original or in direct opposition to the original depositum of faith...that Catholics worship statues of Saints etc. is strictly baloney and anyone saying they do merely admits of not having stopped to investigate. Time and space do not permit me to go into a detailed account of the whole subject...my style of writing would bore you to tears anyway. Any Catholic priest would be glad to give you a couple of pamphlets or even answer personally any or all of your questions. I feel that this is the turning point of my life...I shall probably not even beat you when and if and where we marry. Carol I've never known such peace of mind in all my life...

There had been no silly grin on Carol's face. Unless one grins in a silly way at a trapdoor opening and snatching half of one's life in an instant. At that point faith was the furthest thing from her existence. Paul was still unhappy; he was in the war. There was no alcohol. It must have been too much. Serving as an orderly on a medical ship, with its bleeding cargo of physical and spiritual dislocations, Paul, in Carol's mind, had buckled under the strain, had given up to the Holy Ghost. In Hong Kong they'd grown up in an ambiance of lapsed Anglicanism. Easter and Christmas were the two times each year Carol found herself in church with her family. The Egglestons were more observant, and Paul always more serious, though certainly not about the Church of England. Carol imagined he might end up a Buddhist some day. But hardly a Catholic. If there was one denomination they held in contempt as so much establishmentarian voodoo it was the Holy Roman Church. Of course as Anglicans they were snobs. They had equal disdain for American Protestantism. For Jews they held little of the prejudice (in spite of the attitudes of their elders), but much of the ignorance.

With Paul's "reception" into the Church, and more importantly the Church's reception in him, Carol had suffered a great abandonment and, very briefly, a small awakening. It was impossible to relate to Paul as a Catholic. It was akin to becoming a Communist. In spite of their adolescent scorn for organized religion Paul and Carol shared an unspoken respect for the spiritual. They both believed in God, Carol even more than Paul. With the receipt of Paul's letter Carol felt the lack of substance in the path she was pursuing (which was?) but dismissed this awareness as soon as she was able—in the same way (though it took a bit longer) she finally dismissed Paul. Yet she had never really dismissed Paul, merely run away from him:

Dear Sanborn:

Sorry I missed you when I was in New York...it was to be expected, however, since again I failed to give you sufficient notice. There was so much I wanted to talk to you about. I want you to know that I realize it is I who am responsible for your present outlook. I set you on the wrong track, first, way back in Hong Kong during the summer of 1937. That was sheer ignorance on my part. During the subsequent years, however, when I knew the foolishness of drink and the consequences which must follow in its wake, instead of being an example of perfect conduct, I encouraged you to be as foolish as myself. The summer of 1941, in New York, was the crowning era of a life which I had made sordid almost from the start. And I dragged you with me. Carol don't stay on the path I put you on. Get out on the highway and strike out on your own from there. You're a wonderful woman Carol and your life mustn't be wasted merely scrambling for recognition. You have so much more to offer than that. Your happiness will lie in making a home for someone and all that implies. Leave booze and married men to their own devices. I have no right to moralize...except that I feel deeply responsible for you and must know that you will be happy in whatever you decide to do. Be a real personality Carol and go after the things that really count...live deeply and leave the froth (social prattle, following the crowd, being in the "right set," insincerity as a means to an end, etc., etc.) to those who want nothing else and have nothing else to offer. I have subsisted on the froth. It has not satisfied...merely provoked and disgusted. I must find and hold the body of life.

Am staying at the Maritime Residential Club in Charleston. It was, prior to the war, the most exclusive apartment-hotel in the state. The War Shipping Administration took it over as a place where seamen returning from months at sea, might rest and return to a condition of normalcy. It's a beautiful old colonial home. Swimming pool to match.

Take care of yourself, Sanborn, and don't make yourself any more miserable than I made you. Go after the right things and be sure that what you get is what you want...

Eleven years ago, these letters were irritants. Now, they were cries from a traveler who sees his companion under lowering skies and evening fast approaching persist in taking a path leading to a precipice. She was now officially over the edge, and these memories, whisperings, muffled warnings were like the branches for which a falling person might grasp. But if she would not grasp the few branches still within her reach (for what reason? pride? principle? futility?), there was the ordinary fear of going under forever—that and the loss of her children and what her going away would do to them. Paul was right and she had been wrong. Phil was not an introspective man. Carol recalled a line from Lao Tsu to the effect that a life lived in full appreciation of the surface of things was as profound as the life lived in spiritual search. Was Paul more profound than Phil? The one certainty was that she was the least of them, her only enduring commitment to drink. Blast! And wouldn't another one be just the thing. To hell with all this.

Carol turned and did a somersault on the bed, coming to a vertiginous pause, looking up at the tilting ceiling. She raised her legs perpendicularly and thrust them forward, the momentum carrying her to a sitting position. From there it was a simple matter to stand. Which she did. Where was her little cherub? Her little fuzzy-wuzzy?

"Hey, fuzzy-wuzzy!"

From downstairs, no answer.

A glance at the Westclock. Eleven-fifteen. Empty, lime-sodden glasses, a cigarette burned to the filter, its long undisturbed ash resting in final coherent form, a glance at the mirror, a shudder, a nameless dread and she was at the top of the stairs looking for Mark, waiting for the sound of the little feet. When none came, she descended the stairs grasping the banister, thinking of the time when, several months earlier descending the stairs in the Manhattan brownstone on her way to a late afternoon assignation, Mark, in five-year-old protest of his mother leaving yet again, stuck out his foot at the bottom of the stairs and she'd tumbled in a heap on the parquet floor. The little boy was horrified and screamed pathetically. Emma scolded Mark severely and Eddie watched, stupefied. Carol was fine, actually amused in a way, as if she'd been whacked by a Zen master, bringing her abruptly and unexpectedly from her usual self-absorbed state to something entirely new. She stopped Emma from scolding her son and, after determining everything was intact, went over to Mark and gently soothed him. It was all right, mommy was just going out for a little while, I know you don't want mommy to leave, don't worry, mommy will be back soon, and so on. In fact, Carol had thought of canceling the tryst after crashing to earth but she did not because they were to meet in an agreeable bar on Third Avenue, a thing she had less resistance to than the act to follow, in which, thinking of her children and anxious to return to them, she did not indulge. Mark's foot and her resulting fall had been a signal, very clearly, and for several days after Carol reflected on her state of affairs and where she was headed. If she'd been a little wiser or stronger, she might actually have made an effort. But what? Analysis? Institutionalized dry-out? Some sort of spiritual retreat? If anything, she'd opt for the spiritual. In fact the Bible was very much on her mind lately. Now, descending these stairs at this later date, the possibility of redemption still dimly presented itself. Again, it was Mark, her littlest and dearest, at the bottom of the stairs—her lamb, her innocent darling, her cherub, quietly, instinctively, with humbling profundity offering his salvation. She was the child, descending in supplication to the Kingdom of God. God, in the form of a five-year-old boy sitting Buddha-like on his bed enacting a fierce battle with plastic soldiers, waited in his kingdom. He was content, absorbed in his play, the inert, olive-drab figures at his mercy. He could maneuver them stealthily for surprise attack on the enemy; he could direct a bloody close-quarter struggle with bayonets; he could scatter them to all points of his kingdom with a terrible explosion. Now, as in all theaters of war, there was a lull as he waited for this intruder of special import to enter his realm. He did not mind the interruption. His mother was a marginal, mythical presence in his life, and one he sensed vanishing. The battle on his bed would cease for this visiting, albeit tarnished, dignitary. Mark listened to the sandy footfalls and creaking stairs and watched her legs, shorts, blouse come into view, the hand clutching the banister. And what would this visitation bring? The sudden turn to meanness or abrupt going away? The sadness and silence that he was somehow supposed to make better? Perhaps, he hoped, it would be a few moments of lightness and fun, something that happened even now, occasionally. He didn't want to hear about the glass in her foot. Always there was the dread fear of something wrong he could not understand.

Carol cautiously crossed the threshold of the kingdom. The little potbellied god sat observing his soldiers, Japs and Americans, most of which were dead, or resting.

"Hey, Buster Brown, wanna go downtown?"

Now this was something. A ride on the Lambretta? To Swift's for an ice cream? To Angelica's for candy or a toy? To Segal's for a new pair of Keds? He hoped it would be Segal's. He liked Segal's. The funny man. He liked new sneakers and new bathing suits. He liked Angelica's too. Angelica had a parrot that made grownups laugh. Angelica was a little scary but nice. Her store was dark. They usually went to Swift's at night, before the movies. But they couldn't go without Eddie. Carol's resolve dissipated with the look of hopeful expectation on Mark's face. What had prompted her with this Buster Brown/downtown business? An opener, an ice-breaker, a desperate appeal to the child-God (for what? mercy? love? salvation?) had, to her dismay, been taken all-too-seriously. This would involve an enormous expenditure of energy and will. They had to find Eddie. (How could she face him?) They'd want to go on the Lambretta. She wasn't sure if there was gas. The children would need to be dressed. She couldn't very well have another drink and pull this off. Her foot throbbed.

"Can we really go to town, mommy? On the Lambretta?"

"I suppose I did say that, didn't I?"

Carol smiled at her son and rubbed his sandy head, toppling the rest of the soldiers as she reached for him. He'd nailed her, sure as hell.

"Well, let's go then," she said, trying to smile. "Let's get you dressed, come on, sneakers, socks, shirt, let's go!"

Mark scrambled off the bed, scattering the soldiers. Carol called out to Emma to find Eddie on the beach and tell him they were going to town. Perhaps he wouldn't want to go. Emma, standing in the washroom, pulled hot white sheets out of the dryer. Why the hell didn't the woman get her own son? Something sure as hell was going on with how that boy was acting so quiet and sad this morning. A strange boy anyway, always playing by himself, talking to himself playing ball. The screen door smacked behind her and Emma trudged up the stairs to the deck

In the boys' room, Carol, dizzy with exasperation from trying to get her youngest son ready for the trip to town—the task of changing shorts, finding socks, shirt, sneakers almost too much to bear—was now filled with dread at the sound of the screen door banging and the approach of Eddie's footsteps. She was hoping he'd want to stay on the beach and play by himself. She felt his presence in the doorway and turning around reached out to Eddie as if he were a wild animal she had to win over and before he could turn away her hand was on the cheek she had slapped the night before. He moved his head slightly but allowed her hand to stay. Mark, behind them, was balancing on his knee a soldier in the act of throwing a hand grenade. Upstairs the screen door slammed as Emma entered the house and walked to the kitchen. Mark's soldier dropped to the floor and Eddie ducked under Carol's hand and sat on his bed with his ball and glove. It was no use. Carol told the boys to finish getting dressed and that she'd be down in five minutes to go to town on the Lambretta. As their mother trudged up the stairs Mark finished dressing. At length Eddie bestirred himself and retrieved his shorts, socks, and polo shirt from the dresser, identical, except for the shorts (but everything two sizes larger, a fact that pleased him), to his brother's. They frequently wore matching outfits. Carol, ignoring Emma's obtrusive presence, went directly to the bar and poured herself a glass of vodka and drank it down, gripping the edge of the stainless-steel sink with its black Formica countertop with her left hand for balance, holding the glass above her open mouth, her eyes unfocused on the white wooden ceiling with its obtruding nail points, the last drops of the sweet palliative falling on her tongue. Better. And now, another. In the kitchen, adjacent to the bar, Emma communicated her displeasure by roughly clattering the morning's plastic cereal bowls on the counter next to the old porcelain sink filling with hot sudsy water. She angrily squeezed the remaining flatulent drops of Joy from the plastic bottle into the rising mound of froth, opened the cabinet door beneath the sink, and threw the empty container into the trash. Carol poured another glass, slightly less than the first, and drank once more, again letting the ambrosial drops fall on her tongue. The hell with her fat black clucking and crashing cereal bowls! She let the glass loose from her hand and it cracked on the stainless steel, rolled sideways and came to rest across the drain.

Carol's foot throbbed. This sliver of glass was going to kill her. It seemed to her that it was already beginning its inward progress, now halfway up her heel, not long before slicing into her calf muscle, severing vessel and vein, the pools of blood collecting. She looked out the window at the empty dune, the missing house that had lent so much substance. No more. *For Thou art my rock and my fortress.* Only bits and pieces of the foundation stuck through the covering sand, shelter for the lunatic birds. How they swooped and shrilled and how fiercely they protected their speckled eggs. Mark and Eddie spent hours dodging them and throwing rocks, not completely aware, she imagined, that the poor creatures were fighting for survival.

Would she fight so fiercely if her own were threatened? A familiar thud sounded against the plate glass window of the living room and Carol shuddered. Somewhat unsteadily she turned and walked through the dining room, out the door to the deck. Beneath the window the small brown form twitched on its side. Carol bent over the bird and picked it up, cupping the feathery almost weightless creature in her hands. Standing in front of the window she caught her reflection, her hands suppliant, the dunes and the vast sea-horizon behind her. The small brown eyes blinked and the bird attempted to right itself in her hands. There was a bit of blood at the corner of its yellowish beak. Carol prodded the bird gently, checking for anything broken, but how could she tell, really? The wings, folded in their normal position, seemed all right. She set the bird down in the shade of the eaves and retreated to the dining room door. The bird righted itself, fluttered its wings and took a small hop forward. Then it flew away, darting over the Evans' house, disappearing from view.

Five minutes later Mark and Eddie waited in the driveway as Carol wheeled the red Lambretta out of the garage. There was more than enough gas. The three of them wore smart straw hats with cloth hatbands purchased in Nassau six months ago, the brim of Mark's hat bent from being slept on. The hats were a custom of the trips to town on the Lambretta. Carol wore a loose, long-sleeved blouse with red, orange and yellow rectangles, dark blue Bermudas, leather sandals and her ever-present sunglasses. They were close to a matching threesome. The boys stood close as their mother placed her handbag in the rack beneath the handlebars, turned on the ignition with the small key attached to the St. Christopher medallion and kick-started the scooter once, twice, and the little engine puttered to life, shooting a hot small cloud of bluish smoke at the boys' legs and they hopped out of the way, laughing.

"All aboard!" shouted Carol above the determined muffled clatter of the single cylinder, a rapid heartbeat binding them. "Next stop, Westhampton!" she cried, doing her best imitation of a Long Island Railroad conductor and mounting the scooter. "Westhampton, here we come!" yelled Mark and, as the youngest, hopped on the back seat first, grasping its springs, secure behind his mother. Eddie followed, the seat bouncing, the back of the scooter sagging slightly, and he reached around Mark and took hold of the passenger handle.

"Here we go!" shouted Carol, revving the engine playfully and letting go of the clutch too quickly so that the scooter lurched forward and stalled.

"Whoa!" they all cried. Carol was a little drunk but not terribly so. Be careful, foolish girl, she thought. "Okay, everybody off. Got to start this buggy again. I'm so excited to get to Segal's I can hardly contain myself. I bet there's some new Keds just waiting to slip onto someone's smelly little feet."

The boys clambered off the scooter and looked at their mother with a happiness that bordered on wonder. It wasn't often she was like this. They looked at her and they looked at each other. How long would it last? Carol steadied the Lambretta and kicked three times again. The engine pulsed to life, emitting another cloud of oily blue smoke. Carol swung her leg over and sat, the boys eagerly following atop the back seat, the scooter bouncing up and down.

Upstairs in the kitchen Emma watched the scooter slowly move down the road, picking up speed as Carol shifted gears, a faint trail of blue smoke hovering over the road, the figures on the back in their white polo shirts and straw hats gripping tightly. Traffic was unusually light, a blessing. Maybe it was too hot for folks to drive. Lord, I hope they make it, she thought. The woman was taking a mighty chance. Emma finished drying the dishes and wiped the sweat from her dark chocolate brow with the yellow dish towel. The heat shouldered its way into the empty house, settling into every damp crevice. Emma opened the refrigerator and the freezer compartment at the top with its billowing excrescence and removed an ice tray. She took the tray to the sink and pulled back the aluminum handle and the frozen cubes crackled free. She moved the handle up and down a few times making sure the ice was loose and took the apparatus from the tray, placing it in the dish rack alongside the plastic bowls and jelly glasses and in her thick brown hand grasped a couple of ice cubes and rubbed them slowly all over her round fleshy face, the cooling runnels tracking down her neck to the tops of her large brown breasts and between. A sudden sharp longing overcame her and she looked down at the front of her uniform at her bosom. Would these African breasts ever suckle plump brown babies? At twenty-seven she felt her time running out. Where was her good black man to give her five or six babies? What was she doing in this white world with these sad, strange people? Everything here was white, white, white. The sand was white, the people were white, the houses were white, her uni-form was white. Even the heat, somehow, was white. But the real color was green, and that's why she was here, after all. She was a slave just like everybody else, even white folks. Everybody running around after the dollar. Emma put the ice tray back in the freezer and went downstairs to fold clothes.

"Off we go, into the wild blue yonder...!"

The three of them were singing above the rushing wind and the chattering scooter as they headed towards town, passing the great wooden beach club swordfish and turning left over the drawbridge, over the bay's narrow neck. Going over the bridge was especially fun. The boys had hoped a boat would be coming so the bridge would go up. Crossing over, Eddie liked to look down and see the bay below through the grating. It was mysterious underneath the bridge, cool, barnacled and dark. It echoed. There would be crabs to bite you. People fished under the bridge. Mark loved looking out at the open bay, so big it might be an ocean, motorboats tugging skiers, sailboats going back and forth. Carol, her good spirits durable for the moment, drove the scooter deftly, mindful of her precious cargo but not daunted by it. One went through life as a proper parent this way, mindful and sure, the topmost responsibility to transport one's children from one point to the next in safety and love—in control. They asked you to be in control, didn't they? And if you weren't—if you weren't the proper parent—they suffered for it. Carol sped the scooter down Jessup Lane, the long stretch before town, hurrying away from the beach with a calm fierce exhilaration, mindful of the two behind her gripping tightly, mindful also that they were secure in her at this moment. Their security gave her strength. She turned up the throttle and slalomed the scooter down the road with its flat expanse of sand and beachgrass on either side and occasional house and let out a long yaahooo! that was taken up by the children so that they were all yaahooing by the time they reached Stevens Lane, the abrupt right that in turn gave left to Potunk Lane and then right on Main Street. A right a left and a right, like Sugar Ray Robinson, thought Carol, and then boom! knocked out on Main Street, though it wasn't exactly Gopher Prairie, this chic little burg, with the sly, raunchy Angelica and her lascivious parrot to boot. She felt unaccountably happy. Whether it was the children's excitement or the right mixture of booze and circumstance, she didn't know, but it was real, she felt it, and she wished it would last forever.

Carol slowed the scooter at the head of Main Street by the Episcopal church and told the kids over her shoulder that they were going to Segal's to buy some sneakers. Mark put his arms around her waist and rested his cheek on her back, a gesture so typical and poignant it bid sabotage her euphoria. Despite the heat there was an insinuation of autumn, the cast of light, one's own rhythmic sense of season, and this awareness, along with Mark's gesture, was making it difficult to hold on to what she had, what they all had just moments ago slaloming down Jessup Lane yahooing over the wind and noisy scooter. She would get it back.

"Attention passengers. We're approaching Main Street International Airport, cruising at an altitude of eighteen inches. All frogs please observe the no croaking signs and kindly fasten your seatbelts and prepare for landing. Hummingbirds, please return to your nests. Be sure to stow all alligators under the seats, and kindly refrain from feeding the elephants. On your left we're passing Swift's, home of world-famous milkshakes and chocolate-dipped ice cream cones, not to mention perfume, toothpaste and garter belts—along with other unmentionable items. We will be returning to Swift's in a little while to sample some of their chocolate-covered mousetraps. Now on your left we see the famous Westhampton movie theater, where the favorite pastime of local juvenile delinquents is throwing Jujubes and Chocolate Babies from the balcony at the hapless patrons below. Coming up also on your left is the mysterious Angelica's, home of the piratical parrot and his repertoire of a thousand dirty jokes. Here you can purchase for just a nickel the Scaly News, the No Luck Times, the Herald Baboon and the New York Ghost or, if you'd prefer real sustenance, Hershey bars, Bazooka bubble gum, Pez candies and dispensers, not to mention mechanical pencils, fountain pens, invisible ink, caps and cap guns, comic books to warp your little minds, plus, for an extra fifty cents, Angelica will read your fortune."

"Will she really, mommy?" asked Eddie, leaning around Mark, who wasn't quite sure what reading your fortune was.

"I'm not sure about that but it seems like she should. And now, finally, we reach Segal's, the greatest clothing store, bar none, on earth! All the latest in beach couture directly from Paris showrooms to your town, avidly proffered to you by the inestimable, indefatigable and undeniable Abraham Segal, who cut his teeth as a peddler on Orchard Street while your pilot was no more than a gleam in her father's eye."

"What is a gleam in your father's eye?" asked Mark. Eddie was curious too and leaned forward. He also wanted to know what "cut his teeth" meant.

"It means I wasn't born yet. And now, here we are, world-famous Segal's. Everybody off!" Carol put both feet on the ground to stabilize the scooter while the children jumped off and ran excitedly to the store window, where two limbless mannequins, male and female, dumbly displayed nylon bathing suits and sunglasses. Above the white-papered backdrop Mr. Segal's floating Durante-esque face was smiling unctuously at the boys in pecuniary anticipation, the great proboscis bobbing like a beach ball caught in a rip tide and, spying Carol walking towards his store, smiled even more grotesquely, nodded even more vehemently and motioned for her to come in yes, do come in, yes.

Carol opened the door inward with the boys lined up behind her, Mark stepping on the back of Eddie's sneaker, causing his heel to come loose. "Well, well, look who's here!" intoned the kowtowing dwarf-like proprietor. "My favorite customers! The nicest and chic-est people in all of Westhampton!" He bowed obsequiously, as if one small gesture from Carol might have him beheaded. Eddie, much irritated with Mark, stood on one leg with his forefinger hooked in the back of his sneaker trying to pull it over his heel. Mark stared wide-eyed at Mr. Segal.

"Eddie, Eddie!" cried Mr. Segal, spying Eddie struggling with his scruffy blue sneaker. "Come over here. We got a brand-new shipment of the latest Keds yesterday, just your size and color— blue, right? That's your color. You look terrific in blue. Look at those old beat-up sneakers! Terrible, terrible! I bet that's why you're here, right?" He shot a look at Carol, a typical mixture of shrewd appraisal, false humility, and awkward humor, and saw that he was within bounds. Taking Eddie by the arm Mr. Segal led him over to the shoe section. Eddie shuffled along at the old man's side embarrassed at the attention but excited at the prospect of new sneakers. The old man smelled of Vitalis and made clicking and wheezing noises as he led Eddie to the shoe section, an open square at the far end of the store bordered by racks of shoes and plush seats in which to try them on. Mark followed closely, knowing he too would be getting sneakers. Carol stood with her handbag, amused. There was one other person in the store, a raw-boned younger woman in plain red sleeveless blouse and white slacks—a local by the looks of her, vaguely familiar—who carefully inspected sale items hanging on a revolving chromium rack. She looked at the children and then at Carol and smiled. Carol smiled back. Mark fidgeted next to Eddie by an empty seat, not quite sure whether to sit down.

"Here, here, sit down, son! What are you doing? You both need new sneakers, I can see that. Isn't that right, Mrs. Heizer? Am I correct in guessing you came for some handsome new sneakers?" He looked at Carol and offered a hideous smile that made her shudder. He was one of those salesmen who succeeded through the force of his urgency. He had no charm, no subtlety, but what he did have was the soul of the peddler, fierce, aggressive, indomitable, hawking fruit and vegetables at the age of eleven on his wooden pushcart over the filthy asphalt, ready to kill if necessary to protect his vendibles from the thugs and ganefs who would sweep down like a pack of wild dogs and take everything if he'd let them. Everything about him was the sale. He lived, breathed, ate and slept for the selling. And he could always be counted on to remind Jewish customers of his days on Orchard Street.

"1906 I started selling fruits and vegetables on Orchard Street in a pushcart my father made. My father was a carpenter in

Vilna. He came over in 1893 on a steamship with my mother. Fourteen days in steerage. They were both half dead by the time they got to Ellis Island. Believe me, it was rough in those days."

He had removed both boys' shoes and was measuring Eddie's left foot in the boot-like metal slide rule that was cold on the foot, the front part of which, Eddie felt, Mr. Segal always slid too hard against his big toe. As he measured the boys' feet he talked over his shoulder at Carol who he knew was not Jewish but close enough.

"My father never got to be a carpenter in America, which is what he loved to do. We lived in a tenement on Clinton Street and while I worked from six in the morning till six at night peddling, my parents stayed inside doing piecework, garment work, sewing sleeves on jackets, fourteen, sixteen hours a day they worked, doing the same thing over and over again. It killed my father, *alav ha-shalom.* He died a broken man."

Mr. Segal stopped for a few seconds and stared at Eddie's foot. Carol was never sure if Mr. Segal's spiel and minor dramatics were part of the mercantile strategy. She supposed over the years it had evolved into a package, part salesmanship, part genuine. The boys looked at the old man's shining pink scalp through the sparse, neatly-combed white hair. There were several small warts visible, cousins to the giant that stuck to his cheek like a piece of cauliflower and at which the boys could not resist staring, though they knew it was impolite. Carol took two steps in sympathy towards the kneeling figure with his bowed head, conscious of the absurdity of playing a role in Mr. Segal's routine, attentive should he continue his monologue, interested though having heard it before and knowing it would end in didacticism. The woman at the sale rack also tended to the old peddler's words, at the same time continuing to examine the merchandise.

"Eddie (he invariably addressed his remarks to Eddie, as the elder brother, presumably, something that pleased Eddie immeasurably), something that my father used to tell me I'll never forget to this day: 'Son, don't ever forget that this is the greatest country in the world, this United States. This is God's country. The land of opportunity.'"

The great nose rose up towards Eddie and he thought of Clarabelle, imagining the noise it would make if he squeezed it. The wart stuck out.

"Don't you boys ever forget that—the greatest country in the world! (Carol wondered if that's what his father really felt.) Imagine if you were in Russia living under Communism. Everybody doing the same thing. No chance to get ahead, make a life for yourself, be your own person, make some money. Everybody's poor. Communism! Be thankful you live in this great country, believe me. Do you think you could buy Keds in Russia? Ha! They all wear the same old shoes. They can't even run in those old shoes. Everybody's feet hurt in Russia. Bunions! They can hardly walk. They have to push each other around in wheelbarrows! Communism! Pah!"

The woman and Carol both smiled. The gnomish figure sprang nimbly to his feet and walked quickly to the storeroom, coming back with two boxes of new Keds. The boys looked at the boxes and then at each other. Their old shoes, moments before sympathetic companions and protectors, lay haphazardly on the floor, colorless and ragged, their usefulness scorned—

dead, smelly things ready for the trash pile. Carol would instruct Mr. Segal to put them in the shoe boxes and dispose of them. The first time Mark came in for new shoes he cried for his old ones. Mr. Segal told him they'd be going to shoe heaven where they'd grow wings like Mercury and run as fast as the wind. The old man kneeled, swept the old sneakers out of the way with the back of his hand and threw the clean boxes on the floor, which landed with happy, substantive thuds. He removed the lids and retrieved the stiff, blue sneakers from their rustling paper wrappings, redolent of new rubber and canvas.

"Communism! Here, let me see your foot there, Eddie. No, not that one the other one—atta boy. Did you know there was lots of Communists in the old days?" he turned and looked directly at Carol. "Not me though, never in a million years! There, how does that feel? Not too tight? Good. There was even lots of Jews that moved back to Russia after the Bolsheviks. Can you believe that? *Di alte heym*—the old country—that's what they called it. Now look what they have. Let me see that little foot, son."

Eddie was up and walking around the store with springy steps. He wanted to go outside and run on the sidewalk. Mark, impatient to wear his new sneakers, thrust his foot at Mr. Segal. The woman at the rack had found a blouse to her liking, yellow and short-sleeved, and approached respectfully. The old man, sniffing a sale even with his back turned, called over his shoulder in the direction of the storeroom, "Myra, come help this nice lady who wants to buy a blouse." He has eyes in the back of his head, thought Carol. A short graying woman in a blue sweater and gray woolen skirt walked silently from the room and took the blouse from the customer, calling her "darling" in a quiet deep voice, and led her to the cash register. Mr. Segal tied the shoelaces with a deftness and speed that reminded Carol of calf-roping and Mark was on his feet, hopping up and down.

"Ten thousand miles or your money back," said the old man getting to his feet and wiping his hands like Pilate. He addressed Carol, "Is there anything else? Some shorts? Some nice polo shirts? We have some nice Jantzen shirts that just came in the other day. Anything your little heart desires. Maybe something for yourself?"

"Actually I was thinking of new bathing suits," said Carol, smilingly looking at Mark, who promptly ran over to Eddie with the news and then ran back to his mother. Eddie walked over.

"Beautiful. That's terrific. We got beautiful MacGregor bathing suits, just in." Everything was always "just in," thought Carol. "Red ones, green ones, blue ones, yellow, plaid, you name it—all nylon, very nice."

The boys decided on bathing suits, Mark red, Eddie plaid. Mrs. Segal finished the transaction while her husband took care of the old shoes and busied himself in the storeroom. She put the bathing suits in boxes and, licking the pencil-point, carefully documented the sale (charged to Phil), pulling the receipt from a metal dispenser and handing a yellow copy to Carol.

"There you go, darling," she said.

"Thank you, Mrs. Segal," said Carol. "What do you say, boys?"

"Thank you," they said.

Mr. Segal came out of the storeroom. "Is there anything else you might need? Underwear? Socks? How about some nice cotton socks to go along with those new sneakers?" He rubbed

Mark's head, as if addressing him. Mark looked at Carol inquiringly. New socks sounded nice. Eddie thought so too. Mr. Segal smiled at Carol, all nose, ears and wart. A Jewish gargoyle, thought Carol. A gefiltebat. He should be hanging upside-down in a cave in Vilna. It was true, the boys needed socks, but he'd sold her enough already. That was it. Oh, hell, they might not come to town in God knows when. They were here, they might as well get some socks.

"What do you think, boys, should we get some socks?"

"Socks!" exclaimed Mark.

"Eddie, do you guys need socks?" Carol asked, wanting to confer a measure of authority to her eldest son, trying to make amends for the turbulent scene the night before. A trifling gesture to be sure. Eddie sensed its artifice but understood his mother's intention.

"Yes," he said shyly. "We need socks."

"Can we get white ones, mommy? Instead of blue ones?" asked Mark.

Carol, saddened at what was passing between her and Eddie, nevertheless pressed on, "Should we get white ones this time, Eddie?"

"Yes, Eddie, white ones," said Mark.

"Okay," said Eddie, "let's get white ones."

And so white socks were purchased, another receipt written by Mrs. Segal and one more attempt made by Mr. Segal to sell Carol something else, a pair of slip-on rubber-soled canvas shoes, blue or white, he felt would look attractive on her ("very handy for boating"), at which point Carol's annoyance with the old peddler's wheedling became palpable and she cut him short.

A subtle tide of hostility rose between them—she, the gentile of privilege who never had a care for money in her life, and he, the calculating Jewish merchant obsessed with draining away every last ounce of cash from his customers (their view of each other at the moment) found themselves facing each other across a chasm that may or may not have been peculiarly American. But what of it, mused Carol, as she exited with her happy children. He's probably a decent man. I'm glad his store is here. He has a nice wife and a grown son. His life has been a lot harder than mine, the child father to the man, all of that. And mother to the woman.

"Can we go to Angelica's?" asked Eddie.

"Yes, of course, let's go to Angelica's," she replied. From the Baltic to the Balkans. Angelica with her mysterious Romany-esque ways and appearance. If she was a gypsy she had to be an outcast because there was no tribe of gypsies in Westhampton, that was for sure. Maybe Riverhead. The good Christian folk in these parts would make short work of them. Eddie and Mark sprinted down the block in their new sneakers towards Angelica's. Of all the people on Main Street Angelica was hardest to determine. Her last name, Rose, was no help. The story was she had changed it from Rosenblum (the bloom off the rose?), but no one could say for certain. What was, then, Carol wondered, her first name? Myrtle? Freydel? Bernice? Angelica Rose had a bit of a different timbre than Freydel Rosenblum, especially here on Main Street. The boys were up the steps to Angelica's and she saw them pause and look back at her before going in. Freydel's. Can we go to Freydel's, mommy? They wanted to check that their mother was coming and they were a little afraid of Angelica. She had a bit of the Gorgon about her with her deep voice, sitting immobile and elevated behind the glass counter with the parrot on its perch or sometimes on her shoulder, and the store cave-like and dusty with aisles that were more like paths, leading you behind shelves and racks filled with a myriad of curious things like fountain pens, wind-up toys, paper-weights, playing cards, assortments of rubber balls, toy soldiers, soaps, powders, unguents and more, much more, accreted over the years, dusty and without seeming purpose, piled, stuffed and tucked together, each item possessed of a talismanic quality. If one had the time and patience a thorough search of Angelica's items might yield treasures, though most regarded her collection as mere gimcrackery—a mistake, thought Carol. She'd poked about a bit herself and found some interesting things, including, once, a wooden puppet toy with a bearded white man in top hat and tails kicking a highly caricatured bedraggled black man in the ass, the black man's arms flinging up in the air with every kick. A real bit of Americana, that. Emma would love it. Other things: a package of rattlesnake rattles, miniature brass trophies for "World's Best Lover," "World's Best Drinker" (in the running for that one), and "World's Biggest Asshole" (maybe that, too), plastic whips, handcuffs (not a surprise), packaged tubes of watercolor paint, long since dried, an ancient Brownie camera, uranium samples (she'd have to bring her Geiger counter in), Mexican jumping beans, plastic hula skirts, jars of soap bubbles and wands, ray guns, doctor and nurse kits, Howdy Doody pup-pets, flowering clam shells, plastic musical instruments, gorilla masks, piggy banks, baseball caps, soap dishes, ashtrays ("Steal-ing a kiss may be petty larceny—but sometimes it's grand"—she'd bought that for Phil, a reminder of how things were, once), bicycle horns and bells, miniature boxing gloves, glass wind chimes, tiny bamboo bird cages, carpenter's rulers, marbles, board games, dancing skeletons. Angelica sat like an indolent Romany queen overlooking her emporium with the eye of a raptor. Like any self-respecting gypsy she trusted no one. She rarely let the boys go to parts of her store where they couldn't be seen. Her authority intimidated them and so much remained a tantalizing mystery. Occasionally, if they sensed Angelica was in a particularly good mood, or if she was occupied with a customer, they would slip back into the umbral regions to look at the treasures, but it was always with trepidation as any moment Angelica's stern voice might terminate their explorations.

It was a place of slightly Gothic esoterica and the boys loved it, as did most everyone. Here was where you bought the daily newspaper, a pack of gum, cigarettes, a chocolate bar, a magazine, a soda, a Dixie Cup, a popsicle, a comic book. Eddie liked the way Angelica tossed a book of matches on the glass counter when his mother bought a pack of cigarettes. It was like she didn't care but there was something about it that was friendly. In fact, as scary as Angelica could be, she was really nice. She always said hi to Mark and Eddie in a friendly way and smiled at them, though her smile wasn't very big.

And there was the parrot. The parrot, whose name was Genghis, said things that made grownups laugh, though neither Mark nor Eddie could understand what was particularly funny. They laughed anyway because parrots were funny and because the grownups laughed. Carol and Phil both loved the parrot. Now, when Mark and Eddie entered the store Genghis was nowhere in sight. Only Angelica was present, stolid and forbidding, behind the counter. "Hello boys. Where's your mommy and daddy?" she said somberly.

"Our mother's coming," said Eddie, standing in the middle of the floor, looking up at this Circean presence who seemed to hover above them like a genie. Mark stood silently next to Eddie, also staring. Then Carol entered, the spring on the screen door stretching like some demon harp string and the door banging shut. "Hello there, Mrs. Heizer," Angelica Rose said with the hint of weariness that Carol found so appealing.

"Hello, Angelica. How are you?"

"Fine, thank you," offered Angelica, obviously in one of her less loquacious moods. She had been reading the *National Enquirer* when the boys came in and now she returned to the article about suspected alien insemination of a pig on a Nebraska farm. There had been a strange green glow in the sky and turbulent weather. Three-and-a-half months later a litter of eight piglets had been delivered by Uriah Gantry's prize sow, Bathsheeba. They had huge eyes, scrawny bodies, and exhibited unusual intelligence, scratching strange hieroglyphics in the dirt with their snouts. People had been coming for miles around, professors, biologists, ufologists. Well then, thought Carol, obviously I'm a very important customer. She scanned the dusky interior for the parrot.

"Where's Genghis?"

Angelica looked up. "He's somewhere in the back of the store reading the *New York Times.* Working on his vocabulary."

"I thought he only read the *Daily News.*"

"He's on this self-improvement kick," said Angelica, smiling a bit. "Before you know it he'll be a goddamned liberal."

"A regular egghead," said Carol.

"Just what the world needs, another do-gooder with his head in the clouds," said Angelica, baiting Carol slightly as someone she knew as a *Times* reader.

"We can't have that," said Carol. "Maybe you'd better stop carrying the *Times*. Of course you might lose half your customers." She smiled.

"The better half, no doubt," rejoined Angelica with a twisted grudging smile revealing short teeth in a squat face. The effort of smiling suggested a fiercer disillusion than her usual dourness. Mark and Eddie, under the cover of the bantering between their mother and the dark proprietress, inched towards the tenebrous aisles. The screen door banged and another customer entered, a short, softish man about Carol's age with thinning sandy hair and rough, scrawny legs. He wore a yellow short-sleeved shirt, blue nylon bathing trunks and blue boating shoes, the kind Mr. Segal had tried to sell Carol. He swayed slightly and smiled at Carol. Jesus, another inebriate, she thought. The man stood with his legs apart as if for balance and smiled at Angelica, who nodded back disapprovingly.

"Good morning, ladies!" he announced cheerfully.

"Slip it in!" came an equally cheerful voice from the back of the store.

"So, this is what he's getting from the *Times*?" said Carol, smiling at Angelica.

"He must be reading something else. I try to keep the good stuff away from him. He told me he was going back to read *The New York Times.* I should've known better."

"Oh, baby! Oh, baby!" came the bizarre, high-pitched voice. The words were enunciated with human clarity. The man grinned suggestively at Carol, who smiled back. There seemed something familiar about him.

"Oh, baby! Oh, baby!"

"Sounds like somebody's having a good time back there," said the man, looking at Carol.

"He's writing a novel," said Angelica to the man, straight-faced. "He really enjoys his work."

"Apparently!" he exclaimed, his blue eyes glowing, pleased to find himself in this odd store, and pleased also with this attractive and friendly woman.

"Slip it in!"

With an explosive green and yellow flurry, the parrot burst forth from behind the shelves in the back of the store, navigating its way to a perch next to Angelica. The man recoiled comically and Carol laughed. "My God! It's the novelist!" he shouted, clutching his chest and laughing delightedly.

"Oh, baby!"

Carol, after her initial distaste for this homunculus with his reptilian legs, decided she liked him very much indeed. There was something about him. His reaction to the parrot, his laughter and delight, was appealing. He'd been drinking, obviously, and lord knew he broadcast his suffering like the six o'clock news. Just look at those legs. But yes, she liked him.

In the midst of his laughter at the bawdy parrot, the salacious carnival-Medusa behind the counter, the sun-glassed, probably dipso Lauren Bacall, the two children, their heads poking over shelves in the back of the store, mystified at the unfathomable ways of adults and, finally, this peculiar cave of a store glutted with piles of intriguing things, the man instantly resolved to know this attractive, probably shrewd, and most certainly troubled woman who, behind her sunglasses, seemed to communicate an affinity and even a liking for him. "Can you believe," he said, addressing both women, but the weight of his sentiment directed at Carol, "that in a life of thirty-six years lived in New York this is the first time I've been to Westhampton? And look what I've been missing! I love your store! Are you the owner of this fabulous place?" Though he felt Angelica a somewhat comic character—too much of a type to be taken seriously—his tone was respectful, as he knew it damn well better be. This stranger, in Angelica's mind, was acceptable. She liked his open, theatrical manner, and he obviously loved her store. As for the show of respect, well, it was just a show, but that was all right.

"Yes, this is my place. I'm Angelica Rose. And this is Mrs. Heizer. And this is Genghis." She tilted her head at the preening parrot who, upon hearing his name, looked up abruptly and seemed to ready himself for another outburst, though nothing came.

"Howard Johnson at your service. No finer place for family dining." He affected a little bow. "I'd stay away from the beef tips and gravy though. We're still working on that one. A few cases of salmonella—nothing serious." He looked at Mark and Eddie at the back of the store as he said this. They both knew

Howard Johnson's. Might this be the man who owned all the restaurants? They looked at each other.

"Well," said Carol, "your curried lamb *à la Française* is most exquisite."

"Ah ha, so you've been to our restaurant in Des Moines on route eighty? Obviously, as that and no other carries the curried lamb *à la Française*. I might also recommend the *escargots à la provençale* the next time you're in Bismarck." He clicked his heels and bowed like von Stroheim, clutching an imaginary monocle in his eye. Carol thought this man delightful and determined to know him. Despite the uselessness of everything there were still small spaces admitting of interest. This man seemed such a space. Perhaps a treasure. She thought this as he bowed, noticing Angelica smiling more naturally than she thought possible.

"I would love to discuss more of these epicurean treasures. There's so much about Howard Johnson's I realize I don't know. Perhaps you might join me for cocktails this afternoon and I could learn more about your wonderful restaurants."

Howard Johnson, who had been wondering himself how to effect such a get-together (in spite of the fact that she was married and the children in the store were most probably hers), continued in the stiff manner of von Stroheim, concealing his considerable pleasure in the woman's (Mrs. Heizer—was that a Jewish name?—she didn't look Jewish) invitation. "I would be delighted to spend an afternoon in your charming company. There is much the public doesn't know about our restaurants. I am sure there are many interesting things to discuss." He bowed stiffly once more and the parrot rose up and flapped its wings, clutching the perch with its claws. A small green feather floated over the counter and landed on the worn wooden floor. The bird settled, turned its head, and bit fiercely behind its wing, then looked at Howard Johnson and made a low trilling noise in its throat.

"Well then," said Carol, reciprocating his bow, Dietrich-like, "we will be awaiting your company. Perhaps four-ish?" Howard Johnson nodded his assent. "It's a large pink house about three-quarters of a mile past the Dune Deck—do you know where that is?" Howard Johnson again nodded. "On the ocean side," said Carol, smiling.

"I will be there promptly at four p.m. Until then. Ladies, it's been a real pleasure meeting you—and you too, Genghis. There's an act for you at Grossinger's, I'm sure." He turned to leave, then stopped. "Ha! I did come to buy a paper, didn't I." He picked a *Daily News* from a pile on the floor and laid a warm nickel on the counter in front of Angelica. "It was either the *Daily News* or a pack of Juicy Fruit. Today I choose culture." He was aware Carol might raise a bit of an eyebrow at his selection. "I get it for the sports," he said to her, holding it aloft and displaying the back section as if showing a receipt to a department store detective, "—and the letters to the editor."

"I'm rather fond of the editorials myself," said Carol.

"Well now I'm really impressed. A bit erudite for my taste, I'm afraid." They nodded at each other like Viennese burghers and Howard Johnson left the store.

With the amusing stranger's departure Angelica got up off her stool behind the counter and moved with her stevedore's gait to the back of the store, ostensibly to turn on a large grimy General Electric fan but really to check on the boys, who had disappeared behind the shelves. They were on their knees play-ing with wind-up sports cars, racing them from the shelves to the back wall next to a door that partly opened into a dark room.

"Come on, get out of there," she said in a low brusque voice. She pulled a chain and the scythe-like blades of the big fan began to slowly turn and gather speed and, in a moment, a small hurricane blew from the back of the store. The boys collected the pocket-sized, brightly-colored metal cars and replaced them on the shelf next to Chinese checkers, dried paints and card-board tubes of flypaper, the air turbulent over their heads as the fan turned on high, spun full speed. Always there was the temptation for Eddie to stick a finger in. It was such a big fan and when they stood the force of the air buffeted their ears and nearly blew their hats off. Mark went to the front of the store but Eddie stayed and looked into the fan, its force pushing his hat so that it felt like a bird tugging to free itself of his head and tears formed in the corners of his eyes. He could see through the spinning blades to the back wall. There were two noises—the rushing wind and the humming, vibrating noise of the fan itself. Eddie felt like he was looking into the propeller of a plane and fought the small centipede of fear in his chest. If a propeller went into his face it would cut him into a million pieces. His mother wanted to buy a plane. She would fly high out over the ocean and disappear forever. A tiny speck in the sky, like the jets, so high up it would scare you to look down at the ocean, like the time they flew to Nassau. If he put his finger in the blades would slice it right off. He rubbed his forefinger with the thumb of the same hand. The cage around the fan was dirty, but wide enough to stick a finger in...

"Eddie, let's go!"

He turned. Everybody was looking at him. He expected his mother to be irritated and impatient the way she usually got but he was surprised to see her with a hint of a smile and a subtle shaking of her head. It pleased him somehow that his mother was looking at him in this way. Mark turned his attention to the comic book rack. Angelica regarded him impassively. Carol bought the boys packs of gum, Juicy Fruit for Mark and grape for Eddie and then said good-bye to Angelica, who smiled in her grudging way and bid them farewell and a swift return. The boys tried to make the parrot say something but it remained stubbornly silent. "Good-bye, Genghis!" they said, and, "Oh, baby! Oh, baby!" and when they left the screen door banged shut behind them.

****

After the amusing Mr. Johnson left the store, Carol thought of another man, three years ago in Paris. She'd been there less than a week, living comfortably at the Grand Hotel Bisson at 37, Quai des Grandes Augustins and spending way too much money, most of it Phil's, who was by now desperate to do something about HMS Carol, listing to port and floundering badly, taking on alcohol at an alarming rate. Meandering one cloudy afternoon in Montparnasse she went into a small dive for a drink, *Le Petite Mirage*, and noticed a man sitting at the bar, dining on a bowl of bouillabaisse and sipping red wine. Carol ordered gin and bitters and watched in the mirror the black-bearded man intently work his food into a large mouth with its full Semitic lips. A white starched napkin covered a brown muslin shirt and thin goatskin vest. The rest of him was covered with thick blue corduroy pants and tan sabots. A black beret completed the picture. Carol wondered. Though the clothes were worn, even a bit shabby, they didn't seem quite comfortable on the man. His fingers were pale, long and slender, though strong-looking. Not a workingman's hands. More the hands of an artist—not a painter—there was no sign of pigment anywhere—but a sculptor—a sculptor a bit too obviously in getup, a poseur with a studio in Montparnasse.

He tore pieces of bread from a large hunk and jabbed them into the bowl of fish stew, stuffing them succinctly between the dark beard and red lips. His fingers tapered at the tips, suggesting adaptability and competence, but not purpose. A man adept at feeling his way through the world. After each piece of bread he took a sip of wine. Carol viewed her reflection in the mirror behind the sunglasses and compared herself to the man sitting two seats away. He was, despite the affected garb—if it was affected—clearly well into his role, whatever it was. She supposed, if anything, she played the fashionable mystery woman, the Russian spy in a left bank cafe with nothing to spy on but this artist-looking fellow with his stew and red wine. Well, she was off-duty at the moment. She ordered another drink, downed it quickly and ordered another. The angostura constricted her tongue, but the gin loosened her speech.

"*Êtes-vous français?*" she asked the intently-eating fellow.

"*Non, je suis américain.*"

Aha.

"Well, I guess that makes two of us."

Le Petite Mirage was a very small place. Carol had chosen it for its isolation and lack of Americans. The patron and the one other customer, a young man in a raincoat sitting at one of two tables in the place, conveyed the false inattention of those listening closely. The *patron* resembled a chubby James Joyce—the same thick glasses, an air of shrewd diffidence. Carol had read *Dubliners* and *Portrait of the Artist* but not *Ulysses*. She might get around to it someday. He had spoken some English when she entered so he might understand her words with the American. The young man sitting stoically with a glass of red wine between his hands was a cipher. With a third gin and bitters about finished Carol didn't care who understood English or not.

"It occurs to me that perhaps you are an artist—am I not mistaken?

"You are most perceptive. I am indeed an artist. Jean Loutrel, *à votre service.*" Carol nodded and introduced herself. The man wiped his lips with the starched napkin, reached into a vest pocket, withdrew a white business card and slid it down to Carol with the tips of his long fingers. His name, in lower case and small type, was in the middle. At the bottom left a single word: *sculpteur.* At bottom right a Montparnasse address, also in lower case. The *patron* maintained a serious expression, wiping glasses with a white cloth while looking out the window. Outside a smattering of rain in the late afternoon and people walking with bags of bread. Everywhere people with bread. To walk in the June afternoon rain in Paris protecting one's bread was a thing of great purpose. And her purpose? *Une expédition photographique,* as Phil might say. To essay a few fledgling steps as a fashion photographer, away from Phil and New York. She looked at the mirror behind the bar at the somber face hidden by sunglasses. The *sculpteur* looked at her quizzically.

"Perhaps you'd like to see some of my work. My studio is only a few blocks away. You're drinking gin. I'll buy a bottle of gin." Speaking in fluent French he bought a bottle of gin from the Joycean *patron*, suddenly very attentive. He also paid for Carol's drinks. The young man had left. This Jean Loutrel is very sure of himself, thought Carol. Or am I so abject a spectacle as to give any two-bit artist the balls to try to pick me up like he was Clark Gable or something? This Monsieur Loutrel was way too smooth. But Carol suddenly had no will, felt herself dreadfully lonely, and couldn't take her eyes off the square frosty bottle clutched in the artist's long dishonest fingers. That was okay. She was up for getting smashed and lying in an artist's bed. Let those fingers do what they may.

Jean Loutrel's studio lay hidden in a narrow asphalt-paved street four blocks from *Le Petite Mirage*. It rested forlornly above a dusty tobacco shop whose pipe-smoking proprietor nodded solemnly as they walked through to get to the stairs that led to the second-floor studio. Upstairs, Carol looked out the rain-spattered window across the street at a horsemeat market she'd missed coming in. A huge waxen gray and yellow carcass hung in the window. Something dragged from Verdun forty years earlier. Nicely aged. Monsieur Loutrel's studio was quite barren. In the middle of the room on a large grapefruit crate globs of clay stuck to an armature in the form of a female torso. Jean Loutrel busied himself with drinks by a metal sink. Gin with twists of lemon peel. The piece on the grapefruit crate had unintended interest as an abstraction. Compared with the dozen or so finished pieces on crates spaced around the studio, all done competently in the manner of Matisse and cast in dark-patinaed bronze, the unfinished piece had a disturbing, flayed existential quality, not unlike a bloated Giacometti. Remarkable what thousands of tons of bombs can do. Or the threat of a hundred or so big ones hanging over our heads. A viable aesthetic. Marketable. Get with it, Monsieur Loutrel, thought Carol. The *sculpteur* walked up to Carol with a drink outstretched.

"I have my work in a gallery in the Saint-Germaine-des-Pres. Sorry there's no ice. It's a bit chilly in here anyway. Can I get you a sweater?"

Carol declined the offer. There was a thick blue quilt on the sculptor's unmade bed.

"*À votre santé*," he said. They clinked glasses. "I might as well tell you that my real name is not Jean Loutrel. It's Jack Levine. Jean Loutrel is my *nom d'art*. I picked it out of the phone book. I've been in Paris for three years, after fleeing my family's dry goods business in Massapequa. They were not unsympathetic. I can always go back. In fact, they expect that I will someday. I myself am not so sure. In any case my brother will gladly take over the business when my father retires—which will be never. *Vive la France! Vive la vie créative!*"

He thrust his glass and clinked hers, searching her face—a mask that covered much he perhaps would not want to know—the sunglasses that seemed a permanent fixture, the small remorseless scar beneath her cheekbone covered poorly with makeup, the air of weary cynicism, the years of drinking, obviously. Carol, in turn, looked at the curious Mr. Levine. Massapequa! The only thing she knew about Massapequa was that it came before Massapequa Park, Lindenhurst, Babylon and Bayshore on the Montauk run of the Long Island Railroad, that mournful stretch of track with its bobbing, benumbed commuters. Massapequa. So, there were Jews in Massapequa. Somehow this surprised her. There was nothing remarkable about his sculpture, though certainly it wasn't bad. She knew people who would probably buy it. He was on a lark, obviously. In a few years he'd be back in Massapequa. He seemed about her age. At thirty, one still had a bit of rope left, though not much. He'd soon come to his senses. He was a nice young fellow living *la vie bohème* under the best of conditions. It was nice. She'd judged him harshly. It was she who deserved the judgment. What were her children doing now? Carol raised her glass and forced a smile.

"Vive la vie créative."

After a week of seeing Jack Levine Carol checked out of the *Grand Hotel Bisson* and moved in with the sculptor. She would write Phil and tell him that she'd found a cheaper and infinitely more charming apartment in Montparnasse. She stayed for a month and a half, keeping up the trans-Atlantic charade. She shared a studio for three weeks with a young Belgian photographer working in animal portraits. The man had an impressive amount of work for just starting out. He worked mornings and she afternoons, but it was a tough act to follow. The excruciating array of amateur models, procured through an agency and paid for by Phil, mostly young awkward working girls with high hopes of breaking into the world of *haute couture*, were no match for the morning menagerie. She thought more than once of becoming an animal portraitist herself. There could be something quite good about this, actually, though it was far removed from the world of fashion. She had a vision of people and their animals as she watched the young Belgian go about his amusing business. Over time owner and pet took on aspects of each other. One could capture this, but it was too much. The effort of getting started was too great. It would require an energy, enthusiasm and purpose she did not possess, and though she liked animals well enough, they were of no particular significance in her life. She envied the young Belgian. He was onto something.

Carol, too, was onto something. She and Jack Levine spent afternoons at *Le Dome* drinking Old-fashioneds and taking in the bohemian scene. Paris was unusually rainy.

"The sky is grieving, Monsieur Loutrel."

"Ah, but Mrs. Heizer it is grieving because in two weeks you will be leaving."

In the dolorous streets Parisians walked by clutching their baguettes. Some rode bicycles, hunched over. The statue of Balzac watched over them.

"But Monsieur Loutrel, they want us to leave," she said, motioning to a painted message on a boarded-up window across the street. *Americans go home!*

"You are not the Americans they want to leave, Mrs. Heizer."

In the afternoons *Le Dome* was crowded with artists and too many Americans, whose voices rose in bibulous decibels above the rest. Talk was of the pennant race, which they followed in the *Herald Tribune*, the presidential candidates (most favored Eisenhower), Marciano's punching power. The French talked of Indo-China and Algeria. As the drizzling afternoons stretched into darkness, Carol and Jack Levine rose unsteadily from their cafe chairs and ventured forth to explore the city. Carol had favorites which, in the falling rain and puddled streets, the lamps guiding their way like lucent phantoms, the flickering snatches of the serious Gallic tongue arising from the earth itself through the stout-legged natives, would implant themselves in her forever. This was Paris. Together they walked in the Tuileries silently in the evenings, the Louvre brooding in the background, the rain gently ushering people from the streets.

They had the city to themselves. They and *les clochards* and the cloaked *gendarmes* who walked their beats in officious solemnity and nodded as conspirators of the respectable to Jack Levine and herself and who hustled the disreputable away from their makeshift redoubts in the bushes, bridges and alleyways. In the rain at nights the Champs Elysees, cleared of its usual traffic, took on a hallowed magnificence, the Arc de Triomphe awash in floodlights. Climbing the stairs of Montmartre she was in the 18th century, the dark old buildings murmuring to her. She was a little frightened of the Canal St. Martin at nights. The street dwellers, *les clochards*, hung back in the shadows like trolls. Under the bridge (what manner of mystery?) there was a covered boat that housed a family. She imagined them gypsies though they were probably not. She had no desire to go the Louvre, was content to see the great building from a distance, from the Tuileries. It was too big for her state of mind. Her favorite work of art was the statue of Voltaire at the Académie française. The old genius lay mostly naked in his brilliant sexuality and seemed vastly amused, indomitably vulnerable. There was something awesome about it. They had Coquilles Saint-Jacques and bouillabaisse one evening at *Prunier's* and afterwards she was sick and Jack Levine was up most of the night taking care of her, fearful they might have to go to the hospital.

About her supposed purpose in Paris Carol felt enormously guilty. She lied outrageously in her letters—there were very few —to Phil. It was all a joke, really, surely Phil knew, yet another in a series of half-measures and deceits. And even more than usual, she drank. She drank every day, so much that Paris took on the aspect of an impressionist painting, a Pissaro or Monet. How delightful to live impressionistically, drifting hither and yon with her *sculpteur*, running madly from herself, the return to the States looming like Rushmore, the sanctimonious, granite presidents.

She did try to take some interesting fashion shots. Influenced by Phil's style, which was very much the style of the time, she struggled to add something of her own, something distinctive, a bit of whimsy, a suggestion of parody. This sort of thing was virtually unheard-of in the ultra-serious world of fashion, except perhaps for Avedon. Had she the time, the dedication, and some good models to work with she might have pulled it off. Fashion photography was not such a simple thing. Having the vision was one thing, getting there another bit altogether. Besides, her real talent was as a writer. Nevertheless, she didn't drink until her work was finished in the afternoon. She tried to take her daily routine seriously. Carol had an idea of combining photography with writing, maybe a book someday on fashion. It was an intriguing idea, an idea that helped get her out of bed in the late mornings and gave her the willpower to resist drinking immediately each day, if only for this short period. Yes, a book someday on fashion was a nice idea, but even better the thought of free-lance work combining text and photos, something that might take her all over the world—a niche for herself. Who knew where it might lead?

She had ideas. The world of fashion was a silly but delightful bit of puff. And of course there was the money. There was no helping it, she loved the stuff. Much of what drew her to Phil was his professional success and the perquisites of being married to a man among the handful of better fashion photographers in New York City. She was certainly living in the style to which she was accustomed. And Phil maintained his end of the contract manfully, subsidizing her feckless ways. But she rebelled against this notion of being "subsidized." The only way to become "un-subsidized" was to achieve independence. The way to achieve independence was through vision and hard work. On her better days she was confident of her talent. All that was lacking (all!) was a clear vision and the will to work.

But there always seemed to be too many things to push against. The children. How could she have a successful career and be a parent at the same time? Phil did it. Yet, Phil was hardly a parent. Men were expected to have careers and would be forgiven if the attention they gave to their children was less than perfect. Such a defect was unforgivable in a woman. So she had the worst of both worlds, so behind, so muddled, there seemed no way to make it work. She'd had time to make a go of something, but at thirty it seemed too late. The simplest acts, the ability to make decisions, were almost too much, but what was even more difficult was the will, the desire, to sustain anything. Perhaps those privileged days in Hong Kong as a precocious child of empire were precisely the wrong thing. She grew up with certain assumptions that were not the rest of the world's. As a child she was victim of a disservice. Her talents, her willfulness, her unchecked ramble through her cloistered, exotic world, needed a dose of opposition, of well-meaning governance—discipline. She was an unattended girl.

It was beyond the point of blaming her parents, though there was bitterness. They were not bad people, but preoccupied. Her father, reserved and distant, let it be known in subtle ways that he'd have preferred a male child. As it happened, it was Robert Sanborn's fate that Carol be followed by two sisters. And so the Sanborn name, if not the blood, would be terminated. Carol had perceived her father's disappointment, though he was decent enough not to express it openly, and she strove to please him, knowing that no matter what she did it could never possibly be quite enough. As a result Carol was filled with the usual share of resentment, though it was also the case that she did naturally possess many of what were commonly understood as male characteristics, independence, physical daring, a streak of rebellious iconoclasm. To what degree should she try to magnify these proclivities to gain her father's approval was a source of confusion for Carol. In any case, her personality was not something her parents were particularly comfortable with. She was not the demure daughter of empire, the ideal communicated a thousand ways daily by elders of the company compound. Always the pressure to curb her "hoydenish" ways and cleave to the expected role.

As for her parents' lack of attendance, given Carol's nature, it may not have been such a bad thing. Bob Sanborn was gone a good deal of the time marketing his company's products in south China. It was a job that he loved and one that occupied him to the fullest extent. He was gone weeks at a time. Lottie, Carol's mother, involved herself with the running of the household, delegating responsibility and tasks to the Chinese servants. With the birth of Carol's younger sisters, Deborah and Victoria, Lottie distanced herself even more from the harrying, mundane obligations of motherhood, allowing the nursemaids to take over rather completely. She saw her children when time permitted or when there were troubles, and at dinnertime, where the family gathered properly attired and observant of the decorum befitting their station.

Lottie's parents were stolid middle-class Berliners. She'd met Bob Sanborn on a cruise ship that was also transporting American soldiers home from the still-glistening fields of Western Europe. She'd had training in opera and one night sang an aria from Carmen for the ship's company, her husband-to-be in the audience. Lottie's dream was of the exotic, cultivated life— to shuck the restrictive vestments of an effete bourgeoisie and escape a ravaged German empire. The year was 1920. In Robert Sanborn she found a young, quietly-determined Harvard graduate who was clearly going somewhere. Though they didn't know at the time exactly where, it turned out to be the Far East, in the employment of the Standard Oil Company of New Jersey, which in 1933 merged with the Standard Oil Company of New York (Socony) to form Standard Vacuum, one of the great oil empires of that day or any other. Life at the company compound, high on the "Peak" overlooking the harbor, was festive and formal, the very thing Lottie had dreamed of. All of the homes in the compound had servants. There were cooks, laundresses, gardeners and cleaners, including water coolies who climbed ladders at the back of the houses to change the heavy toilet bowls twice a day. In special care of the children was a certain kindhearted Mrs. Peng, their amah, the only servant the Sanborns felt had genuine loyalty and concern for their well-being. Lottie Sanborn took full advantage of this trust in Mrs. Peng to spend her days in idyllic fashion, reading, playing the piano, and helping to organize the activities, outings and parties for all the families of the compound. Every Wednesday afternoon many of the Peak families (Lottie, Mrs. Peng, the children and Robert, when home, were regulars) clambered aboard the company launch for picnics in the cove with ginger beer, cakes, cookies, swimming, and diving contests from a springboard that Carol invariably won. There was also aquaplaning, yet another thing at which Carol excelled. In addition to the regular Wednesday picnics there were frequent swimming parties at Repulse Bay with its nipa palm dressing-huts, in which on more than several occasions Carol and Paul met in furtive excitement, their innocence slipping away.

And so Carol had free rein. It was, in retrospect, her misfortune to be a little quicker, a little bolder, a bit contemptuous of those around her. Boredom was an insidious, corrosive companion at an early age, its natural correctives, struggle, challenge, abiding passion, lacking. Neither was Carol possessed of a particularly compelling imagination, at least not of the sort to serve as mainstay and primary companion. She was a social child, an extrovert who came alive through contact with others. An expanding force, her very life depended on breaking through the genteel prison of her childhood. Had she not, with Paul's help, encountered alcohol at fifteen, gripping her ever more tightly with time's passing, she might have had a chance.

For fun one day when the rain had stopped Carol and Jack Levine went to a show at *chez Dior* on the right bank, the couturier's mansion on a wide street canopied by grand old trees. After weeks submarining through pluvial Parisian twilights and evenings, walking the warm and sun-dappled sidewalks was like waking from a dream. Pedestrians in this part of the city were marvelously snooty, a mingling of elegance and superior conservatism. Carol and her companion were a mismatched couple, she, fashionable in dress and hat bought in Paris especially for such occasions, and he, in his usual goatherd's costume. There was enough of the snob in Carol to be slightly embarrassed being seen with such a *déclassé* fellow. She had a way of communicating to the men in her life a subtle disapproval, something Jack Levine became quickly aware of but chose to ignore. This was, after all, a dalliance. There was no point in taking things too seriously, a response Carol reacted to with typical ambivalence. She was aware that her snobbery and dissatisfactions were not affecting him, which she respected, but at the same time it was an acknowledgment of the transience of their affair. By not taking her attitudes seriously he was not taking her seriously. He had no intentions of allowing anything emotional to arise between them. Nor did she. But how was she to explain the sadness his stance evoked, a sadness, among many others, salved over and over again by the continual drinking, starting each day promptly after the abysmal photo sessions and lasting throughout the night until passing out on the sculptor's iron bed, barely aware of making love or not.

The show at Dior's was a lark, Jack Levine grudgingly admitted and subject to supercilious disapproval throughout. Carol, with four Bloody Marys under her belt, was amused and delighted to be at the epicenter of the fashion world, even if it was a minor, transitional display. The beautiful people were not fully represented—it lacked the tension and excitement of an important show—but the attitudes and formalism still prevailed. Thin, elegant mannequins walked the runway stiffly to murmurs of approval. In keeping with the mid-season frivolity, samba music played from an ornate wooden console. One of the svelte attendants, dressed in a dark suit and red tie, scratched the record badly at the beginning of one of the runs and an amused censorious ripple passed through the crowd. The mannequins had some trouble getting into the swing of the Latin rhythms while trying to maintain the expected aloof composure. Some did it better than others. A few were bad enough that Carol had to bite her lip to keep from laughing. At this point, her stay in Paris at an end, Carol had given up any ideas of a career as a photographer. She'd been with Jack Levine almost a month and except for the few hours working in the afternoons she'd drunk steadily, drowned by the rain, the feeling of entropy crushing down more forcefully than ever, the damnable conflictions of being with a charming Jewish dry goods merchant posing as a Montparnasse sculptor. From Massapequa, no less! She had no intentions, of course. The whole thing was an irresponsible adventure. After all, Paris was to be enjoyed with a lover, even if a temporary one. Her eyes were wide open. Monsieur Loutrel was an amusing companion and guide. How could one be serious about such a petit bourgeois fellow?

As for Monsieur Loutrel, despite his own open-eyed detachment he found himself increasingly under the spell of this mercurial, complex, inebriate, likely-doomed woman. The two of them, with every intention to the contrary, had arrived at something. The realization of this descended upon them at Dior's when, smiling at the scratched record, they looked at each other and the harsh sound became the ripping of a veil between them, so that they perceived each other not as if for the first time, but in a different way. Surely it was a marvel how two people so dissimilarly placed in the world found themselves by chance together, their multitude of aspects by some alchemy of time, location, and spirit, for the moment, at least, merged in recognition. But what was the nature of this recognition, and was it not again just another illusion? A tympanic resonance of the soul-membrane or mere projection on the blank screen of a stranger one's own cellular longings? The ripping record also dredged up other things. For Jack Levine it was tearing fabric and his family's store in Massapequa and knowing that he would, sooner than later, return, rebelling against the small world of all that it was, but comforted too that it was there, the warmth of home, the tense, exasperating, doughy trap of Jewish love and family. He would find himself a girl and be like his brothers and, thinking that, felt sadness for this woman in front of him on eternal diaspora. Could he not, perhaps, convince her to go back with him for a secure, contentious, stomach-churning Jewish merchant's life together? The absurdity of this made him smile. For Carol, the ripping record was a ripping record, reminding her of the many times she, or others, in drunken states had scratched records trying to set the needle down. It was usually comic but became less so when she discovered recently that it was a difficult task even when sober. She remembered when she'd scratched one of Paul's Bix Beiderbecke records on an afternoon of drinking at his house at the compound and she had laughed and laughed again at his anger until it got out of control. It was days before Paul would speak to her. Half of Phil's records were scratched because of her drunkenness. If a record was a life, a thing of wholeness and beauty—a symphony—then she was the rip across the grain. And this man, tall and serious, looking at her now, really a fine and sensitive man, a solid man, with his steady sculptor's or merchant's hand, molding clay or measuring fabric, cutting cloth, counting change, balancing the books, paying the bills, taking care of her when she was sick, good salty chicken soup with matzo balls, latkes, kissing her warm brow, tucking her in and coming to bed soon after turning off the lights and securing the manor—all these things this man would do, she was certain. Was it the unconscious recognition of these things that prompted her to speak to him at *Le Petit Mirage?* His long fingers were not in the least dishonest; it was she who had chosen to see them as that. She realized now that indeed there was something about this man she had recognized immediately. An alternative. An impossible alternative.

***

Howard Johnson pulled up at exactly four p.m. in a baby blue 1953 Mercury convertible. Carol saw him from her bathroom window on the second floor where she had gone to brush her teeth, remembering she had not done so that day. The only problem was she couldn't find her toothbrush. She searched under the lion-pawed cast iron tub, behind the toilet dubbed Charybdis with its constant gurgling, poking through the dust and cobwebs, behind the sleeping pills (don't wake them!), ointments, and aspirin bottles in the medicine cabinet—to no avail. Giving up, she used Phil's, a beachcomber's treasure with its worn and splayed bristles. If only for some whiskey-flavored toothpaste. She and Mr. Johnson could spend the afternoon brushing their teeth together. The first dab of pink paste fell off the brush and stuck forlornly to the sink bowl close to the drain. She applied another bead, lesser than the first, not bothering to wash its fallen comrade down the drain. It was thus, while brushing her teeth, her lips foaming pink, she spied Howard Johnson pulling into the driveway.

"The saucy fellow!" she exclaimed. Upon her return from town she'd been drinking vodka tonics (new supplies purchased at Bohack's), one after the other. The children were on the beach, the disgruntled Emma standing guard. Howard Johnson rose unsteadily from the white pleated upholstery of his blue convertible and stepped out, grasping the door for support. He was wearing the same outfit, the yellow short-sleeved shirt, blue bathing suit and blue boating shoes and, in addition, a sailor's cap. He stood holding the door of his car and looked down the road from the direction he'd come for several moments, as if checking to see if he'd been followed.

"What a curious fellow," said Carol, watching the toad-like man in his sailor's cap grip the car door while peering down the road. He resembled someone scanning the horizon for a reassuring landmark from the deck of a pitching vessel. Carol emptied her mouth and rinsed twice with tap water, pushing the fallen bit of toothpaste down the drain with her finger. Now she was fortified with the three Ss: Squibb, Smirnoff and Schweppes. She pulled up the window.

"Howard Johnson, ahoy!"

The man turned around and after a moment's search spotted Carol at the window and waved.

"Ahoy there!"

"Come on in, sailor!"

Carol watched amusedly as Howard Johnson's unsteady posture reanimated—almost as if he'd given a little hop—and he slammed the car door and stepped determinedly on his spindly legs towards the front of the house. Her mood was high.

"Welcome to the Leeward Islands, Mr. Johnson!" she shouted, thinking of the approaching hurricane, going down the stairs to greet her peculiar visitor, visibly swaying as he peered through the screen door. Carol proceeded cautiously, gripping the banister. She was almost wildly happy to have this funny, clever, drinking man at her doorstep. She wished for wind and running drunkenly down the beach with Mr. Johnson trailing a couple of dodging kites, collapsing and releasing the swiveling sky-birds into the ether (where would their journey end?), but as she stepped carefully down the stairs the no-wind was dreadfully there, the dull afternoon smothering like a steam-towel. One more reason to exhilarate in the face of demon circumstance. She thought of Phil, probably still working, the people in the city, sweating blood, everything blood.

"Welcome, *mein kapitän*," said Carol, opening the door for her visitor, who touched the bill of his cap and bowed at the waist in his von Stroheim manner.

"Frau Heizer."

She bent forward and pecked him on his puffy red cheek with its road map of venules. They were the same height. He smelled of gin. Clearly delighted by her kiss, he gave a little hop and entered the house. She'd seen correctly. He *had* hopped at his car.

"Do that again and I just might turn into a prince."

"Obviously you are already a prince, Mr. Johnson." Was he aware of his toad-ness? "Please come upstairs and have a tonic and something with me. By the way, I saw you looking down the road. Was somebody following you?"

"Actually, I was afraid a cop might be following. He was parked at Pond Point. I was going a bit fast when I passed him, nothing too outrageous, maybe forty-five. Then again, this hasn't been the soberest of days. I thought for sure he was going to get me."

The two of them trudged up the stairs. Howard Johnson was panting when he reached the top. "Don't worry about the cops," she said. "We give them steaks and booze for Christmas. The chief of police loves my husband. They look alike. They joke about switching jobs."

"Well, I'm jolly lucky then, aren't I?"

Howard Johnson paused at the top of the stairs and looked around the living room while Carol walked ahead. "What does your husband do?"

"He's a fashion photographer. He's got a studio on fifty-fourth street in Manhattan. That's where he is now, no doubt slaving away. I've been drinking vodka tonics. Would you like one? With lemon? You'll become even more prince-like. Maybe we'll go for a swim. Would you like that? I've been thinking of swimming. It's so bloody hot. How do you survive in Brooklyn? Are you a Dodgers' fan? My son adores the Giants. Arch enemies, aren't they? I know nothing about baseball. I'm not a communist though. Are you a communist, Mr. Johnson? What am I saying! How could Howard Johnson be a communist! Did you say yes to that vodka tonic?"

"Yes, a vodka tonic would be delightful."

Howard Johnson walked through the living room in the direction of the bar, where Carol stood mixing their drinks.

"Now, do tell me about those *escargots à la provençale*, Mr. Johnson."

"Please call me Howard."

"Howard."

"The truth is," said Howard Johnson, walking carefully through the living room, looking out the large window at the sea, "I've never had snails in my life." Howard Johnson had been in Germany at the time of Hiroshima and Nagasaki, a private in the Army, part of a detachment that had liberated Buchenwald. After the waste and horror he'd seen in Germany the dropping of the bombs on Japan did an extra bit of damage that never seemed to quite heal. Images of warfare consumed him. Now there were hydrogen bombs. Looking at the sea from the living room he saw the Bikini atoll, the massive column of water, the tiny ships, like toys.

"What a beautiful view you have here," he said, seeing the colossal explosion in his mind's eye. The atoll with its warm waters, colorful, unsuspecting fish, the pristine coral reefs. Try to imagine such a thing right here, in front of this house.

"Yes. But you know when I like it best, Howard? In the winter, when there's nobody here and the wind howls and the snow comes down like death."

Howard Johnson stood next to Carol and accepted the drink she handed him in the plain glass heavy with vodka—the undersized ice cube retrieved from the dwindling supply in the freezer, piece of lemon, dash of tonic mere adjuncts of decorum. This woman would just as soon drink straight from the bottle, as would he.

"To the Dodgers," she said.

"I hate baseball, Mrs. Heizer. But I will drink to your health." They clinked glasses and took hearty swigs. Howard Johnson swirled his drink. Carol looked beyond him, out the window.

"I feel bloody good, Mr. Johnson, don't you? Let's go outside and continue this fascinating conversation. Perhaps we can analyze your aversion to baseball. My oldest boy would look upon you most disfavorably. But it might be worse if you were actually a Dodger fan. This Duke, or Count, or whatever he is, he particularly dislikes."

"That would be Duke Snider."

"Yes, Snider. What sort of name do you suppose that is, Snider? A most disagreeable name, don't you think?"

"I have no idea what sort of name that is. But you know my mother used to say, 'as quick as Jack Robinson,' and now he plays for the Dodgers. I always pictured him as some mischievous little fellow in green pants and striped shirt darting around corners. You could never quite catch him. Apparently, he's just as hard to catch running around the bases."

"Not exactly a little fellow in green pants."

"Not exactly."

At this point Carol recalled Howard Johnson had claimed in Angelica's he bought the *Daily News* for the sports.

"Well now, Mr. Johnson—Howard—if you don't like baseball, what sports do you like?"

"My abiding passions, believe it or not, are hockey and horseracing. There are no greater creatures on this God's earth than Nashua and Gump Worsley. I am also partial to a round of golf now and then. I suppose I would also add Ben Hogan to my list of royal creatures. My temples are Madison Square Garden, Dyker Beach, and Aqueduct."

"Dyker Beach?"

"A Public golf course in Brooklyn. Seventh avenue and eighty-sixth street. Par seventy-one, six thousand-three hundred and seven yards. My best score, ninety-six, two weeks ago."

"Ninety-six is not terribly good, is it, Howard?"

"For me, my dear, it was transcendent. The first time I'd ever broken a hundred. In fact, my best previous score was one hundred and seven. I celebrated for a week. Of course, one of my problems is that I tend to celebrate a bit much, even while playing."

"I don't suppose that helps your score very much."

"No, but it makes the triple-bogeys infinitely more palatable."

"Triple-bogeys, imagine that. How often do you go to the race track?"

"Every Thursday during the season. I never miss."

Howard Johnson and Carol finished their drinks while talking and Carol mixed two more. There certainly was something about this man that delighted Carol. He certainly was odd.

"Do you bet?"

"You bet your life I bet. I've lost several fortunes at the wet duck."

"The wet duck?"

"Aqueduct. The high point though was losing five hundred dollars on Native Dancer two years ago at the Kentucky Derby. It was worth it. I fulfilled a lifelong dream going to the Kentucky Derby. Every Moslem needs to go to Mecca. For me it was the Kentucky Derby. Of course, I barely remember a thing."

Carol handed Howard Johnson his drink and led him by the hand through the dining room to the deck. They were both rather drunk, and happy in each other's presence. There was no breeze. The sun, westering, a dull Moloch pressing down on them. The wet duck. Silly. Still, a clever fellow.

"I doubt I would remember a thing if I went to the Kentucky Derby either. Phil is interested in race horses. He and one of his associates talk about buying a horse. Jesus, it's bloody hot. I suppose better here than Brooklyn. No offense, Mr. Johnson." It seemed so natural to call him "Mr. Johnson."

"Not at all."

They sat on the canvas chairs at the round table under the umbrella. The usual fishing boats were gone, the ocean a simmering metallic soup, the flittering pipers, restive and shrill at cooler hours, subdued by the heat. A lone gull tugged at something by the water. The boys and Emma were not in sight.

Thank goodness for that, thought Carol. If only they were not here at all. It was too much.

"Is your name really Howard Johnson, or have you taken it on to better identify with this marvelous culture you seem to love so?"

"I'm afraid Howard Johnson is a very common name. There were twenty-eight in the Brooklyn directory alone the last time I counted. It has proven to be of no use whatsoever, not even for a free cup of coffee in one of those abysmal restaurants. As for this culture you seem to think I'm so enamored of, it's the New York Rangers, horseracing, and a round of golf now and again. That's about it. You can have the rest of it. Except for Kurt Weill. The only civilized person in the universe—well, he and Gump Worsley, that is."

"Well, I'm not inclined to disagree about Kurt Weill. His music is marvelous. But this Worsley fellow I'm not so sure about."

"The Gumper? Oh, you must see the Gumper! He's the goaltender for the New York Rangers. Rookie of the year in 1953. Five-foot-seven inches of pure poetry. A prince in pads. A penguin with a purpose."

"I wonder if he likes Kurt Weill?"

"Who knows? Anything's possible with the Gumper. I'm certain though that if Kurt Weill had ever seen Gump Worsley play he'd have written an opera for him. Brecht would love him. They look alike. He has this wonderful quality. He's completely engaged."

"I suppose he'd better be."

"I mean more than just while the game is being played. I love to watch him while there's a lull in the action. He's observant of everything. He converses with the fans, he cleans the ice, adjusts his equipment, talks with players, talks with the referees—and all with this quality of absolute awareness. I suspect he must be extremely intelligent. And then he has lapses—you know, the game is so fast I don't know if it's fair to call them lapses. There'll be a flurry and whoosh! the puck goes by him in an instant, you can't even see it. And you don't know if the Gumper was napping just for a second or if no human being could have possibly stopped that puck. These things go a hundred miles an hour, you know. And what's so wonderful is that in those moments the Gumper is everyman. You really see that he's five-foot-seven and just a bit dumpy. Gump. Dumpy. Because when he's playing brilliantly you don't see that. What you see is an acrobat, a ballet dancer, a wizard, a philosopher. But when he fails, and that would be about three times per game—it would be less if the Rangers had better defensemen—we all love him a bit more, in spite of our disappointment. He's all of us, he's everyman. The Gumper."

How odd to be talking about an ice hockey goalie in August under the demented sun with a perfect stranger. What a curious man!

"My dear Mr. Johnson, I somehow get the feeling there is more to you than sports. What do you do for a living? Forgive my crass curiosity, but you strike me as an interesting man."

"Believe me, I'm of no interest whatsoever. I'm ashamed to say that I'm a failed writer and have abused what little creative talent I have to eke out a living writing advertising copy. I'm a very small person in a very small Brooklyn firm very far away from Madison Avenue. My latest masterpiece was writing an ad for the Circle Line Statue of Liberty ferry. I expect if you have occasion to wait in the doctor's office you might find it in a recent *National Geographic*."

"How wonderful you're not in television. Putting dreadful words in Betty Furness' mouth or some godawful thing like that. Detergent jingles. How very noble and literary to write Circle Line ads. It's rather Homeric, I think."

"Yes, an odyssey on the Circle Line. Every man an Odysseus. Come home to Penelope after a trip on the Circle Line. Or take her with you! Splendid. My dear woman, you are the one who should be writing ads for the Circle Line."

In fact, several years ago, before her trip to Paris, Carol had written brief, witty fashion articles for *Park East*, a short-lived publication of breezy sophistication that billed itself as "the magazine of New York." Like so many hopeful newborns, it lost its way in the city's raptorial canyons. There was a brief silence. Then Carol spoke.

"I think the war robbed us of the ability to laugh."

"I think it's life that does that, but there are a few things to make it amusing at least, on occasion."

"Like Gump Worsley?"

"Gump Worsley is God."

"Noel Coward is God."

"Ben Hogan is God."

They raised their glasses.

"To Worsley."

"To Coward."

"To Hogan."

"Worsley, Coward, and Hogan. Sounds like a law firm," said Carol.

"Or an ad agency."

"Or an undertaker's firm."

"Now my dear, let's not be morbid. Drink up and let's get a couple more."

They rose shakily from their chairs and turned in the direction of the bar.

"We mustn't forget Kurt Weill," said Carol. "He's God too."

"And Bertolt Brecht. We mustn't forget Bertolt Brecht."

"My God, I think you must be a communist. How do you get from Glump Worsley to Bertolt Brecht?"

"Oh dear. It's not Glump, it's Gump. As for getting from Gump to Bertolt, every moderately-informed New Yorker knows that Gump Worsley went to see *The Threepenny Opera* last winter. He enjoyed it immensely. Besides, they look alike."

"Oh, you can't tell me that Glum Parsely or Plump Ghastly, or whatever his silly Canadian name is, ever went to see, much less enjoy, *The Threepenny Opera*. Please, Mr. Johnson, I simply will not swallow those escargots."

"Well, it's quite possible he went. I know I did. At least I think I did."

Carol surveyed the beach. There were people about but in her condition it was difficult to determine if Emma and the boys were among them. Everything was distant. This was the preferred way. This funny little man standing next to her also looking at the beach was distant too. But close enough to enjoy. As long as he kept the correct distance. He made certain of that on his own account. The beach was very much out of focus. It seemed people were just walking around. Aimless, half-naked beach. People found their own amusements. Anything to continue putting one foot in front of the other. She looked down at her feet and thought of the piece of glass. It was still in there, somewhere. She was slightly splayfooted. Always had been. Feet were ridiculous things. No pain from the glass.

"Shall we get another?" said Howard Johnson. He'd been watching her, sensing her drift away. She was drunker than he was. He amused her, he knew. He amused lots of people. This was his job, to amuse people. If only he could amuse himself. This woman was not amusing. She carried some ineffable burden. Hard to say what it was. She hadn't seen what he'd seen. The parchment sacks of bone shuffling in their miserable filthy cotton striped camp uniforms, beseeching, tugging, screaming noiselessly like an imprisoned tribe of Munchs. And could anyone ever understand the stench, having never experienced it? It hit them more than a mile from the place. The wind carried it. Buchenwald. As if what lay ahead were a passageway to hell, opened up amidst the destruction and carnage that lay now commonplace. Amazing what one could be conditioned to. War was quite literally hell, certainly, but also a historical commonplace. One rarely, perhaps never, had occasion to see and smell the distillation of evil as had Howard Johnson and the men he accompanied as they trudged reluctantly towards the rictus of the death camp, as if it were a sulfurous cave that led them to a confrontation with something they'd known all along but never admitted. War was beastly and horrible and a tragic capitulation to baser means—but the reality of the death camps was a horror and shame they wished not to face. The Germans, like they, were human.

In particular there was the nightmare of the children. One tugged silently at his leg, a boy of indeterminate age, very small. Perhaps he was 12, but he looked like an old man. He dropped to his knees and put his arms carefully around the creature, a thing of bones and hair and cotton as ragged and insubstantial as if he were embracing smoke or a column of decaying threads, and though he did not sob or moan or manifest any of the audible and honored signals of grief and sympathy, the tears ran down his face like water seeping from a fissure in a canyon wall. All this in silence, a silence so dreadful and unmitigated that it became at the same time holy, as if the patient and all-knowing angels hovered above them. There could not be, it seemed to Howard Johnson, something so dark as this without its complement of light nearby, or perhaps closer, perhaps immediately present, *immanent.* At least he hoped so. At the same time that he felt this he also knew that he would never recover from it, that his life would be made less durable from it, as if some cane cutter of prodigious strength had hacked away a piece of him.

"Yes, let's do get another," answered Carol.

II

At twenty thousand feet she flies above the hurricane's eye, the little plane bobbing like a petrel on the cyclone's crown. She feels the tugging at its skin, the world below succumbed to a riot of magnetic forces, pulling and pushing at the underbelly of her vessel. Gasping, she reaches for the oxygen mask, an elephant's snout, and pulls the straps of barbed wire over her head. She breathes, feels the barbs piercing her skin, hears the storm whispering. In the mirror the elephant face turns into her father and the little plane plummets a thousand feet towards the storm before she can gain control, gripping tightly, the troubled currents bouncing the plane, its wings flexing, the plane itself elastic, the storm's susurrations louder, more insistent. The image in the mirror is replaced by that of a young girl with scratches on her face as if scored by twigs and branches—she has fallen from a tree—and now she notices the cut on the girl's chin and the crying, tears flowing down the mirrored face and pooling in her own lap, a great warmth and relaxing, the source from underneath the plane, from the eye of the hurricane, a massive upwelling of humid breath, a whirling cauldron-beast calm in the middle breathing into her sex, and miles below, the blue ocean, placid but for the innocent blooms of white that she knows are the crests of one-hundred-foot waves, waves that await her. The great eye stretches below, a blue amphitheater fifty miles across, the walls of the hurricane swirling counter-clockwise two hundred, three hundred miles an hour, impossible speeds. All at once she is aware of how weary she is, and of the sadness that emanates from the moist spiraling surge of the eye, enveloping her plane in grief. The storm is aware of her, whispering, pulling her down.

Now a shock hurls the plane sideways and she cries out, fighting to gain control, skidding over the dizzying abyss of the eye as if her plane were sliding on a tongue of ice, flinging out over the blue chasm. The horizon pitching, she fights and cries for help, cries for her children. Hurtling across the blue eye she is pinned flat, unable to move anything but her eyes, helplessly taking in this unreasonable turn of events. She gives a low, frightened moan and the plane catapults into space and all goes weightless in the cockpit. She floats to the top, bumps her head and begins to somersault, watching through a hole in the bottom of the plane the planet slipping away. For a moment, a peacefulness envelopes her. But then she sees, outside, her children seated at a large console with glowing blue dials and intricate, looping antennas, intently eating cereal from an oversized bowl. The cereal and milk float above the bowl and the children are biting at it like animals, wearing their blue bathing suits with the white piping. She grasps a handle to steady herself and knocks on the cockpit, but the glass is yielding, putty-like, and makes no sound, retaining the imprint of her knuckles. She cries out. The children don't look, nibbling at the floating mass like delicate pronghorn or impala, secure for the moment, but they would fly at the first hint, the smallest disturbance.

Now she is afraid of the hole at the bottom of the plane, of falling through and being sucked into the hurricane. Though the planet is far away and moving quickly, the storm's whirling, centrifugal force is palpable, more powerful where the hole is, as things fall through and slip away in a stream, food, tools, white detergent spilling from boxes, smudging the darkness. Outside, the children are gone. She begins to close the hole at the bottom of the plane by turning a crank attached to her ribcage, but not before some object that has traveled inside the length of her body dislodges itself from her foot and shoots back to earth in a glistening line. This brings a momentary sense of relief: something dangerous has been expelled. But she understands that her troubles are about to multiply and, directly, pieces of the plane begin tearing away. Her children, somehow part of the plane, cartwheel back to earth, calling out as they fall. The crank detaches from her side and floats in the cockpit, pulling a hemp-like cord from her body. She feels herself diminishing as the line pays out, and she attempts to break it with her hands, gnaws at it, to no avail. The plane is shuddering and more pieces fall away with ripping noises. The tail section flies off, leaving a ragged opening in the cockpit that she stuffs with crumpled sheets of newspaper. The plane drops. She is terrified that the newspapers will fall out, but behind them is a curved, rusty surface. She is inside a barrel, with handles, which she grasps. The barrel tumbles in the direction of the storm. She can't see anything. Yanking on one of the handles she crawls through an opening into the back of her station wagon, which is spinning in the darkness. It is night and the car is a thousand feet above the sea, buffeted by the winds, falling, windshield wipers clocking back and forth, motor rumbling, the dials of the dashboard bathing the interior in cobalt. Rain batters the windshield. She struggles to get to the wheel, crawling over the seats. The car is at the surface, the black cresting waves rising above her. She is at the wheel, driving. Something is behind her, gaining. She pushes the accelerator to the floor, trying to escape. A light flashes, illuminating the waves, a deep translucent emerald, the patterns of the foam pulsing like veins. The thing behind overtakes the car, silent, fast, towers a hundred feet above her, then, underwater, sinking towards a distant light at the bottom of the sea.

Lying in bed Carol listened to the rhythm of the crickets, a steady undulating line that filled the morning darkness with consciousness: cricket consciousness. How vile the jabberings of humans compared to this purity. Really, there was only one message in life and the crickets expressed it eloquently. How had we missed it? The blessed crickets' call submerged by our own riotous babble. God gave us crickets and we trod them under foot. She imagined the great crackling web of communication alive at that very moment, fabulous radio waves in a thousand tongues skipping around the world, ship to shore, continent to continent, person to person, crazed, supersonic, incessant. On one level, thought Carol, this was our own cricket-call. In spite of the cacophony, the yearning, even heartbreaking attempts at communication were a kind of ultimate symphony. Yet, what a din! You couldn't hear the forest for the trees. Drifting out over the abyss what was left was the steady music of the crickets and the steady beating of her own heart, the pulsing of two billion hearts, the faithful forgotten rituals of circulation and respiration. She thought of the whirling craziness of Hong Kong, the glass moving up her leg. She heard the train sounding from across the bay, shuttling back and forth, Montauk to Manhattan, Manhattan to Montauk, trailing its plangent call, adding its own voice to the others, the crickets, the radio waves, the beating hearts. And now the sky dimly waking from the east. If only the nights were longer, she might be able to think. But there was never enough time. The days advanced on top of themselves. There was a wild, headlong out-of-control quality to her life and at the same time a dreadful collapse, as if she were rushing madly along like some mid-town express but utterly devoid of anything resembling purpose, or energy. A terrible fear would remind her of where she was heading. These were the few moments, just before dawn, when the world cooled down just a bit. She lay feeling her leg throbbing in rhythm with the crickets, the gentle thump and wash of the waves.

As now the case each morning, Carol had difficulty remembering the evening, or even the day, before. How had she ended up in her bed? Had there been sex? There was an unusual feeling of, not happiness, but warmth, somehow, in association with the previous day's blurred memory. Ah, the funny man, Howard Johnson. What a ridiculous name. They were very drunk. The children were frightened. Emma took care of them, thank God. How Emma must hate her. Some vague recollection of Howard Johnson and his dreadful experiences in the war, poor man. He'd gone down to the beach and walked into the water fully clothed for his, what did he call it, ritual of purification—and how she'd followed him into the ocean proclaiming her own ritual, whatever it was.

The feeling from the dream came back and Carol was frightened. She pulled the sheet up to her chin and stared at the familiar patterns on the ceiling. There was the necromancer with his crooked beak. When she had decided that particular shape to be a necromancer she couldn't recall. And just what the hell was a necromancer anyway? Something to do with reading the signs of death. Next to it the hammer with the spot of blood. Howard Johnson had cried after going into the water. She was afraid that he was going to drown himself when he swam out quite far and she'd followed him certain that even in her state she was a stronger swimmer than he and that she could save him. They talked of drowning together and it was only partly joking. That's when the children appeared with Emma on the shore and cried out to her, knowing that she was in the condition that so distressed them, Mark crying, Eddie on the verge of tears, and she angrily yelling at them to go away. A dreadful scene ensued where Emma used her iron strength, gripping their small wrists and pulling them back to the house as they cried and pleaded for their mother. All that Carol wanted was for them to go away and leave her alone, and when Emma had dragged them halfway to the house and Eddie broke free and ran back to the shore, calling for her, a small figure waving his arms and mouthing desperate entreaties she heard only dimly, she fought the impulse to swim ashore and beat him and instead swam farther out in the ocean that was warm like bathwater, so that he became very small and silent and she watched as Emma came up and snatched his wrist again, this time succeeding in forcing them to the house and out of her sight.

She remembered little after that, vaguely recalling a long, agitated walk west to Moriches inlet, the sand like hard wet cement flowing beneath them. She had a sense of walking on a treadmill and everything around her moving, this strange but sympathetic man letting loose beside her, now relating more images of horror, perhaps from the war, she could barely tell, now laughing maniacally at the small absurdities of his own existence and the larger ones of the world, now opening up the secret compartments of his life that seemed to reveal—again, she could hardly tell, given her condition—the most harrowing emptiness, now railing against the usual agents of venality and worse, the politicians, sellouts, hucksters, red-baiters and so-on, and once or twice in the middle of some harangue or other he stopped speaking and began to cry for no apparent reason other than it was just in him, a reservoir of grief that simply spilled over, as if the intake of alcohol had raised the level of sorrow, causing it to overflow.

Carol tried only half-heartedly to follow Howard Johnson's extraordinary monologue. She was way too drunk to make sense of much that he said. She did feel however the strength of him, the reality of his experience. In some ways Howard Johnson was a kindred spirit—certainly a fellow drinker—but in other ways he was not. There was an animating force in him that she did not possess. In spite of his suffering and all that he had seen, there was something that kept him going, more than simply the will to survive. Look at the way he dressed. A sailor's cap, no less! Why did he wear such a thing? Surely a sense of absurdity, which he had in abundance. But was it also a bit of vanity? Nobody wore things they felt made them look ridiculous or ugly. So there was vanity. She had her share, always careful to wear the right clothes, to make sure her appearance was up to snuff—now there was a word—though God knew she looked a dreadful mess lately. Well, Howard Johnson had a vanity that was endearing. The fashion world was the essence of vanity. How disgusting, really. Though she took whimsical delight in its absurdity. But there was this deadly serious obsession with style, appearance, class—money. Howard Johnson had something else. She could think of nothing else to call it but spirit—the breath of life that was but the merest of dusty whisperings in her. He had it, though he was engaged in the systematic business of shutting it off. With alcohol. Out of control, now. He was one of those rare characters whose spirit obstinately persisted. Maybe he was born with a stronger dose than others, only to be doused with the disease. Would Howard Johnson live to see forty? Would she?

Carol recalled returning from the beach with Howard Johnson, well into the evening. Upon reaching the inlet and deciding they'd become too sober, they'd walked down Dune Road and had several gin and tonics at a small weekenders' club, *The Whitecap*, Howard Johnson paying with soggy bills pulled from a wallet engorged with seawater. She remembered a quiet house with one dim light burning in the living room and the children retreated to their rooms with the door closed (Emma in the room next to them, her door also closed), carefully stepping down the stairs with Howard Johnson so as not to attract the children's attention and walking to his blue Mercury with its gleaming white upholstery. Say good-bye to Howard. Howard Johnson. Would she ever see him again? Funny drunken man full of sorrow. Somehow, she'd gotten into bed, though she remembered nothing of it. And then the terrible dream followed by the still and warming morning, thinking of nothing and all things, feeling as if she were sinking into a soft, endlessly receding hole and then, a knocking on the door, firm knocking, not a child's knocking, and the morning was warm and it was later, much later, some leap of hours here, thinking, and then, Emma's voice, informing her that she could take no more, that she was gone, leaving, finished, the cab already on its way.

Carol lay quietly, staring up at the ceiling. They were jumping ship on her. And who could blame them? A slow panic began to rise, like an incoming tide bringing dead animals. She heard the heavy steps going down, the pause at the landing, the front door opening and the screen door slamming. And so, this chocolate brown stranger was out of her life. She never liked Emma, and she didn't know her. There was something like doom however, in her leaving. And now the whole day with nothing to stand between her and the children. Another impossibility. There wasn't a hope of her going through the day and remaining sober. She thought of tying them up or locking them in their rooms. She could see how it could come to that. Angelica would read about her in the *National Enquirer*. A car pulled into the driveway and Carol pictured Emma walking in her stolid manner towards the cab, gripping a suitcase in her strong fleshy brown hand, probably sweating, trying to imagine if the driver would get out to help. There was a long pause and then three shutting noises, the first the muffled sound of the trunk and then the crunching finality of the two doors. Long day's journey into night. Then came the sound of the cab backing out of the driveway, another pause, and then driving off and Emma was gone, relieved, thought Carol, and never looking back, down the road of these white summer people with their rich homes and golden tans. Emma would be thinking ahead to the city and her own struggles, the bouncing gritty ride into the stewpot of Manhattan, the subway uptown to the projects. And then? More work for the same distant, superior whites, resentful and growing bitter with each passing year girdled in her white uniform waiting on Mr. and Mrs. and their alien children. Carol felt sorry for Emma, but within a minute the brown woman from South Carolina was out of her thoughts and she found herself staring at a ceiling that was moving. The fabled necromancer nodded his head and the beak, already attenuated, stretched even further and there appeared small dark spots moving in the nostrils. So, now we are here, she thought. The dots multiplied and swarmed, threatening to drop from the ceiling, onto her. A cold fear swept up her back and out to the tips of her fingers. She sought to reassure herself: This can't be. I'm not even drunk. She managed a certain detachment. The dots swarmed across the ceiling, covering the menacing face. There was no question of their existence and yet she knew she was producing them. Jesus Christ, I've got the D.T.'s. The fucking screaming meemies. And indeed, she did want to scream, and fought the impulse. Nonetheless a moan pushed its way up her throat and through her clenched teeth. She knew the dots— the bugs, the ants, whatever they were—were not real, but Carol felt their numbers increasing and she flung the sheets aside and wrenched herself out of bed and stood against the door, rubbing her eyes, producing fantastically-hued bubbles bursting behind her eyelids. She sensed the dots dropping in clumps onto the bed and spilling over the side to the floor. With her eyes shut she groped for the glass knob and yanked the door open and closed it behind her. Standing in the living room, her eyes still closed, Carol yearned for Emma's return, for the cab to turn around, for the brown woman to come back to take care of her and the children, downstairs in their rooms, now at the mercy of whatever angels might watch over them. Cautiously, Carol took her hands from her face, opened her eyes and looked at the crack beneath the bedroom door. Nothing. The house was still. She stood quiet and without clothes. A lone bird's delicate song sounded outside like crystal, the same three notes over and over, as if the release of an auditory spirit of something precious, now shattered. In a minute the bird ceased singing or had flown away.

Phil awoke unusually early for a Sunday morning. The day before he'd worked until seven-thirty in the studio, a tense and sweltering day with balky air-conditioning, high-strung models, an incompetent darkroom man hired for the day who ruined a crucial set of negatives that had to be re-shot, sending Phil into a rage, the phone ringing off the hook with nervous, harrying clients, his ulcerated stomach feeling like a sack-full of razor blades, his blood to the boiling point with worries of the money lost on this jinxed account, and always, gnawing at the back of his mind in the circus of his involvements, Carol and the children.

He went directly after work to the *Black Angus* on 50th Street, walking slowly down First Avenue, working off the strain of the day in measured steps, breathing deeply, letting the approaching evening work its way with him, trying to settle down. He walked past his own block on 51st Street and headed west on 50th. The shift in the city's energy soothed him and as he crossed Third Avenue the thought of the restaurant looming ahead, a quiet haven of scotch and good meat, leavened his spirits. He was a regular customer at the *Black Angus*—at least once a week—and he knew he'd be given a good table and preferential treatment. He'd taken a bath on this last assignment. But then it was fortunate the whole goddamned place hadn't burned down. The insurance would cover the electrical problems. Maybe he'd break even on the job. It was okay. He had all the work he wanted and more. Too much work. All that was fine. He was one of the best, no question. The agencies were always looking to get Phil Heizer to shoot for them. Knock 'em dead, Phil. He had this town by the balls. Imagine that. To stroll into the *Black Angus,* order a couple of scotch on the rocks, a shrimp cocktail, some lamb chops or a prime cut of red meat with a salad or some fresh garden peas, or maybe the asparagus vinaigrette salad. He was entitled. And all of it would be good but for the trouble of his wife and children. Something always there to knock you down a few pegs. He didn't know what to do with her and he foresaw nothing but tragedy. He wished he could escape it, somehow. The woman's troubles were beyond him. He'd tried, in his way. Jesus, life was hard enough.

Clarence, the short, light-skinned Negro *maître d'*, showed him to his favorite corner table in the dark, air-conditioned restaurant, busy with murmuring customers feeding on their meat and baked potatoes. Phil would not order the baked potato. He did order a double scotch on the rocks right away, Cutty Sark, drank it quickly, and then ordered a single. With the drinks he relaxed, loosened his tie a bit, and surveyed the room. The drinks braced him, insulating his concerns for the moment. He felt comfortable here, in company with others who were in some sense very much like him, more than mere survivors in this crucible that had been home all of his life. He was proud of his strength and resourcefulness. The pressure of the place brought out the essentials. A couple of tables away sat friends he hadn't noticed in the dim interior. The woman ran one of the largest modeling agencies in the city and was respected as decent and highly competent. For being head of such a glamorous enterprise she was aggressively ordinary in appearance, not uncommon among the bigwigs of the fashion world. But her qualities, those essentials the city brought forth, transformed her plainness into something appealing, if not attractive. Her husband was a very American guy who looked like English royalty, tall, pleasant, dark-haired, always formally attired, and a bit dull. He had some real estate dealings and served as a quiet factotum for his wife. They were a nice couple, good friends, and Phil liked them. They noticed each other at the same time and exchanged warm smiles and discreet pleasantries, and then retreated to their privacy.

Phil ordered shrimp cocktail, lamb chops, and the asparagus vinaigrette salad. The heat and tension of the day had drained his appetite but he finished his food, something he always did, and with it two glasses of red wine. His friends were still eating when he got up to leave, and he stopped briefly at their table to make light of his troubled day, which indeed, he had already begun to forget. None of the models had been from his friend's agency. Phil and her husband spoke vaguely of playing tennis soon in Westhampton. He glanced at the clock on the dark wall as he left the restaurant. It was eight forty-five.

The day's fiasco was memory. At least the job had been finished and the pictures decent enough. Not great, but decent. The evening heat pressed around him as he walked to the brownstone on 51st Street. He dreaded it, but he would have to call Carol. He should have been out there, with her, helping with the children. In all likelihood he would have to drive out in the morning and then return to the city that evening. He had an assignment at nine o'clock, which meant arriving at the studio at eight. The streets were quiet for a Saturday night. A cab and red convertible had scraped fenders on Second Avenue and the two men were talking quietly and exchanging information. It seemed too hot and the wrong hour to get worked up. In a matter of minutes Phil was opening the door to his apartment, which occupied the first and second floor of the brownstone he'd bought five years ago. In forty-eight years he'd moved less than two miles northeast in the city, but it might as well have been another planet. The apartment was cool and dark. He turned on the green-shaded lamp on his desk and, drawing a deep breath, dialed the Westhampton number with his left fore-finger, gripping the receiver tightly against his ear. The ensuing conversation with Emma confirmed his fears but also reassured him: Though Carol had been drunk most of the day and all evening in the company of a man who was a stranger to Emma, she'd gone to her room after the stranger had left and as far as Emma knew, was sleeping soundly. The children were okay.

Phil didn't pretend to understand the troubling labyrinth that was his wife's behavior, and his response was to retreat further into his own enterprises, his developing career, serious investments in the stock market, the formation of a Potemkin real estate company for tax purposes that he called "Arol Reality" (after his wife, which she quickly dubbed with her usual wit, with a bit of Orientalism thrown in for good measure, "No C Realty"), the enlargement of his modest but respectable art collection. Fashion photography was taking off and Phil Heizer right along with it. He considered himself among the handful of best in the city. As his wife's troubles multiplied so did the extent of his avoidance, nicely disguised by the legitimacy and demands of his pursuits. And everything he did was justified by the fact that it made money or was in the nature of investment and would someday yield results. He worked himself hard and was generous in meeting his financial responsibilities. But he knew that while no one could fault him for what he provided his family, the other side of being a husband and parent fairly overwhelmed him, especially the job of trying to deal emotionally with his wife, the volatile, insistent demands of her darkening life.

Not only had Phil awakened early for a Sunday morning— it was seven o'clock—he'd slept poorly, in fact, hardly at all. It was clear that his wife was fast losing ground. There was no alternative but to go out to the island and somehow take control of the situation. But how? He dreaded the thought of another commitment, a repeat of the trauma three years ago when Carol had returned from Paris in a severely depressed state, drinking excessively, culminating in a scene at a friend's house on a full-mooned, ill-begotten November evening, Carol drunk and out of control with a rambling monologue of alien visitations followed by an embarrassing denunciation of Phil, and then the violence, the glass-breaking and threatened suicide.

Carol had to be subdued that evening until she finally calmed down, and Monday morning, before Phil went to work, the doorbell rang and Phil greeted Dr. Campbell from the East Hill Sanatorium, a private institution located in a small town on Long Island about halfway between the city and Westhampton. Dr. Campbell, absurdly looking the part of the earnest, tweedy, pipe-smoking psychiatrist, a little older than she, perhaps forty, bearded, just the right degree of dishevelment (my Van Helsing, thought Carol, come to rid me of the twin-headed vampire of alcohol and madness), invited Carol to sit with him at the dining room table, a choice with less clinical associations than the couch in the living room, for which Carol marked a point in his favor. Phil, without being invited, joined them. It was, of course, Phil's decision to call Dr. Campbell and, unbeknownst to Carol, it had already been decided that she be committed. Carol, depressed and still shaken from the madness at their friend's house two evenings before, much of which she could not remember, succumbed wearily to the gentle therapeutic murmur emanating from the psychiatrist, his words washing over her like some pacific but inevitable force. She barely listened, resigned to let things go where they may, understanding the import of what was happening, however, with the sharpest clarity. Dr.

Campbell was there to take her away. She didn't particularly mind. A few days might be okay, though not drinking would be difficult. Halfway through his spiel Carol cut the psychiatrist short, announcing that she was ready to go and saying also that wherever it was that she was being taken she wished to stay no longer than three days, and that she would like a drink before she left. Phil made her a rye and soda. The psychiatrist said that they would try to accommodate her wishes but that there could be no guarantees. Carol felt curiously happy and relieved.

Carol spent two weeks at East Hill Sanatorium, chain-smoking, medicated, staring solemnly through her window at the late-autumnal trees and the grass hill covered with brown and yellow leaves, sloping towards the institution, and in the background, mostly obscured by the trees, the top of a water tower with the letters ILLE discernible. She went for a session in Dr. Campbell's office every other day, accompanied by a large Negro woman in a white uniform who called her "honey," and grasped her gently by the arm, as if guarding against escape. Carol allowed the woman to guide her, disinterestedly aware of herself shuffling down the brightly-lit hallway in her green terrycloth hospital gown and ludicrous fluffy pink slippers. Her feet and hands perspired all the time but the rest of her was continually cold, a chattering affliction of the marrow she could not escape. Dr. Campbell was sincere and intelligent, but their talks never made much headway. Perhaps it was the pills they gave her. She couldn't seem to think very well. Time passed as a shivering, muddled dream. She tried writing letters but was never able to get beyond three or four sentences. There were books on shelves in the hallway that were of no interest. At any rate she lacked the concentration. She had little conception of time and no appetite for anything but sweets. When Phil visited on the weekend she felt nothing, as if he were a vaguely-remembered colleague, and when after thirteen days he came to take her home she felt no emotion but a subtle tightening of her stomach and a *soupçon* of dread at the bottom of her feet, as if she were walking across a chasm on a layer of glass.

Phil knew that this time things were worse with his wife. He decided to call Dr. Campbell and reserve a room for her at East Hill. She wouldn't go so willingly. He might have to sedate her, somehow. He arose wearily in the cool darkness of his bedroom, the hum of the air-conditioner filling him with unease. Four days ago he'd marked his forty-eighth birthday by himself (Carol and the boys had called in the morning and together sang happy birthday) with dinner at *La Cave Henri IV*, on 52nd Street. He'd had his usual pre-dinner scotches and ordered filet mignon brochette, rare, and a couple of glasses of the house red wine. Sitting by himself in the close, candle-lit restaurant he reflected on the irony of his success. The more money he made, it seemed, the less control he had over his life. It would not be so, he decided, but for the stubbornly self-destructive ways of Carol. But he hadn't the wherewithal to cope with it. He admitted his weakness. Thank God he had the money, at least, to try to make up for his shortcomings. This was much of what drove him. His whole life was about survival, the challenge to show the world— and the world was New York City—that he, Phil Heizer, son of parents who'd met in steerage, the small tailor from Lublin who devotedly read the Talmud in all of his spare moments, and the gentle woman from Pinsk who died soon after he was born (to be replaced by a virago who adopted an unrelenting, unreasoning dislike of Phil from the moment she entered the household), was as good as any man and better than most, and if you doubted it he'd knock you down to make sure you understood. This was a difficult burden, this attitude, but it had defined him since he began to work at the age of eleven, his entire earnings from a job loading bins in a vegetable store at six a.m. before going to school handed over to his scowling step-mother. At 18 he'd reached the city Golden Gloves quarterfinals as a welterweight. One provided for one's own and asked for nothing.

***

Eddie awoke first, hearing the screen door close, the car idling in the driveway, the slamming of the trunk and doors and the driving away. It was unusual and troubling. He thought it might be his mother. It spoke to his biggest fear, this going away. She always talked about it, threatened it. Mark was asleep on his back, his head turned sharply to the side as if having received a blow, his left leg thrust outside the covers. Eddie lay listening to the quiet house and the bird just outside his window trilling the same three notes over and over. Then the bird noise stopped and there was a shuffling upstairs and he heard his mother's door shut. He got out of bed and went into the bathroom and tried the door to Emma's room. It was unlocked. He opened it cautiously and saw a carefully made bed in a barren room. He realized that the car had taken Emma away but this abrupt leaving was puzzling. Maybe she was going for her days off, but why would she take all her things? He opened the closet and it was empty. Some part of him was aware that Emma had gone away, that he might never see her again, but this wasn't easy to understand. She'd been with them for a long time. How could she just be gone? He didn't like Emma and was a little afraid of her, but this going away made him feel like something was wrong, that the house was now very empty, and that he and Mark were alone.

Eddie knew his mother was in her room. He wanted breakfast but was afraid to go upstairs. He went into the bathroom and peed, pulling aside the leg of his bathing suit. Mark stirred. Eddie flushed the toilet and went to the head of his brother's bed, looking down at him. Mark opened his eyes.

"Get up. Emma's gone. Let's make breakfast."

"Where's mommy?" asked Mark.

"She's in her room. Sleeping, I think." Eddie knew his mother was probably awake but it seemed better to tell Mark that she was sleeping. He hoped that she really was asleep. Sleep meant that they possessed her and that they were safe from the ways she'd been acting. Yesterday evening was even worse than being slapped. She had swum so far out it seemed she might disappear. She was with the man from Angelica's. Howard Johnson. And then Emma dragging them away, a brute force he would have destroyed if he were capable. The overwhelming powerlessness and fear they felt. It was better to have been slapped. At least then mommy was there, as mean as she was and as much as it hurt. With her so far out in the ocean with a strange man and Emma pulling them away it was like a nightmare where there was nothing you could do because everything was so much stronger. And it was worse because mommy had her clothes on, like the man. He thought he heard movement in her room.

"Come on. Get up. I'll make us some cereal."

Mark rubbed his eyes, got out of bed, and padded to the bathroom. Eddie went to the foot of the stairs and listened. Then they went upstairs to the kitchen. Their cereal bowls, spoons, drinking glasses and straws were on the table, with a box of Cheerios, the same way Emma always had things in the morning. This made Eddie think that she'd just be away for a little while. But why was everything gone in her room? Eddie told Mark to get the milk. Mark went to the refrigerator and brought the cold bottle to the table with both hands and then he turned and shut the door. Eddie shook cereal into both of their bowls and then, holding his hand over the top of the bottle, stopped with its paper lid, shook it up and down several times to mix the cream. Mark sat watching him as he poured the milk into the bowls.

"Where did Emma go?" asked Mark.

"I don't know. Maybe she went on her day off to the city. Do you want some toast?"

"Uh huh."

Eddie went to the metal bread bin and retrieved a loaf of Wonder Bread with its colorful circles that reminded him of circus balloons or clowns, set it next to the toaster and fetched a stick of butter and some grape jelly from the refrigerator.

"Get some orange juice," said Mark, his mouth full of Cheerios and a runnel of milk on his belly. Eddie searched the refrigerator but could find no juice.

"There isn't any."

"Make some. You know how."

Eddie opened the freezer, thick with odd-smelling frost. It was empty except for an ice tray, in which sat one cube.

"There isn't any," said Eddie, who went to the counter and put two slices of the soft white bread into the toaster and pushed down the handle. Little black ants marched in a line at the back of the counter and Eddie watched them go down behind and disappear. Absorbed in the ants Eddie was startled by the toaster's report. One of the pieces had burned slightly and he scraped it into the sink the way he'd seen Emma do. He buttered the toast and spread the jelly and laid one piece next to his brother's bowl. Mark put down his spoon and began eating the toast. Eddie sat down, took a bite of his toast, set it on the table and commenced eating cereal.

"Let's go down to the beach and play war today," said Eddie. "You can be the Americans. I'll make an island with tunnels and stuff. We'll play Iwo Jima." Eddie had an idea about flame throwers, using matches to burn the entrances to the caves that would be covered with dried seaweed and bits of wood. The Japs would surrender, like in the movies. He didn't mind being the Japs and losing because it was fun to build the caves and tunnels. And as the oldest he would light the matches. Of course he'd have to sneak them down to the beach. He hoped his mother would sleep for a long time. The idea of playing Iwo Jima excited him and he became impatient watching Mark slowly eat his food. The sooner they got down to the beach the more time they'd have to play with the matches before possibly being discovered.

"Come on, let's go," said Eddie. "We don't have all day."

From her bed Carol could hear the boys in the kitchen. Their voices were admonitory echoes, conspiratorial. They were, of necessity, binding together. She had a moment's notion, that she knew immediately to be absurd, that they would, in this coming together, be able to take care of themselves. In some small sense she was possibly right. They would, in whatever ways they were capable—and even this she knew to be a tenuous proposition—bolster each other in spirit. But they were just as likely to fall apart. Again, the marvelous delusional capacity. To think even for a second that her disintegration might somehow be beneficial to them. Howard Johnson was gone and she'd probably never see him again, this curious toad-like, stricken, spirited man, who, while not in the least attractive, nonetheless caused something to come alive within her, a strike of flint in a dank cave. But even if there was a spark there was no dry tinder, nor the will. The ticking clock and now the secretive feet, quiet near her door, on tiptoe, and down the stairs. Purpose in those padded footfalls. What were they up to? She put her hand between her legs and squeezed her thighs. A warmth and measure of feeling. The swarming mass on the ceiling was gone, but there was still movement up there, on the ceiling mind, just under the top of her pickled skull. Her numbskull. She thought about the dream and shook her head to banish the image. There were fresh bottles of vodka in the liquor cabinet. Surely negotiating this day was only feasible with the buoyant raft of alcohol. Just what the hell was that light at the bottom? An H-bomb in the abyss. Her foot throbbed. She got out of bed and quickly opened the door to the silent living room. There was no sound from the boys' bedroom, but a palpable sense of awareness emanated from below. Carol felt some sort of line had been crossed and the boys knew it, and from now on she would be, even more than before, the stranger in their life with so much power to hurt them, and though Mark and Eddie certainly would grow apart as years passed, for now they were closer, and it was because of her.

She retrieved the white terrycloth robe from a pile on a wicker chair in the corner. Feeling a subtle difference in the atmosphere as she put on the robe, she paused. The air was cooler than yesterday. A breeze stirred the beach grass. She looked at the barometer on the wall in the living room. It was down slightly. Outside the living room window the ocean at first glance seemed no different from the calm of the past week, when it lay sluggishly. Now the barest of agitation roiled below its surface and Carol detected it. Fifteen hundred miles away, veering off into the Atlantic, approaching the Tropic of Cancer and gathering fury, the hurricane turned its massive, spiraling, moist body in Carol's direction. Whether the membrane that separates the surface from the true intuition of things had dissolved under the corrosion of drink, or if this was a moment, one that she sometimes had, of a deeper perception, Carol was unsure. It seemed to her that the pullulating mass on her bedroom ceiling indicated a dissolution of that membrane, that she had brought about a permanent state of liquid madness. Yet she could sense the ocean's rippling agitation and coming fury. There seemed now a communication between her and the whispering underworld more vivid, more articulate, than ever before. If only Howard Johnson were here. He would be one to share this with. Certainly not Phil. He would take her as crazy. Goddamn, she wasn't crazy!

Carol heard the children quietly exit the back door downstairs and was momentarily deflated. Her connection to the mystery world existed in them and they sought escape. How could she blame them? A whole life sundering ties with everything that mattered. Let them go. She existed in them and they in her as surely as the wind soughed through the forests in God's mad world or fish swam in the seven seas. Let them go. Carol peered between the glass louvers of the door that opened to the deck as Mark and Eddie descended the steps to the beach, holding their war toys carefully to their bellies, slightly doubled over, almost as if wounded themselves, clutching their viscera. God, let them not go to war, she thought, and felt the deep blood-spilling fear and pain of maternity, and she thought of all the mothers since their time in this world began and their agony and fierceness. Why had she hardly ever felt this way? How could this profoundest of human emotions have visited her so infrequently? Well, it was never too late, was it? To resuscitate this mother-agony. On top of all the other agonies. She couldn't let them go!

Carol tied the belt of her bathrobe and went to the bar and fixed a vodka tonic, squeezing into it some drops from a dried lemon slice left overnight. She drained the glass and lit a cigarette, inhaling deeply, letting the smoke go in a jet stream that clouded the dining room, and as the light was diffused by her smoke so the tightening in her gut was soothed. It was too late and it was too much. Or was it? Leaving her cigarette on the edge of the bar she went out on the deck and then down the stairs to the lower deck, where she was able to walk out on the sand and climb carefully up the dune so that she might observe her children without being seen. Approaching the crest of the dune she dropped to her hands and knees and crawled so that her head peered over at the two figures at the water's edge, the smaller one sitting, readying his soldiers for an assault on the fortification the other on hands and knees intently constructed. Three or four pipers circled above their heads, shrilling, but none swooped. One fishing boat, farther out. A lady bug landed on the back of her left hand and made its way to the knuckle of her ring finger—the ring she sometimes threatened the boys with selling to buy a plane to fly away. What possessed her to utter such cruelties? No, she'd buy the plane and take them with her, to the Caribbean, back to the Bahamas, back to the cabana next to Harold Rosenberg, and this time she'd be more careful, more attentive. She wished she might go down there and play with them or somehow just be there, but of course this would have been impossible, especially after yesterday swimming out with the strange man and Emma dragging them away. And now Emma gone. And just a few hours before that ridiculous scene they'd been happily together on the Lambretta going into town, and the great fun and silliness of Mr. Seagull, the gefiltebat, the Jewish troll, and how happy they were with their new sneakers, bathing suits and socks, and how good it was to be there with them, to give them something, and it wasn't really the stuff she'd bought that was given. Life was so utterly simple, wasn't it? You gave and you gave and you went into it as deeply as you could. Whatever you did you did with everything you had, which meant that you couldn't let your own petty, foolish self fuck things up. You couldn't allow your own childish cravings to drag you back to some tit-sucking, diaper-soiling, masturbatory level that obliterated everything around you, at the same time enshrining your own monstrous, devouring ego that controlled your life like some deprived martinet. And the justifications one came up with! The rationalizations one conjured like some fiendish alchemist—out of thin air! What good have I done? she thought. What have I contributed to this world and my children? Where has the time gone? I don't even remember my life! Jesus! Carol rolled onto her back and stared up at the pale sky, and the rocking world told her that a few more drinks would set things right, quell her torment and self-recriminations. What was the good in beating oneself up? She could control it. Just a few drinks to set things right and that was it. No more embarrassing, contemptible scenes. She couldn't do it all at once, nor did she want to. But somehow she had to get back—get her life back, her children back. Though that was a place she'd never been. Back. What was back? Forward. That was where she needed to go. Forward to a place she'd never been. Into the wild blue yonder.

Carol rolled onto her stomach and looked at the boys, still readying their field of battle. They had no idea of the horrors. Paul and his conversion to Catholicism on the hospital ship. Her foot ached as if in sympathy with the maimed and the dying. She remembered falling out of a tree at a very young age and the jagged branch digging into her leg, the pinkish meat of her thigh turned out like the inside of one of her dolls. Magnify that by a billion times in gore and suffering. God, let them only play at war. Let them never see what Paul had seen, what her father had seen, captured by the Japanese in Hong Kong at the beginning of the war, spending six months in prison camp, nearly starving, losing most of his teeth, never really recovering from the experience. Or Howard Johnson, Jesus, poor Howard Johnson, what he'd seen during the war and then, Buchenwald. Poor Howard will never recover.

She watched Mark move his troops, advancing on the structure Eddie had built, both bombing with clots of sand. Eddie hunched over, and in a minute wisps of smoke rose above them and they moved back, sitting on their haunches. So, this play was getting more serious. Eddie had gotten some matches, obviously, and was burning dried seaweed, from the looks of the yellowish smoke that was thicker now, carrying down the beach with the breeze. The wind shifted and blew the smoke at Mark and he scurried out of the way on his hands and knees. The smoke lessened and Carol could see the small blaze flare up as Eddie moved away. Both of them stared at the fire for several seconds and then Eddie jumped to his feet and quickly searched the beach for more seaweed and pieces of wood, pointing at the sand near Mark, who got to his feet and began also to look. Soon a white column of smoke rose higher than the boys' heads and carried down the beach. They stood back and both glanced in the direction of the house as Carol ducked reflexively. So, they were thinking of her, and in some way with the lighting of this fire, declaring something. Eddie was in charge of the fire and Mark a willing accomplice. Under different circumstances she might go down there and scold them, smother the fire, snatch the matches from Eddie's hand. But she watched, fascinated, her children looking like aborigines tending a fire on some Tasmanian shore. They'd have lizards and fish to bake, wrapped in wet seaweed. Both of them were fully capable. They would survive without her. There was noise from the Evans' deck behind her and Carol turned and saw Marge, arranging a lounge chair, holding a drink in her left hand, squinting against the smoke from a cigarette held tightly in her withered lips. She seemed oblivious to Carol oddly encamped on the dune next to her own house. Downstairs, she heard Marge's husband hammering on one of his do-it-yourself projects. Issues of *Popular Mechanics* lay about their house. He'd just completed a doghouse, though they had no dog. Maybe now they'd get one. To hell with the Evanses. Carol rolled over and watched her children, who were foraging for wood to stoke their fire now burning brightly. A stout man (for one lurching moment she thought it was Stanley Golden) stood nearby, watching them, as if about to intervene, then walked off, saying something to them as he passed. Eddie had an armload of driftwood and Mark a smaller pile. Their battleground had turned to Hiroshima. Unless they'd been evacuated, the plastic soldiers were melted. Verisimilitude. The skin melted like wax. They dumped the wood on the fire, which diminished momentarily and then gradually rose to their waists. She'd read how the sand had vitrified at Alamogordo. She'd left her cigarette on the counter. The hell with it. The house would go up like nothing. What a sight that would be. Show them a real fire. On the beach the flames grew higher and the children stood back in uneasy contemplation. Earth, wind, water, fire, all the elements and their product, her children, lay before Carol, who felt a sudden rush of giddy excitement: How fabulous they were, these young creatures! They'd started a fire for play and now stood in a kind of nervous rapture, not certain of its meaning but feeling the power of it. Carol saw it as a gesture of defiance and independence—and perhaps effigy. Perhaps they were burning her, exorcising the demons that prowled their world, growing more formidable. They needed some sort of weapon. They would surely like to burn the creature she had become, and then hope for a different version to rise out of the ashes. The incinerating purity of flame, cleansing her fouled bones, then thirty-two pieces gathered like the milk teeth of angels in a soft hempen sack tied with umbilical cord, divided evenly and planted in the warm humus of the sixteen great moments of their lives. Providing a life had sixteen great moments.

The breeze shifted and blew from the south, moving the smoke in her direction. So now they're smoking me out, she thought, my signal for another drink. Just one more to calm down. My young Prometheans on the beach. Proud of my little cave-dwellers. My little aborigines. Carol backed down the dune on hands and knees and then righted herself, turning around and looking at Marge Evans, reclined comfortably, drink in one hand, cigarette in the other, waving lazily at Carol, as if it were the most natural thing to see her neighbor crawling around the dunes in the morning. Carol waved back and walked into the house and up the stairs to the bar. Her cigarette was ashes—another burn added to the collection that scored the countertop like notches on a gun handle. One more moment expired, forgotten. Could she but remember the story of each ugly melted wound on the black surface. She counted the marks. There were twelve. One for each apostle. One was deeper and uglier than the rest. She ran her finger back and forth in its jagged trench. Judas. And she of course the Christ. A sponge with some vodka, that would do it. She was sweating and went to the freezer for ice. One cube left. Carol rubbed the chunk on her forehead and then put it in her glass, which she filled to the brim with Smirnoff, eighty proof. She walked to the living room window and looked out. The boys were obscured by the dune but smoke still rose from their battlefield. She wished to go down and raise the fire to great heights so they might stand together exhilarated, babble in some heathen tongue, festooned with shells and seaweed and circle the fire in rhythmic steps. They'd get Marge to come down and drum for them. And Marge would dance too and then fall into the fire, a fabulous pagan *flambé*. For that matter Carol herself would be advised not to get too close. She finished the drink in three swallows. End of ice. Though the day was cooler she was sweating profusely. The belt from her bathrobe had come loose and the ends hung like limp divining rods signaling a sort of sapless perdition. The open terrycloth robe exposed her body in a thin slash down the middle that reflected back in the window. A stranger, slack and bones. One of Howard Johnson's walking dead. The elements consisted of energy—mysterious stuff, that, and their mingling produced life, another sort of energy, and the pinnacle of that energy was consciousness. And then we turned around and produced another kind of energy that destroyed everything. The anti-energy—whether it was Hiroshima or eighty proof vodka. The smoke from the beach was no longer. Perhaps the fire was out. Energy had a particular life span. Maybe the children were counteracting her entropy with the fire. And the fire, like their own parcel of energy, their own allotment, would end a dry, cold heap of ash. And so, the purpose of each fire was to burn according to its nature, whether it smolder in longevity or flare incandescently. The point was that each force not be circumscribed or squandered. That would constitute a kind of betrayal. Maybe this was the meaning of sin, this thwarting of the natural luminescence. One could sin against oneself, or others. In any case, it was a sin against God, because God was the all-encompassing. God was everything, whose purpose was the creative realization of all its energy-aspects, and an affront to any of those aspects was an affront to him, it, whatever God was. Ergo, by deliberately destroying her own energy-force (and hurting the children's, and everything around her) she was going against that which was natural, that which strove to be. This was the meaning of sin, surely, and she, a sinner outright.

A sinner without ice. *Sin hielo*. A sin to be without ice. At least she might attempt to make some. Nice to have cooler drinks in the afternoon. Carol tied the belt of her robe and went to the kitchen, retrieving the empty trays from the freezer, returning the dividers abandoned in the dish rack, filling the trays with tap water, noticing the bowls, glasses, spoons and straws left in the sink by the children. How astonishing. A line of black ants moved from the counter to the wall, bearing crumbs scattered about the periphery of the toaster that loomed over them like some chromed Kaaba. Inside the electric fires of the damned. The anti-Kaaba. Everything in opposition. Well, she could make ice to counteract the fire. It was either fire or ice. Excluded from the temperate zones in this lifetime. And outside, the boys cultivating their own inferno. She set the trays on the table and opened the refrigerator, a larder bereft, some butter, jelly, milk, three eggs, ketchup, mustard, an almost-empty jar of relish, something wrapped in tin foil. The empty freezer was encrusted with stale-smelling thick frost like some forlorn arctic cave where a doomed explorer might spend his last frozen hours slipping into eternity. She tried to insert both trays at the same time and the water overflowed. I am a shaky specimen who has squandered her time on this earth. Paul would be disgusted with me. Where is now Paul? Married in Westchester with six children, attending mass each morning before commuting to the city and his job at the Department of Welfare, his dark-haired wife, devout, ex-nurse, home taking care of the children. Irene her name. Paul and Irene. Good night, Irene.

The breeze picked up, the beachgrass swayed. Carol went to the bar and poured another drink, opened a fresh pack of cigarettes and lit a kitchen match on the underside of the bar, a piece of sulfur flying off and landing on her foot.

"Shit! Fire and brimstone!"

She bent and slapped at the top of her foot and as she did so the phone rang.

"Maybe it's Howard Johnson, the escargot man." Carol hoped it was. How she would enjoy him now, to share her thoughts with him, the sad sympathy of his company. His intelligence and experience were dear to her already, though she hardly remembered a thing from the day before. How unlike Phil he was. She took a drink, set the glass and cigarette down on the bar, and walked briskly to the bedroom, calling out, "Coming, Mr. Johnson. I'm coming, my little captain man, toad-man, captain toad. Don't hang up, I'm coming!" And when she put the phone to her ear and issued her greeting, the voice at the other end was Phil's. He was in the city and leaving for Westhampton right away. He would be there in less than two hours. Traffic would be light. The receiver was saturated with the weary resolve of his voice. It seemed to take on a liquid weight, as if a hard, portentous sponge. Something was up with that tone. It unsettled her.

"Shitfire. They're coming to take me away."

She could run. She could get in the station wagon and drive away, maybe forever. They hadn't spoken much. He'd asked about the kids. They were fine, of course. Carol had spoken as soberly as possible, a dead giveaway. And he didn't know the half of it—Emma gone, the kids setting fires on the beach. She hoped their fire was still going, for it meant something. It gave them strength and knowledge. How one's understanding could increase by simply lighting a fire was quite mysterious but it was true. It spoke of the duality in everything, didn't it? The opposing primal forces. I should burn down the house, myself in it. That would traumatize them forever. I'll have a fire of my own. Of death and new beginnings.

Carol went to the fireplace in the living room and crumpled some newspaper from a pile, threw the wad into the grate and placed several pieces of cannel coal from a metal bucket on top and then doused the whole thing in kerosene from a small can, which was Phil's preferred method as self-anointed fire-starter of the family. I'll do it his way, but better. She sloshed some extra kerosene on the pile and lit a kitchen match from the box next to the bucket and threw it into the grate. It ignited with a hot con-cussive force that took her breath away. The flames leapt up and out of the confines of the fireplace and feathered menacingly at the white brick mantle, already smudged from previous fires but now blackened instantly by the oily smoke beyond the grayness that was before. The smoke went up the face of the wall and filled the ceiling's cavities. On the beach Mark and Eddie saw the black smoke rising from the chimney of their house and looked at each other, puzzled. Their own fire was ashes and a few dying embers. The black plume removed them instantly from their battlefield and flames, now extinguished. It spoke of an adult intrusion, serious and ugly, and since they knew it was their mother a kind of dread came over them. Carol stood back from the fireplace, the flames along with her initial fear and excitement subsiding, retreating to their more ordinary boundaries, the small bituminous chunks beginning to burn brightly, sending a stream of dark gray smoke up the chimney. She put two large hunks on the fire that quickly ignited, cracking fiercely, the flames and smoke flowing upward. The room turned warmer, then hot. Excited, Carol went to the bar to retrieve her vodka and cigarette, which was just beginning to burn the countertop. She emptied the glass in two determined swallows and poured another drink, her hand shaking. She drank once and took the glass with her cigarette into the living room, standing for a few moments looking at the intensely burning fire and the fireplace itself that seemed too small to contain the roaring yellow flames. An idea formed. Carol looked at the wooden table of pale, varnished elegance that stood in front of the fireplace and one by one removed the objects from its surface and fed them to the fire. The first to go was a week-old *Life* magazine. She placed it on the fire and it began immediately to smoke. The gamine's face on the cover furled redly and burst into flames, curling back, wickedly devoured. Poor Audrey. The pages peeled away, individually burning. An ad for S.O.S—no Marconi would save it now. The article on Audrey appeared and disappeared, page by cindering page. Then, a *Sports Illustrated* from the same time. On the cover Swaps caught fire, its equine thew of no avail. She saw flaming sailboats in blue water. Holocaust! Conflagration! Requiem for the recreators! And Swaps again, brute beast mutely bellowing, his story in ashes. The magazines were followed by a wooden box filled with small sea shells that burned vigorously compared with the ponderous, unsatisfactory periodicals, the red-flamed pages turning slowly, as if inviting final, mournful review of their contents. A cracked maraca with most of its beans missing issued a small jet of smoke from its bulb and then burst into flames. Carol finished her drink and went to the bar for another. The bottle was almost empty and she fetched a fresh one from below and twisted the cap, the breaking seal resonating pleasingly in her palm and she lifted the bottle to her nose and inhaled. She was happy and determined. There were lots of things to burn. God, it was hot. A kind of sexual excitement surged within, her body damp with sweat, a palpable urging between her legs. She felt her vagina and discovered that she was damp. Carol took the other, near-empty bottle and licked its top and slid it around her labia. It felt good but the urge for drink was strong and she emptied the bottle into her glass and then filled it to the brim from the new bottle. If they're taking me away I'll give them good bloody reason. Carol drained it and poured another. Back to work. There were three items left on the table: an ashtray that wouldn't burn, obviously, a clamshell, another inflammable, and Hemingway's *Death in the Afternoon.*

Mrs. Macomber alive and well, thank you very much. She placed the book carefully in the flames and watched with pleasure as the hated author's bloody, cockish maunderings smoldered and then caught. So long, Hem, you creep, you impostor. The book burned more readily than did the magazines, and before long it was consumed and indistinguishable from the coal and remnants of other things. Carol looked at the table and was pleased with its near emptiness. She went to the bedroom, and while it seemed to her that her mind was almost preternaturally clear and focused on the correctness of what she was doing, her body, like an elephantine blimp suddenly blown loose from its moorings, had abandoned her. She had the curious sensation of extreme bloatedness, as if she were some helium-filled character at a parade, and not only was she in danger of floating off, her body had become so enlarged that she thought she might not fit through the doorway of the bedroom, and once inside felt there was barely space in which to move. I've become way too big for my britches, she thought, but I must carry on. Carol scooped the pile of clothes from the corner chair into her arms, sucked in her gut, and squeezed through the door. Walking carefully in the living room lest she knock things over with her girth, she dropped the armload of clothes onto the table in front of the fireplace. Starting with this pile she would burn every item of her clothing except for her robe. And she might burn that, also, so when they came to take her away she would be as the day she was born, bloated, liquid and helpless. Let them drug her, let them shock her, let them take her apart, she would comply.

Carol began to sort through the clothes. There seemed to be a preferred order in which to burn each item, but it escaped her. She thought, I'll douse them with kerosene first so they'll burn more quickly. She retrieved the can and sloshed the pile of clothes with the liquid. As she did this an alarm went off in her head or, rather, as if from some distant point an alarm sounded and flew very quickly inside her, insistent and fraught. Carol paused to listen, clutching the kerosene in her right hand, her face rigid, as if held together with wire. The alarm sounded four, five times and Carol realized it was the telephone and she replaced the can and, carefully, because she was huge and clumsy, walked to the bedroom and stood over the phone, whose ringing now that she was next to it was weirdly muted and distant. She picked up the receiver and listened to a dim voice whose words were unintelligible and sounded as if washed over by waves and all the more urgent because of it. Carol tightened the ridges of her brain in concentration—it sounded like a man's voice—to no avail. Maybe it was that fellow from—was it yesterday? What was yesterday? What did it mean, yesterday? A name connected with this, Fulgard, Florencio, Jospin. What was it? The voice was less demanding now and took on a beseeching tone and words seemed to come haltingly or intermittently. Then silence. Carol held the object to her ear for a long moment and then placed it in the cradle of the phone. Howard Johnson. A whisper of memory and, yes, an image attached to that name, comical, forlorn, stick-legged, batrachian, a captain's cap. Think now, woman. Friend or foe? At what point in the murky past did that image invest itself in your crusted soul? She stood dumbly, a giantess in the shrinking room, and the phone commenced again, this time not with a far-away ringing but a small bird's chirping—Mr. Sparrow come a-calling. She would answer the call. Howard Johnson, Howard Johnson. She picked up the phone and again listened without speaking. It was the same voice, more deliberate, and she could pick out certain words, but the meaning of it all was indecipherable. Finally, she spoke. "Is your name Howard Johnson?" The voice paused and then started, rapidly taking on the urgency of the first time it spoke. It couldn't be Phil, he was coming to take her away. "I believe they're taking me away," she said into the phone. The voice halted again, in silent reaction to her words, and then the earnest jabbering redoubled and just as abruptly Carol heard the click of hanging up, as if the receiver were a pistol held to her ear and someone had cocked the hammer. She put down the phone to go the bathroom—she had to pee like mad—and, walking, was aware of some troubling thing behind her in the living room, but all was troubling things and so paid no attention and went to sit and pee in the bathroom and from her seat and for some while looked out her window across the road at the bay and its frolickers, the sailboats and water skiers, trailing their wakes, buoyant like plastic bathtub toys, a world so far removed she might as well have been on another planet. She thought of the happiness of the creatures out there and said the word aloud. Happiness. She, the aquaplane queen of Repulse Bay, watching the happy termites skid over the bay's rippled surface. Absorbed and happy little termites in their recreation. She was a happy little termite once, wasn't she? Carol bent to wipe herself with a fistful of toilet paper and saw that part of her robe hung in the water, and as she stared between her legs at the soaking end of white cloth the troubling thing she'd been dimly aware of made itself apparent. She looked up and saw it. A thin layer of smoke hung in the bathroom that was connected to a thicker body yet in the bedroom, and she saw in her mind's eye the living room somehow ablaze, and even in her corrupt state she understood: The crackling cannel coal had launched a missile onto the pile of kerosene-soaked clothes, now ablaze like a city of the damned. She thought of the children immediately and hoped to Jesus God they were still on the beach absorbed happily or seriously, whatever the case, in their own war play and all about the world death and destruction and she but one insignificant manifestation of this brutal truth but significant enough at this particular moment in this particular world: She really was going to burn the house down.

Carol ran to the living room that was filled with smoke and the sight of the burning pile of clothes transfixed her and she stood with her mouth slack, the soaked end of her robe dripping onto her foot. Surely this was extraordinary. Damn! The popping coal! She hadn't been on the phone and in the bathroom that long, had she? Then again perhaps she had. Maybe she'd blacked out. She had no idea. The coal cracked loudly and sent a piece skidding under the table. Carol watched as the floor began to smolder. It occurred to her she might do something. She went to the kitchen, filled a large blue enamel pot, its brimming contents spilling to the floor as she labored, but then tripped on a leg of the kitchen table and fell, the pot clattering, water everywhere. It seemed she may have hit her head. She lay for some time, mildly chagrined at the wet floor, aware of something she was supposed to be doing. The burning house. She righted herself, staggered to the sink and filled the pot. Good Jesus, am I shaky, she thought, and, straining with the weight of the pot, she commenced the journey—it seemed to take forever—to the living room, to the table, where she poured the water on the pile of clothes, still burning, and as she did there came a determined knocking on the front door downstairs that confused her, and then her name called out perhaps two or three times and something else. The pile was a sodden disrupted creature, its smoking guts charred and spilled outwards. She took a wet piece of it and picked up the ember beneath the table that hissed like a small asp and threw it into the fireplace, then took another wet piece of something and rubbed the charred spot on the floor. The screen door creaked open and banged violently shut and steps ascended.

"Carol! Are you all right? What's burning?"

Howard Johnson reached the top of the stairs.

"What in God's name—"

The woman stood before him, a ghastly creature dully startled in the midst of something terrible, bent over the reeking carcass with a piece of it in her hand. She looked at him with bare recognition and a glint of triumph, as if passed over to a place beyond the understanding of ordinary citizens. She threw the piece into the fireplace and turned her back to him, looking out the big window. A strip of metallic ocean lay between the dunes and the cloud of smoke in the living room. A puddle beneath the table was filled with bits of stuff and the water came over the side in a thin stream. He could hear the sound of it meeting the floor, a slender trickle of madness. The room smelled vaguely of something from the war. And here was a lone survivor in her robe mutely staring out the window. He'd seen more than he'd wanted of those staring survivors. And in this land of the victors there were more of these sorts than people realized. He ought to know. The room was hot. Sweat rolled from his armpits. He didn't know what to do.

"Carol. Are you okay?"

As Howard Johnson spoke, he moved to the fireplace and placed the folding screen in front of the brightly burning coal and then bent to pick up a handful of newspapers from a bucket with which to absorb the water under the table, wincing from the wicked heat of the unnatural flames and keeping an eye on the forlorn figure nearby. In times like these it was the practical that one attended to. He was thankful he hadn't anything to drink yet, a little unusual, and also that he'd called, though not without a feeling of guilt as his intent had been to explore the possibility of drinking the day to oblivion with her, an easy mark, really. And here she was already there and dangerously so. He wondered about the maid and the children. Surely this was at least as disturbing as swimming out to sea fully clothed, though a different variety of catastrophe. He laid the papers out on the puddle. The date on the top piece read August 12, 1954. Almost exactly one year ago, another universe altogether and altogether meaningless. What wasted expenditure of energy had entertained him then? Extraordinary that he knew virtually nothing of this sunburnt world and its summering people, surely of course not all like Carol—not many like this one—but she emblematic of a certain condition, and though he was not part of the scene he shared some of the symptoms. The alcohol was bad stuff, that which brought out all the other bad stuff, ultimately, though the paradox was that you drank to keep it at bay. It didn't work. Madness and destruction were the only outcomes and he momentarily appraised this now very strange woman as an object lesson, another in a long line of object lessons that in the end had no effect, and as he stood from placing the newspapers two desires burned wickedly through his mind—to get blitheringly drunk himself and to have sex with this besotted madwoman naked in her loosened bathrobe. The old ravening impulse. One would have thought it beaten out of him by now, with all that he had seen, and indeed the thoughts burned through that part of his mind as quickly as a magician's incandescent paper flares and vanishes. The provenance of those impulses had been rightfully chastened and disarmed, but the irony of it was that he was none the better for it, at least emotionally. A different person, but not a better one. In fact, Howard Johnson often wished for a return of the old full-on predatory instincts as their withering signaled an emasculation of sorts that he did not enjoy, an emasculation that in some ways betokened a loss of spirit. He'd known people in the war who had responded in the opposite, people whose spirits flourished in the midst of depravity. He'd loathed these people and yet in some ways envied them, their force and physical courage, the way their existence seemed to reach some kind of pinnacle of fulfillment that most people would never hope to glimpse. Yet surely now they were no better off than he. Probably much worse. No, maybe not. Maybe these were the ones who, after all, ruled the world in all its insane glory.

These thoughts were on Howard Johnson's mind as he finally moved to Carol, still unsure of the proper course to steer through these dismaying currents. The captain's hat he wore mocked him but it would have been a ludicrous gesture to take it off now. Carol felt the figure approaching and had a vague sense of who it was, a benign presence, certainly, and an understanding one who would know about the mysterious forces of energy that ruled the world and their countless manifestations and the myriad ways they expended themselves. She felt an extraordinary power and warned in her mind this fellow, Howard Johnson, to be circumspect in his approach. To get too close might be dangerous.

"Careful, Mr. Johnson, I might incinerate you. I am very dangerous at the moment. Quite flammable. I think we'd be advised to partake in a frosted martini, don't you? But, of course, I have no vermouth. You know I've discovered something today, Mr. Howard Johnson. I think you'd be one of the few people who might understand this." Carol continued looking out the window at the deck, the dunes, the sea and sky. "I've discovered that we're all bits of connected energy, and that what we call soul is really this fabulous, fiery consuming force that is what we really are. When we finish, when we are consumed—" Carol sighed deeply, still looking out the window. "When we are consumed it is the residue of the force that once was us that we call soul. It's like a ripple effect. Some of us are boulders thrown into a pond. Others are like pebbles thrown into an ocean. I am one of those pebbles, Mr. Johnson."

"That's not true."

"It is true, and it's all right. You've a much larger soul than I. I don't know what I've done—I can't seem to remember anything. But I know that today for the first time in my life I understand that I am part of something—though a very small part. But still, I am. I believe the universe is something with consciousness, with purpose, and its purpose is energy itself. Its purpose is the consuming of itself. I know you don't agree with that, Mr. Johnson. I know you think it's all a pile of meaningless—"

"That's not exactly true, but go on."

Better to keep her talking, he thought.

"Now this does sound trite, but all of it is what we call God. And every bit of it in the process of consuming itself—like the sun, for example. Think of all the societies that have worshipped the sun. They all knew, at least unconsciously, that the sun was in the process of consuming itself. Look at the Aztecs. They were so afraid the sun would lose its power that they cut people's hearts out as offerings. They knew the sun was consuming itself —in the same way everything does." She turned toward Howard Johnson. "And what is God's will itself but energy? And does not this energy also consume itself?" She paused, looking at her feet. "And then, darkness. But there is light, somewhere—I've seen it." Carol was thinking of the light at the bottom of the sea in her dream. Its translucent, veined, emerald pulsing presented the final enigma. She looked expressionlessly at Howard Johnson. "Is it light everlasting?"

Howard Johnson was not given to think much of light everlasting. What he'd seen was insanity, cruelty and darkness. Yet Carol's words had some sounding with him. Hers was the clarity of desperation and the obliteration of the mundane, done away with by alcohol and a suffering he still couldn't fathom. Though he tended to think more of darkness everlasting there was the inevitable residual of faith, hope, optimism and an occasional moment of wonder in the face of it—life, nature, the consciousness of his own existence. And, of course, there was this woman standing next to him. He had to admit that his motives were not "pure," but then, they rarely were. He was sure he was like most people in this. Probably the greatest saints were those with the strongest instincts and "impurities," who struggled the most in overcoming them. But he didn't believe in the purity of anything, not even children—not even the child he put his arms around at Buchenwald. And he'd called first not out of any concern whatsoever for Carol, but rather to drink with her, and if things took an interesting turn, well, that too. Complete and utter selfishness. Not that he didn't like this woman. He supposed that he did. She was attractive and interesting enough—from what he could remember. But then her condition over the phone had concerned him. At first, he was disappointed. Consorting with this woman today would likely be out of the question. But he felt the burden of complicity. There were the children. She might be in real danger. Under most circumstances he would hang up the phone and go about his business, his inebriate business, this person with whom he'd shared a few scarcely-remembered delirious hours rapidly receding. But something, much to his surprise, worked on him differently this time. He supposed it was that he liked her—liked her from the moment they met in that strange little dark store with the spooky, leering Romany woman and the towheaded yearlings peering from the back. Imagine! Still, something stirred within. How ridiculous, how hopeless it was. What did it matter? And yet, apparently, it was his role to give succor to those in the most abject circumstances. In some sense this was another Buchenwald—this woman victim of a self-created concentration camp. At the rate she was going she would not be a survivor. And what did it mean to survive? A succession of days, one much like the other, a few odd (indeed) moments of recreation, much of everything forgotten, the solitary, onward trudge.

On the beach Mark and Eddie had, by unspoken consent, decided to delay as much as possible their return to the house, where they knew something fearful awaited them. They'd taken the soldiers, half of them charred and ruined like their formerly animate counterparts on Iwo Jima, and stashed them beneath the beach stairs. They had a brief discussion on which direction to walk, towards Moriches inlet or towards the Swordfish Club, and again, through a process that was largely inarticulate, though logical—the walk to the inlet less-traveled and a bit strange—they decided on the more familiar direction of town and the beach club with the great wooden swordfish in the front and the vast sparkling saltwater pool that itself was like the ocean where "big" kids dived and swam and roughly played, their piping voices echoing, ascending, then lost in the greater vastness surrounding. The boys walked slowly and somewhat forlornly in the direction of the sun, which, not yet overhead, cast their shadows behind them. Before long, the distance they'd walked caused them to be uneasy. They were not used to being on this part of the beach by themselves, and while they fled from the strangeness of their mother, they also sensed they were abandoning her and, as well, that she might be distressed over their absence. Nevertheless, they continued, the irascible sandpipers swooping down inches from their crew cut heads, the ocean, less calm than the day before, pushed shoreward by a stiffening breeze that troubled its surface. The few people they passed looked at them with solicitous smiles. Then they were at the Dune Deck with its more crowded beach, the lounge chairs and brightly-colored umbrellas, the great white lifeguard stand upon which sat as if on a throne that species of male far surpassing the big kids who played with unselfconscious abandon at the Swordfish Club pool, bronze, unapproachable tutelary gods with their zinc oxide peeling noses whose glance brushed thrillingly and dismissively across you. They inhabited another realm altogether, seated with such authority in their wooden aeries shaded by umbrellas much bigger than anyone else's. Though it was conceivable that someday you might become a grownup, it was far less likely you would ever be a lifeguard. They hastened past the Dune Deck beach, diffident at the authority of the place and numbers of people, as well as apprehensive they might be suspected as runaways. Ahead lay an empty stretch of beach, and beyond that, still out of view, the Swordfish Club.

Howard Johnson followed Carol to the bar, where she poured them both vodkas, hers straight and his with a dash of tonic. They'd opened the doors and all the windows and the smoke had mostly cleared. Carol's head, too, had cleared. An immaculate calmness possessed her. She wondered if Howard Johnson sensed her new power. Her head felt three or four times larger, along with an almost giddy sensation that everything—the universe itself—was contained within it. She wouldn't have been at all surprised to find that, viewing herself in a mirror, she looked like one of the Venusians of popular imagination, all forehead and bulging, omniscient eyes. In her mind's eye she saw the children on the beach playing in the tide pools, digging tunnels, creating inlets and small new bays, just as an inlet had opened for her, creating a great new bay of consciousness: The Bay of Fundy. Where was the Bay of Fundy? The Bay of Profundity. Nova Scotia, wasn't it? Nova Scotia. A cabalistic ring to it. The magical utterance. My mind has taken a Nova Scotia turn. Also, an excellent toast. "Nova Scotia," she said, raising her glass to Howard Johnson. "Nova Scotia," he said, raising his own. They looked at each other over the rims of their glasses as they drank. What Howard Johnson saw was a set of hazel eyes transformed from the wild distraction of a few moments before. They were now coldly sober, glisteningly opaque and aggressively rational. A disturbing transformation. One didn't move from drunken, destructive madness to the objective balance of Madame Curie (even if she had fatally irradiated herself) in a matter of seconds. Nevertheless, these misgivings quickly succumbed to the iddish bubblings of his brain. Here was an attractive woman in her bathrobe, seemingly in possession of herself, who had been a moment earlier clearly mad from alcohol and God knew what else. He glanced briefly over the rim of his glass at the cleavage beneath the bathrobe and drank the vodka in three determined swallows. Carol understood the look but dismissed it, not as base and trivial but as an impulse less important than the vivid image that filled her mind, a seraphic crew of inward-smiling, white-robed carpenters busily measuring, sawing, hammering— constructing a staunch and splendid edifice that reached to the heavens, indestructible to the ravages of misery, ignorance and decay. The Toad Captain's desire was not at all a trivial or loathsome thing, but it was a subset of a much larger—infinitely larger—what? It wasn't necessary to know what it was, only that it existed. More real than anything she'd ever known. She was certain of it. The Captain's longing was touching and poignant —and completely acceptable. She might under different circumstances respond (although in her past "condition" or "blindness" it would have been an exchange born of despair and nihilism, carried along, of course, on the rattling, careening *carreta de la muerte* of alcohol), but she wanted very much to hold on to the vision that so exalted, buoyed her in a manner unprecedented. There would be nothing wrong or sinful in making love to this man but to do so now would move her away from what she was feeling. Imagine the sweating, grappling and moaning (all of it good, was it not?). Where would her Bay of Fundy be then but at stagnant low tide between her legs? This revelation, or awareness, or whatever it was, was a fledgling thing, precious and requiring of nurture. It seemed to her then that if there was a dark aspect to sex it was that its power took you away, and if you weren't fortified with something more substantial it rolled you under like a giant wave crushing you to the bottom. And, again, there it was, the emerald light at the bottom, still a mystery, but less so. The light had to be connected to her different consciousness. All of her life roiling rag-doll without a sensible thought in her husk-stuffed head, those vacant Raggedy Ann eyes fixed stupidly on selfish purpose alone. No, she couldn't make love now, it was too important to hold on to this new, powerful thing.

Phil had talked to Carol at ten o'clock and a half hour later he was in the Chrysler on the East River Drive headed towards the Triborough Bridge. Of the several routes to Westhampton this was his favorite. There was something about the bridge that he liked, its expansiveness, perhaps, and the fact that it fed into the Grand Central Parkway, more expansiveness that passed La Guardia and Flushing Bay, part of a grand arterial system that never quite functioned as planned, invariably choked with traffic, but not today. It was something to have grown with all this and to be a part of it. The city with its magnificent intelligence and industry, its vanguard civilization, the progress the whole world regarded enviously, was his no less than anyone's. If one could be said to have an organic connection with soot, concrete, steel, relentless jackhammer-mad destruction, jostling incorrigible crudity, and limitless creativity—all of it impelled and sustained by the intoxicating promise of opportunity and fortune that ran through the veins of the place and its people like a golden, adrenal drug—then Phil surely had. Crossing the Triborough Bridge was flying to freedom, towards the well-deserved rewards of the Hamptons, the blue ocean, the white clean sand, the tennis and waterskiing, the self-assured company of others like him who had made it. For the price of a quarter he could fly across this magnificent bridge (Moses' route to the promised land) one hundred and fifty feet above the East River, foot pressed comfortably on the accelerator of his powerful red car, left arm resting on the door, steering wheel gripped firmly at twelve o'clock, the top three buttons of his Brooks Brothers shirt opened, exposing the hair of his sturdy, prideful chest, warm wind rushing violent through the windows exploding in his ears drowning the whining of his Goodyear tires (it's been a good year, many good years) spinning unimaginably, headlong. He'd talked with Dr. Campbell before leaving. Preparations had been made for a room at East Hill. The question was—actually two questions—What kind of shape would his wife be in? How would he get her to go to East Hill? Phil drove the Chrysler more slowly than usual, filled with a sense of dread at the coming scene. He'd taken this route because it made him feel good, and he suspected it might be some time before he'd feel good again. There was virtually no traffic. The big car, its forward progress reluctant yet inevitable, rolled down Grand Central Parkway past the airport and the bay, the boats carelessly shuttling back and forth like Central Park miniatures. In a short while he was on the Van Wyck and then too quickly the Belt Parkway and finally Sunrise Highway, the force of the city diminished to the whisper of memory and the destination ahead roaring like the bottom of Niagara or a train rushing head-on to meet him. It seemed hardly fair. Well, he wasn't going to let it derail him. He supposed it was a mistake to have married this woman. But it seemed right at the time. And the children an extra burden. At least Emma was there to help. And if not Emma, a million like her. He had the money. The money took care of everything. And now the expense of admitting Carol to East Hill. He sensed the thought that occasionally showed its pale underbelly swimming in the darker part of his mind: It would be better if she were dead. Frankly, what good was she? A drunk, a drain on everybody, a continual sadness. She was more harmful as a parent than anything else (and what was he?), and long ago their relationship had foundered. It wasn't entirely her fault. He was, he supposed, difficult, in his own way. He passed the town where East Hill was located. If he pushed it, he could be in Westhampton in a little over an hour. But he wouldn't. He'd keep to the speed limit, an appropriate, measured pace, slower than he usually drove, the pace at which he correspondingly navigated his life. Of course, there was the need to slow down—he had the bleeding ulcer and the caffeinated nerves to remind him—but there was a lot to chew on, his property, his possessions, his children's schools, the vacations, the whole fabric of his life—his wife—the continual drive to prove that the lefty Jew from Hell's Kitchen with the diminutive, reticent old-world father and bitch of a steamrolling stepmother, could cut it, shit, more than cut it, excel, in the frothy, glamorous world he'd chosen. He didn't believe in anything like fate. Opportunities presented themselves and you either took advantage or you didn't. Of course, you had to sweat the hair off your balls if you wanted anything to come of it. This wife of his was not cutting it. But then, look where she'd come from. All that Anglo-Saxon, genteel, Ivy League bullshit. She was spoiled. A spoiled alcoholic. But, hell, the "real" blue bloods were killers, cultivated cutthroats. They ran things, didn't they? He would barely admit to himself that he hated them, those insufferable, murderous snobs. And it was more difficult still to admit that he feared them, their easy assumption of privilege and power, the exclusivity that made one always feel bloody inferior. And a Jew on top of it all. But he wasn't doing too badly. He'd made some money, hadn't he? Not the real money like them, but enough to get some respect from the bastards. But fuck it. He was, he knew, in their minds, an *arriviste,* and a Jew. Never a chance. Once a Jew, always a Jew.

Anyway, to hell with them. They were as boring as dried dung. How he wished he was going waterskiing today instead of taking his poor wretched wife to a sanitarium! How had it come to this? Wasn't there something they could have done? Together? Poor, poor Carol. Yes, thought Phil, I could have, and should have, done much more. Perhaps it wasn't too late. But the thought of her rehabilitation was powerfully daunting, the effort like some family Manhattan Project. It would require a complete upheaval of their lives and an absolute refocusing of energy. The expense and time and emotional effort would be monumental. Everything would have to be centered around Carol, and with work as demanding as it was, and the children needing to be cared for—his responsibility! And this for a woman he'd stopped loving years ago, for a woman who had given up on herself long before they'd met, as he'd come to realize. Maybe now, with a long stay at East Hill and help from the earnest Dr. Campbell (boy, was he making some money) there might be some kind of breakthrough. But they couldn't keep her there against her will and he doubted she would want any part of it. Even if she were thoroughly drugged it would be hard to keep her there. And how much could he afford anyway? No, this was an impossible dilemma. No way out. Divorce was a possibility, but that would mean giving up much of what he'd worked for. She'd drive a hard bargain, that was certain: the alimony, child-support, loss of property, the stress and time consumed going through the proceedings. And then the small matter of the children. She was not competent to care for them, but that would mean proving, in a horrendous scene, certainly, her alcoholism and more. It would be out of the question for her to have primary custody of the children. But how much better off would they be with him? He could physically provide for them, but, as he'd admitted to himself some time ago, he wasn't cut out to be a parent. He loved them but they were far from the focus of his existence. He met his responsibilities and beyond. If he didn't give them the attention they needed, he was sorry, but he couldn't be something he was not. And he refused to feel guilty about it. Look what he'd grown up with. Their life was infinitely easier than his had been. He'd seen to that and he would continue to see to it. He was doing his goddamned job. She wasn't doing hers. It was too much to think about being both a father and a mother.

Without realizing it Phil had increased his speed to seventy-five. He slowed down, carefully pumping the brakes. Patchogue just ahead. More than halfway there. Things were advancing too quickly. There were cops on this road. He'd gotten a speeding ticket a month ago, not too far from here, from a young Suffolk County cop who'd followed him over a mile, clocking him at eighty miles per hour. A young, trim guy with pale skin and dark aviator sunglasses. Very respectful. He remembered his name. O'Shaughnessy. He'd had more fights with the Irish than any other group as a kid. The cop's respectfulness irked him, it was a sham, the deliberate way he filled out the ticket and then carefully pointed with his clean fingernail pressed against the paper where Phil was supposed to sign. The warfare continued at all levels. The cop hated his "fancy" car and he hated the cop's arrogant authority. The mick bastard ticketing the Jew bastard. Well, he'd lost the battle but he was winning the war. It was unlikely the cop would ever get much farther east than Oakdale, much less spend the weekend at the beach in

Westhampton. In essence, the cops were working for him. That was the beauty of it. You could make something of your life if you wanted to. If you had the wherewithal. In this country. But no two ways about it, it was a struggle. They were everywhere, nipping at your heels. And then as if it weren't hard enough you had the demands and struggles of emotional life, where things like Carol and the children interposed themselves, insisting on being accounted for. A balancing act. His own childhood had been a joyless, dingy business, home no more than a place where something rank boiled dark and continuous, whether a blackened metal pot on the stove filled with soggy cabbage and potatoes, so repulsive after time that he chose to go hungry and light-headed, growing thin when he should have been blossoming robustly, or the mood of his parents, weary and frustrated with their lot, his father simmering and stoic, his stepmother at an acid temperature, scolding, caustic, domineering. And they, his parents, did nothing to discourage his alienation. His father, bent over his treadle machine fourteen hours a day, an unwilling guilty accomplice to his wife's unceasing harshness directed at his oldest son. In spite of the contributions he made, they were pushing him out. But it was a long miserable time before he actually left. He sometimes felt that the decision to become a photographer was a reaction to the dark, sour, cramped physical conditions of his childhood—the two small bedrooms (he and his step-brothers shared one of them, gloomy, with peeling walls that were never painted—the walls through which the cries, the shouts, the everyday patter of other families in the building could be heard, unending, echoing in his dreams at night), the kitchen, the heart, stomach and lungs of the apartment where everything happened, the constant susurrus and tacking of his father's machine, the bubbling pots on the coal stove, the bulky figure of his stepmother bent over angrily stirring the lifeless vegetables or, in a larger pot, the family's dirty clothes, his two younger brothers at the table helping with something manageable, cleaning or mending, only rarely doing something that was "fun," like reading or drawing, and the whole time a quiet, desperate tension weighing on them like a moldy, foul-smelling tarpaulin that only occasionally lifted, sometimes but not often for the Sabbath, holidays, the children's (but not his) birthdays. The other room in the house, the bathroom, the one place to go for privacy, was bitter compensation, the rusting cast-iron tub that was too small for a real bath (the water heated on the kitchen stove), the forlorn, stained, gurgling toilet, the tiny sink above which an ancient mirror cast sad reflections back at the household. There was neither heat nor cooling. Baths in the winter were taken with the door open for warmth from the kitchen, but the worst was the heat of summer, which gave no respite to anyone at any time. There was a shaft directly behind the bathroom that led to the ground, and from this in the summer's heat the rising effluvium was a potent reminder of everything dolorous and shabby about their lives. Photography was, above all, for Phil, a matter of space and light, the very things his home had lacked. (The separation from his father, though, saddened him deeply. He grew slowly to regain some of the respect he'd lost, understanding with time and distance the difficulties the man had faced. As for his stepmother, he never thought about her, though he'd called his father with condolences years later after they'd moved to Los Angeles when he'd heard from one of his brothers that the woman had died of cancer.) Phil was completely and uncritically American, believing in all the country's virtues and convinced that its faults (and most of these, in his mind, were faults of individuals, not the country itself) were correctable. The proof was his success. Though he respected the hard work and sacrifice of his parents, he disdained their cautious village mentality (although the fact of their coming over was hardly cautious) and distrust of the fast, alien new world, their painful ambivalence towards it. For him there was no ambivalence. It was there for the taking, or, as he had come to realize, some of it was. At least there was enough to satisfy the ambitious man like himself, providing the talent and drive were in supply. Phil's evolution from old world son to new American man, much more radical than his half-brothers' path, was felt by him on a visceral level to be a rejection of darkness in favor of light, from the joyless servitude of the humble immigrant to the yonder clarity of the brilliant American sky.

He'd risen towards photography as if by some heliotropic instinct, detesting any sort of defeatism, neurosis or self-pity, those things that throve in darkness. If he could escape the oppressive conditions of his upbringing then why couldn't anybody? It irked him that Carol, born into privilege, should have such difficulty, be so mired in inertia. Yes, it was the alcohol, but was it not something else as well? Why had she become an alcoholic and her sisters not? True enough, by the time her sisters came of age family circumstances had changed—the Japanese attack, the war, the move back to the states. The genteel life at the compound, the casual drinking, all that had vanished with war. Before the move to the states then, Carol had already been drinking. But why had it grown so? What were the conditions of her being that allowed the disease to take root and then, like a cancer, creep its way into the core of her and to the very fingertips? Why some people and not others? Who didn't have suffering, sadness, struggle, tragedy—all that shit! And who didn't take a drink now and then? Why some and not others? Why Carol?

He hadn't seen it. Or, if he had, he chose to gloss it over with those aspects that were so appealing—the wit (a bit caustic at times), the sophistication, her physical beauty, the strong attraction that had existed between them. She'd had a touching, almost childlike loyalty to him and his career that struck an ambivalent chord, resonating at once grateful, puzzled and slightly hostile. He'd never had anyone close openly champion him as she did. For that matter he'd never had anyone close. He couldn't accept it fully and questioned its authenticity. They had some terrible fights about it. He was unreasoning and a bit cruel, he knew, but he couldn't help himself, and he succeeded in pushing her away. He believed, however, that in the end she would have lost enthusiasm for acting the eager satellite to his career, not only because she seemed to ultimately loose enthusiasm for everything she undertook, but because it would have simply bored her. She was smart, very smart—in some ways, he would allow, smarter than he—and almost desperately in need of some absorbing, intellectual challenge, something of her own. And she had tried, in her half-hearted way. The stint with *Park East* (the magazine failed but she could have continued with her fashion writing), the abortive attempt at photography in Paris, a brief foray into acting just after college. Ironically, the happiest he'd ever seen her was in the mundane role of shopkeeper. She and her friend Simone, the wife of Geoffrey Winward, a writer she'd met at *Park East*, had a small place, *Beachcraft*, on Main Street the summers of '53 and '54. Simone, whom Carol adored, had an instinct for the *objet trouvé* and a gift for constructing whimsical collage-like pieces that were not without a touch of mystery—much like her personality. Carol dubbed her "Simone de Cornell," a conflation, typically Carolinian, of philosopher and box-maker that had the usual virtue of being apt. Simone had the French philosopher's independence of mind and spirit and the mystic of Utopia Parkway's unerring eye for the lost, the found and magical.

Their husbands paid the rent for the shop, which included beachwear (fashionable, yet affordable), paintings and sculptures by local artists (little of the usual seascapes and fishing boats), Simone's own curiosities, and even a couple of oil paintings by Carol, portraits on wood done in impasto style. They held drawing classes on Mondays, painting on Wednesdays and crafts on Fridays, attended mostly by the children of friends. A nominal fee was charged and the classes were taught by themselves or the occasional invited "guest" artist. Sometimes Mark and Eddie came, usually for the crafts, which was their favorite. Simone's children came more frequently, her teenage daughters helping with the classes, her son, Eddie's age, an eager, energetic participant. Carol and Simone were a good team, one the compliment of the other, and though Carol drank she managed some control, her days busy with the novelty of running a cheerful business. It was pleasant and it was "healthy," and Phil hoped that somehow this would make inroads through the haunted terrain, that the landscape might be nurtured, the ghost towns re-populated, but Geoffrey's finances took a turn for the worse. Phil couldn't handle the rent by himself and the store closed.

There was always the possibility, even with the closing of *Beachcraft*, that Carol might try a similar venture, but on her own. Phil had encouraged her and offered to help with expenses, but the willfulness and independence that seemed such a salient aspect of Carol's personality had begun to sag. Perhaps it had always been a bit of a pose, this rebellious singularity. Certainly, she'd depended on him ever since their marriage, most obviously financially, but in subtler ways as well. His success, Phil felt, gave her excuse to retreat from the demands of pursuing her own career goals. She refused to conform to the role of ordinary woman/wife/mother, but it seemed this rebelliousness was at least in part affected, that beneath the toughness was something delicate that sought to be cared for, that in fact she was quite overwhelmed with the prospect of having to make it on her own in a world dominated by males who seemed to go about the rugged business of competition and survival so matter-of-factly. Then, of course, after the children (and neither she nor Phil in their innermost hearts were, to this day, even sure they wanted children), Carol's difficulties compounded. Here was, then, something enormous and life-altering. Choices had to be made. Phil would go about his career and providing for the family. It was the expected role. But Carol's expected role had suddenly, profoundly, changed, and she was just as profoundly ambivalent about it. Having children was something of a death sentence. Having children meant that any hope of clearly defining herself had become that much more deeply troublesome, and her response to this reality had been to drift into an increasingly formless world, away from concrete connections to anything except alcohol, which became, then, in a way, her salvation, as other people might turn to religion. It relieved her from more difficult choices. It relieved Phil as well from more difficult choices. They might muddle through their lives in much the same way the Evanses did, somehow surviving, coexisting with the troublesome family member. Only there was a great difference between Carol and Marge, and also the families. Marge was homely and harmless—she didn't even drive. Carol was none of those things. The two daughters were old enough to take care that nothing disastrous happened (though imagine the burden, the unhappiness this caused them). No such conditions existed in his family. Indeed, it was the opposite. It was the children who needed caring for as much as the mother. And yet Phil could think of no alternative but to stumble along with hope against hope that nothing terrible happened. It was true, Carol was like a dead person. A walking dead person.

Phil was driving through Center Moriches on Main Street, Montauk Highway, which continued through East Moriches, Eastport, Speonk and on to Westhampton, then the right hand turn down Mill Road, through six corners to Potunk Lane past Main Street, to Stevens Lane, Jessup Lane, over the bridge and then—Dune Road. Doom Road. These small towns, Center Moriches, East Moriches, Eastport and blink-of-an-eye Speonk had, in the dead of summer, a languid, hermetic lushness that seemed, to Phil, much like the South—though he'd never been to the South—evoking the claustrophobic dread he imagined in such towns with names like Natchez, Greenwood or Leland, the spooky, humid verdancy that covered one's footsteps in new growth by the time the sun had set, the kind of devouring heat that would dispose of a body in days, leaving the bones for the terrible insects. These towns were death—the slow, smothering pace of life, and the equally slow, smothering mentality of those who lived there. And yet there was a kind of comfort driving through. For one thing, it meant that he was getting close to Westhampton, the beach, the ocean, the limitless, open sky, the nurturing elements of salt water, sand and sun. Driving through these towns with their gentle names, Moriches, Eastport, Speonk, in some way spoke to a part of his ancient, inarticulate past, haunted intimations of dark wooded places, people speaking in a strange guttural tongue, close upon each other, protecting, a small resolute fire flickering at the edge of night.

But now these towns spoke only of dread. In less than half an hour he'd be at the pink house, having to deal with God-knew-what sort of situation. He was, reluctantly, ready for anything. Thank goodness Emma was there to help with the children. Carol was going to end up at East Hill. How in the hell was he going to get her there? How in the hell did one do anything? Somehow, you managed. If one intended to move forward there was really no alternative. You simply, somehow, did it. But now he wished he had help—a squad of white coats to storm the house and subdue her, a shot of something in the arm, tie her down, take her away. He wished it had already been done and he would drive to East Hill in a week and visit quietly with his wife and she was calm and undergoing treatment and hopeful of coming home in a month or so and her life to begin anew. Why, indeed, hadn't he made arrangements for Dr. Campbell and company to take her away? He supposed it would have been the wrong thing to do. As painful, as horrible, as the situation was, it remained his situation. His responsibility.

Phil's stomach churned and twisted. He'd had only coffee and grapefruit before he'd left. He thought of his own father, sitting in the same spot hour after hour, year after year, stoic and quiet, in the dark corner, his machine whirring and clacking. His own father, ultimately, an enigma. And the sadness of never really knowing him. He used to think of him as weak, in submission to the imperious demands of his wife and to the grim realities of his station. But the small man must have had great strength and wisdom, hadn't he? In comparison Phil felt his own life, in spite of his material achievements, to be shallow, devoid of the inner qualities that so fortified his father's. Virtually his whole life given over in pursuit of the bitch goddess. And she had obligingly lain with him. Had he seduced her, or she him? In any case, her allurements, while sweet and intoxicating, in the end, he suspected, left one in a bin of ashes, some of which he could already taste. In spite of everything—everything!—all the work and sweat and agony of jangled nerves and bleeding gut, it amounted to a lonely, fretful drive on a desolate Sunday morn- ing to once again clean up the wreckage of another domestic catastrophe. He wondered if his father had felt any of the same things, the sense that really, after all the effort and sacrifice, his life had turned into some kind of sad joke, dark-cornered slave to his sewing machine, under the dominion of a hard, unhappy woman and material circumstance. His father had, perhaps, experienced a few years of happiness in the new world, in the beginning, married to Esther, Phil's mother. A few times when Phil was a child, his father, always careful to make sure his wife wasn't around and even then, in hushed tones, had spoken to him about his lovely mother with the soul of a poet and "eyes as deep and blue as the ocean." She'd died of tuberculosis just after Phil's first birthday. There was no picture of her, nor did Phil have any recollection of this gentle and poetic person. Imagine the wonder and happiness his father must have felt meeting such a woman—in steerage no less! Imagine their first years, in love and struggling together in this hard, strange country that offered so much promise—and not the least of that promise the thought of surviving together, raising a healthy family, becoming grandparents to beautiful American children. Max and Esther. Poor Max. Life played one of its wicked jokes. And then by necessity came Bertha into their lives, blustering, booming Bertha. Big Bertha. She was aptly named, firing her bitterness at will, terrorizing everyone, driving Max to his corner in silence and stoicism, his only comfort the Talmud, kept open on a table next to his machine. It was Bertha who insisted, barely three months into their marriage, that they change their surname from Grossman to Heizer. Well, Phil and Carol had been briefly happy, this beautiful spirited woman, the world his oyster, all of that, and then the children, the drinking, the darkness settling in, and he saw himself as no different than his father, hunched over the treadle machine in a gloomy corner. Of course, that wasn't really true, his life was much better than that. Good lord, so much better, wasn't it? But something nagged at Phil, something subtle that suggested that perhaps he wasn't so much better off after all. Though it hadn't much crossed his mind he now felt regret at not knowing his father, of not being close to him, and of course this was precisely what was happening with Mark and Eddie. He didn't know how to be a father. It was certainly a father's job to provide. He did that much and more. His own father had worked valiantly at that. But the enduring image of his father was of a small balding man with his back turned, bent diligently over his work. And did he not spend most of his time bent over a camera? Father and son, bowed over their machines.

He was through Speonk without even realizing it, on the last leg of the drive. He would make an effort to be closer to Mark and Eddie, to spend more time with them. Ironic how he'd intended to make everyone's lives so much better than his own had been and, in some ways, yes, very important ways, they certainly were. But in other ways—in ways he never foresaw—their lives were not that much different, or better. A red truck with sideboards, laden with watermelons, pulled out in front of him and proceeded slowly, at first angering Phil, but then he was grateful for the delay. It was a little cooler than it had been for the past week, thankfully. He sensed the ocean for the first time, a looming, sentient presence. Intimations of the approaching hurricane. Connie. The truck turned off the highway and a stretch of open road lay before him, normally an invitation to step on the gas and feed the powerful engine, feel its satisfying, compelling response, the landscape flying past. But he maintained the workmanlike pace the truck had established.

He was not ready for this dreadful moment. And then, much too fast, he was passing the restaurant with its dueling musketeers, past Beaver Dam Creek, and then turning right on Mill Road, inexorably and damnably, as if some demon magnet were now controlling his car, pulling it towards the pink house.

And now, though he was driving slowly, the high school was upon him and then six corners, everything oddly deserted, and though, somewhat absurdly, he wanted nothing more than to stop and get out of the car and walk around the town (something he almost never did), to observe closely things he hadn't paid much attention to, but of course he did not, and there he was, slowly down Potunk Lane, past the goy country club to his right, the Episcopal church on his left, past Main Street, just as deserted as six corners (where the hell was everybody?), as if Westhampton had suddenly been struck by some biological or radiological catastrophe (there were a few cars and people about, the sort that didn't know, or refused to flee), and then, alas, the right turn to Stevens Lane and abruptly left to Jessup Lane and the long shimmering stretch at the end of which loomed the bridge and beyond. Dune Road. It occurred to Phil that this slow, reluctant but unavoidable journey was much like his own life, or any life, for that matter. He dreaded this confrontation with Carol as much as death, and to be in this vehicle he drove was the like the passage of one's life. And how fast he usually traveled. One just went like mad, racing around. He never really stopped, did he? Even "recreation," or "leisure time" was a sort of breathless dash, with some preoccupation or responsibility looming, casting its deadening shadow over the present. And only now with the dreadful moment at hand was he driving slowly, yearning to get out and look around. Perhaps if this latest ordeal were negotiated successfully, he might get something important out of it for himself—if he would even remember these thoughts. Slow down, Philly boy! Slow down with your life and remember. Forty-eight years old! And as he was thinking about the blink of an eye that constituted those forty-eight years the car rose abruptly upwards, crossing the drawbridge where out on the bay he saw that no catastrophe had befallen the summer town, the water busy with the usual sailboats, water-skiers and assorted revelers intently packing as much of the fading weekend's recreation as they could, as if into trunks and suitcases, preparing for, indeed, an evacuation about to happen. He recognized the pitiful absurdity in all this and understood that he was no different and wished at the same time that he were out there sailing or water-skiing like the rest of them, that his life was normal and that it was a normal week-end. The car nosed down off the bridge, pointed directly at the Swordfish Club and he thought of the marlin he'd caught once on a three-day fishing trip. The scintillating leap out of the blue water, the splashing reentry. He was actually relaxed on that trip. Did it take an ocean voyage to do it? Chuck it all for a life at sea. Sailor Phil. The club's parking lot to his right was full. They were out in force, all of them. This was reassuring. Though he was far removed. It seemed a movie or a dream in which this very scene repeated itself endlessly, that he was forever driving off the bridge and looking at the beach club and thinking about the fish he once caught thirty miles off shore and remembering those few moments of excitement, and there was the beach club parking lot, the great innocence of everything, and how much he wanted to be a part of that, but could not, at least not now, and down the road to the west, only darkness.

***

Mark and Eddie cautiously approached the beach in front of the club, having forgotten for the moment their anxiety at being far from home and the troubles of their mother, although they were aware now of a shift in their lives that felt different from other things. It was as if the world itself had abruptly turned and faced a new direction, one that they'd never seen before, casting upon them a subtly altered light, a denser atmosphere, a stronger gravitational pull. The change, somehow, seemed permanent, and Eddie, older than Mark, perceived something about life he'd never really thought of, though there had always been the feeling. Perhaps Emma's going had triggered it: People disappeared. Just like the man walking past them who asked where their parents were and told them to be careful with the fire. Eddie had watched him go down the beach until he was out of sight. He'd never seen that man before and he'd probably never see him again. Emma was a part of his life and now she was gone and he realized that he'd never see her again. Such a thing was possible with his own family. Mark, or his father or his mother might suddenly be gone. Or he could be gone. He could be kidnapped. Such things happened. Or Mark could be kidnapped. Eddie watched his younger brother walking slowly, staring absently at the ocean. He would have to keep an eye on him and make sure he didn't get lost or no one tried to take him. He didn't like Emma but he was a little sad at her leaving and hurt that she hadn't said good-bye. She never liked him, for some reason. But sometimes she was nice, the way she cooked for them and made sure they had enough food, or the way she'd sometimes dry their hair after their baths, humming deep in her throat as she did.

The boys walked close to the water when they got to the Swordfish Club beach, surrounded by a mass of splashing, running, yelling people, families, lots of children, many his age, and Mark's, some looking at them curiously, a few in a more challenging manner, as if they wanted to fight. Eddie avoided their stares and whispered to Mark did he want to go up and look at the pool. They walked back a bit in the direction they'd come and circled around the throng, walking as unobtrusively as possible up the great wooden stairs, their heads turned down hopefully not to be recognized as strangers but their very demeanor marking them as such, anticipating at any moment a lifeguard or some adult stopping them and ordering them away. At last they arrived overlooking the vast sparkling pool. The marvelous Swordfish pool! The only bigger one they'd seen was at Coney Island, but that had so many people it seemed more like a huge bathtub than a real swimming pool. The boys stood quietly, their shoulders touching, and stared at the limpid, dancing salt water glistening silver and green and the unimaginably deep end where big kids dove from the high board. There was no question of going in. Even if they had been members the thought of swimming in the Swordfish pool was daunting, its vastness, the strange children, and something more, a forbidding quality they couldn't identify. Even the people who belonged to the club didn't seem to use it very much. Eddie wondered if it was because they felt the same way as he did. There was something about the pool that was similar to his feelings about people disappearing. After a few minutes they became uneasy—though no one paid them any attention—and they turned and went down back to the beach, thinking that they'd better go home, reluctant to do so yet anxious now they'd been so long. They angled off from the crowd and headed directly to the shore and then back in the direction of home. The ocean was rougher than yesterday when his mother had gone swimming with that man and they both had their clothes on. The ocean wasn't rough at all then. But now there were waves and the distant water was choppier. It was cooler too, and cloudier. Yesterday there were lots of fishing boats and today not so many. Eddie, looking at the horizon, stepped on a piece of tar and it squished between his big toe and the one next to it. There was turpentine and rags in the closet downstairs to clean it, a small closet next to their room with cans of paint and bug spray (Flit!) and other things for the house. It was hot in there and it smelled. Emma said once that it was going to blow up and burn the house down but he thought she was kidding, although sometimes he wasn't so sure. He knew well enough that it would be a bad place to light a match. He wondered what it would be like if he did. He found a stick and scraped as much of the tar away as he could. They were always stepping on tar. He wondered where it came from. It couldn't be part of the sand, could it? The beach was always different. Yesterday there had been little pools and islands and today they were gone. There had also been more rocks and shells and bits of softened colored glass. Sometimes when there were lots of fishing boats close to shore there would be different kinds of fish washed up and the seagulls would eat them. His favorites were the sand sharks with their rough skin like sandpaper and little mouths underneath and the sharp teeth, and also the sting-rays that he and Mark would flip over with sticks and now had finally gotten up the nerve to pick up by their tails. Those days when the boats were close to shore were best, when the sky was deep blue and the water calm. There were a few times when men in smaller boats would come and put their huge nets into the water and then from shore drag them in, catching hundreds of fish. They were rough men in big boots and the way they spoke was hard to understand. A lot of them had beards. One of them had once shown him an octopus. He supposed it was dead, and he felt a little sorry for it. When he left, he saw the fisherman throw it into the water in a high tumbling arc, its tentacles flailing, and it landed in a small silver splash beyond the waves. The boys often saw dolphins, sometimes very close, and once a dead whale had washed up on shore. There were lots of people looking at it and touching it. It was big, but not as big as whales he'd seen in pictures or movies about whale hunting. Some people were afraid of the whale and wouldn't go near it, but Mark and Eddie went right up and touched it and stayed close to it for a long time. The next day the whale was gone.

The boys walked along quietly on the hard sand next to the water. There were more people on the beach and the day was getting warmer. They passed a man and a boy about Eddie's age having a catch with a new baseball. Farther down a man and a woman were attempting to launch a kite and it dove and skipped along the beach behind them. Ahead they could see the Dune Deck beach and all the people, though not as many as the

Swordfish Club. They walked along and neither wanted to go home, though they knew they must. Eddie looked at Mark, not certain if his brother's thoughts were the same as his own. He thought perhaps not. Mark walked with his head down seemingly looking at his feet. In a few minutes they were walking through the Dune Deck crowd. The people were older and there weren't nearly as many kids. No one seemed to pay any attention to them and soon they were past the Dune Deck and onto the stretch that, after last year's hurricane that had washed houses away, including the Goldens', seemed lonely and strange, with pieces of the houses still in the dunes, bricks and pieces of wood and also glass and rusty nails you had to be careful about. Ahead they could see the great empty space where the Goldens' house used to be, and they could see the sandpipers swooping and turning and, faintly, the noises they made. There didn't used to be so many of these birds but after the Goldens' house washed away there were hundreds of them, almost magically appearing. He and Mark quickly discovered the fun of going where they lived and being dive-bombed, but they didn't do it too often because it meant walking on the dunes, which was against the law, and also because the birds were really scary, coming so close you thought they might peck your eyes out, and sometimes they would even poop on you. Now the sandpipers swarmed in agitation and the boys saw two people walking over the dunes near where the Goldens' house was, oblivious, apparently, to the birds that swooped down at their heads. Eddie marveled at how close they actually came: They might really hit you. One of the people, a man, it looked like, raised his head and swung his arms at the birds, which only seemed to make them angrier.

The other person was a woman, it seemed, walking with her head down and arms folded, a vaguely familiar silhouette wearing a white bathrobe, and it began to dawn on him with a sick feeling in his stomach that it was his mother. The two figures disappeared behind the dunes and all the boys could see was the birds rising up and hovering and others flying out in a circle as if gathering speed, then coming back and diving at the unseen couple. Straight ahead another person came walking at them down the beach, a stocky figure striding purposefully, oddly dressed in long pants and a white shirt rolled up at the cuffs, and now he was waving his arms and shouting. It was such a strange sight it took a moment for them to understand, but then they did and the strangeness of seeing their mother disappear behind the dunes, the outraged sandpipers swarming and diving at her, the other person with her whom they did not recognize, became even more strange and also frightening with the addition of the agitated powerful presence coming towards them, coming after them, and they knew they were going to be in trouble for going so far away, but perhaps not too much because they sensed that the most serious thing of all was the strange way their mother had been acting, and in comparison to that their going away wasn't quite so bad. They slowed their pace almost to a standstill as the figure approached, hearing his tone of voice which was more concerned than angry, the world now a mixture of familiarity and strangeness, of safety and fear, and then they stopped altogether. "It's daddy," said Mark.

"Listen, Carol," said Howard Johnson, a few steps behind, ducking as the fierce, angry birds plunged inches from his head. "I think Phil is right. You need a break, some time out, some rest." He flinched, and flailed his arms. "Jesus! These fucking birds are insane! It would only be for a little while. A chance to dry out a little bit. Hell, I should do it myself. We're both crazy anyway, drinking like this. There's too much to lose. You've got two beautiful children who need you. You owe it to them—and yourself. Carol! Do you hear me?" Carol spread her arms and did a kind of pirouette and then stood as if opening herself to a downpour after a drought, her head tilted back, only it was not rain she invited but the malevolent pipers with their dart-like beaks to pierce her like St. Sebastian. At first she closed her eyes but then opened them, willing herself from blinking as the pipers wheeled and pumped their small furious wings rapidly and accelerated in a beeline towards her upturned face, banking upwards at the very last possible thrilling second, emitting a singular, wrathful shriek as they turned, as if the concentrated anger of the sound itself was enough to drive her away, circling around and coming in for another run at these oafish intruders who threatened their fledglings. The birds that did not circle raised themselves over the trespassers' heads and then dropped like stones towards them, at times almost colliding with the ones that circled, that flew clockwise and attacked from the north-east. Aware that her robe was loose she continued to stand with her arms outstretched feeling doubly thrilled, presenting herself as some feral child of God welcoming the world of man and nature into her sexual body. The birds kept circling and diving, their fury increasing. One let loose a stream of excrement that landed on her thigh and bathrobe.

"Carol! Come on! Let's get out of here! These fucking birds are going to kill us. For Chrissakes! And tie up your bathrobe. You're making a spectacle of yourself." And as Howard Johnson stood behind her saying this he flinched and ducked as a man on stage dodging rotten vegetables hurled by irate groundlings, at the same time coldly enraged at these wicked, brazen birds, wanting nothing less than to kill them with stones or sticks or anything lethal he could get his hands on, but constrained from such action by the sheer stupidity of it and the priorities at hand. This was a damnably absurd situation, pleading with a woman he hardly knew, half-naked and out of her mind, while being at-tacked by maniacal, shit-flinging birds as the woman's husband, whom he'd just briefly met in one of the most awkward and embarrassing situations of his life, walked on the beach nearby, frantically looking for his children. And to think that he'd almost not called this morning, debating whether to go back to Brook-lyn early to beat the traffic (not really wanting to stay any longer as a guest of a couple he'd met at a party three weeks earlier) or, more out of boredom than anything else, to call Carol for a pos-sible day of drinking and perhaps (very small chance) something else. Exercising the merest of arbitrary choice, he'd picked up the phone and dialed her number, only to be, because he had a bit of conscience left (try as he might to get rid of it), drawn into her desperation, and now a situation that was getting stickier and more dreadful by the minute. He felt like Br'er Rabbit grabbed hold of some existential Tar-Baby. He felt a fool and he certainly felt he had no business being there. But there he was and there was no getting away. There was a kind of mocking justice to it. He was getting what he deserved. How extraordinary to be in the middle of a family drama and not know anyone in the family! Thank God he wasn't drunk, for despite the chagrin he felt at being trapped in this situation, and the absurdity of it, his heart had softened and he felt pity, and he resolved that since he was here he would do what he could (in a temporary, barely significant way) to help them and he would stay, if needed (though the husband might order him away as soon as the children were found), for as long as they wanted him. He would see this to the bitter end and he would marshal all that was decent in himself. He would do what he could to bring this woman back to the world—bring them all back to the world, if not to each other.

Carol, meanwhile, stood as before. The silliness of the birds was irksome. Didn't they understand? She proposed to stand like this for as long as it took the birds to get it. She was one of them—of the same fabric as everything that was. Her arms grew tired and she lowered them to her sides. The birds kept coming, though they, too, seemed to tire and relent, if only slightly. Some flew off a short way and rested on the ground. They were so well camouflaged she couldn't see them once they'd landed. Others continued circling and diving. Their diminishing hostility led her to think that they might be becoming attuned to her nature, her woman-nature, this body that produced its own fledglings, like theirs, this body that could fly too, like they, and would fight too, if necessary.

"Carol?"

She made an easy backwards motion with her left hand intended to quiet and reassure him. "Shhh," she said. "It's okay."

"Tie up your bathrobe at least."

"Shhh!" She made the motion again, this time with some impatience. Carol was beginning to feel herself a bit of the Great Mother and, if anything, wanted to take the robe off completely. She pulled at its sides to open it a bit more, exposing the front of her body more fully, her breasts, stomach, pubic hair, thighs, open to the birds, the sand, the sky, the passing cars. She was the birds, the sand, the sky, the passing motorists, the one who begets and nourishes, and through her all the world was begetting and nourishing, a busy copulating swarm of energy —self-begetting, self-nurturing abundance! A perpetual energy machine and she the font, the outpouring motherlode and all of creation, a dancing warring, frenzied ceremony of obeisance. How few of them understood! And all the death, the violence, the wars, murders, mutilations, the Hiroshimas and Nagasakis, all of it the unconscious sacrificial bloodletting in honor of the Great Mother, the decay, the blood, nurturing and soaking the earth in which her feet took root—she the giver, the dispenser of grace. The sacrifices were necessary, she now understood. It was part of giving birth. And neither was she anything particularly special, though a kind of grace had been offered and gratefully received. It was not even necessary, perhaps, for most to understand. In fact, few ever did, and this was natural. The rest a childlike divine innocence. She would be content to know and to observe, rooted in the Great Mother Realm at the earth's center, her body the vehicle for the creation of ever-new elements granting in some distant future access to the planets and stars, communing finally with the others, those who had undergone the process—the air, the light, the fire below, the cyclic order spiraling upward through the loins and spine out through the chamber of the heart—Bleeding Mother!—the serpent-fire bursting forth, incinerating illusion and fear. The birds rose again in agitation for no discernible reason and began to dive at them, and she felt the force come up through the earth, from the Great Mother, through her spine, seeking egress. The birds dived with renewed fury. The sizzling pressure rose up along her spine to her neck and she felt the top of her head open and a flash of light shoot forth as if she had suddenly added her own current to the world's field of electricity. Then a huge, weary sadness pressed down upon her and she slowly sank to the ground, the remains of her energy-force draining away, invisible but palpable down into the sand, dispersing down and away from her, as if her whole body was liquid poured from a pitcher and she sat finally in a kind of useless heap, unbearably sad and enervated.

Howard Johnson came to her side and knelt, taking the edges of the bathrobe and drawing them together and then, reaching under her limp arms for the ends of the belt cinched them as tightly as he could without constricting her. Carol slumped forward, her legs haphazardly crossed, her hands resting beside her on the sand, a defeated and distant expression on a face whose animating muscles seemed to have gone into paralysis or shock. From the energized other-worldly conviction of a few moments before she had lapsed into a kind of catatonia—all the better, thought Howard Johnson, for now we might be able to deal with her. Perhaps she would allow herself to be coaxed or more easily led into the car and driven to the sanatorium. It was the first thing her husband had said after sizing up the situation, understanding that their maid had left, seeing the sodden mass of burned clothes on the living room table, like some hellish, unrecognizable ruined animal, the floor beneath sopping wet, the man he'd never seen before, his missing children: "You're going to East Hill whether you want to or not, and that's all there is to it! As a matter of fact, there's already a room for you. So, get ready. I'm going to find the boys." His anger and conviction were powerful and imperious, but there was also an element of bravado, a mask for the fear and shock he surely must have felt. He was not an unlikable person and Howard Johnson felt a sympathy for him. At the same time, here was a man out of touch with his home, perhaps not wanting to face up to the depressing, overwhelming reality of his wife and the problem of the children. He couldn't blame the man for feeling overwhelmed but there must have been a shortcoming there as well, not pulling through, somehow, on all fronts. So many were like him, their lives in not-so-tidy compartments, each separated from the other, a kind of stupid acceptance of the conventions of the time where daddy went off and worked himself dry and weary and trusted wifey and the children to happily thrive, nurtured by the pipeline of his sweat and material harvest, each trusting the other to do the job correctly, the result a happily-balanced equation brought to you by Westinghouse or Pepsodent or Pepsi-Cola. Yes, he was a fashion photographer and a hip fellow, but the scene was convention itself, recapitulated *ad nauseam* throughout this deluded country—convention itself. But he was not a disagreeable fellow, despite the fact that for a moment, when Phil was taking everything in, in his shock and outrage, recognizing the catastrophe that was his home, his wife, his children, Howard Johnson feared that, when the man's blue furious eyes lighted on him for three or four burning seconds, he might have to physically defend himself and, giving no outward hint or sign, prepared himself for a possible assault, not a pleasant thing to consider as this husband was a powerful-looking man and justifiably filled with righteous temper and, to be sure, a sizable portion of guilt. With some very fast talking, Howard Johnson more or less convincingly put himself in the position of honorable man befallen by circumstance, admittedly no saint, who on impulse called this morning and recognizing the seriousness of the situation rushed over, etc., etc. Phil wasn't buying, but his anger was overshadowed by obviously more pressing concerns and Howard Johnson's moment of physical apprehension passed.

"The blessed little birds—"

Carol spread her fingers and pushed her hands into the sand, moving them around, the grains gently abrading her skin. Somewhere she heard leaves rustling and a deep thrumming as if from the center of the earth. The great beating heart like an enormous hand playing the same chord over and over on a guitar with strings as large as bridge cables, portentous, re-assuring, connecting her to the essential, what she had recently discovered—though it was something she'd known all her life, what everyone knew, if only they—

"Carol. Sweetie. We need to think about—"

"We surely don't need to think—only listen. Mr. Johnson—that can't be your real name, you've been putting me on the whole time—what a funny man you are—very sweet—I like you very much. Mr. Johnson, America's family restaurant man—

avatar of wholesome promise. You and I, Mr. Johnson, we've been—oh, dear, it's hopeless. It can't be explained. You think I'm crazy, I'm sure. Just like Phil. He wants to take me away. Maybe not such a bad idea. But I won't let then drug me, no sir. I've found something I will not allow anyone to take away. The world spins a bit faster, Mr. Johnson. Can you feel it? Can you hear the sound of the great beating heart beneath us, all around us? Have you ever looked at the stars and felt someone, something, looking back? They are, you know. They know so much more than we do. There's no hurry, really, but then all of a sudden, I'm terrifically impatient. I want to know, Mr. Johnson, I want to get there. The thing that hurts is leaving my children behind. But they'll get there too, some day. They're already there and don't know it. Maybe they'll remember me. Don't hate the birds, Mr. Johnson, they are very precious. They recognize us for the stupid oafs we are. Just trying to wake us up. Don't you love the fishing boats, Mr. Johnson? There's not so many today. The ocean is different. Can you feel it? Can you feel the world spinning a little faster? It is spinning faster—I can feel it. I think I'm going very far away. I can fly, did you know that? I mean of course not literally, but I can fly a plane. I've had lessons. It's the first step, isn't it? Flying lessons? My guru, the flight instructor. How marvelous it is up there, streaming through the ether, the engines droning like some wonderful purring tiger, angels sitting on the wings playing their celestial lyres, the yonder blue wild—all this civilization, Mr. Johnson, it's just a sham, just— and now we fly to get away from all of it. Isn't it marvelous? Soon we'll be casting our seed into space, interbreeding with other seeds and ova. I won't be around in this body, but I done seed it all already!"

"Carol—"

"Have you read *Flying Sausages Have Landed*, by Leslie Adamski? Oh my! Flying sausages! Don't you think so? That they've landed? I had a classical education, Mr. Johnson. Did you know that? And now I scan the sky for flying sausages. Out of the flying pan into the fire. Those were Joan of Arc's last words, you know. She was looking for flying sausages. The universal light, Mr. Johnson, it's what I've been seeing—the essence of things—but for most people it's darkness, going through their lives in selfishness, stupidity, back and forth, back and forth, like the Long Island Rail Road, such bitter, malcontent lives, so bitter they have to ignite their own feeble flames—industry! commerce! war! Hiroshima! Nagasaki! Their own pathetic way of getting back to the light. And of course it kills them all, like dumb moths flying into a candle flame—"

"Carol, I like what you're saying. It makes sense to me, but—"

"Jack be nimble and Jack be quick. Here, help me up, Mr. Johnson." Carol suddenly felt very afraid that if she sat much longer in this desolate place what was left of her spirit would drain completely away, that her body would melt, leaving a frightful, putrid mass beneath the bathrobe, and in her mind's eye she saw the bathrobe as time passed, decayed, mottled with sandpiper and seagull shit, becoming the sand, disappearing. Death, her own death. Palpable. A presence that closed around her like something dark and iron, a dreadful medieval torture device, a Bloody Mary, Iron Maiden, Queen Elizabeth—what was it called? Leave this place at once. She raised her hand in the air. "Help, Mr. Johnson, I'm mhe-hhelll-ting!" Howard Johnson rose to his feet and, taking hold of Carol's limp right hand, pulled her body, heavy with collapse, to a tenuous, standing position. He looked closely at the small, tense, weary face, the scar beneath the cheekbone especially livid, her hazel eyes distant and glazed with resignation and fear, vaguely reminiscent of certain expressions he'd seen in war. Her eyes were bloodshot and for the first time he noticed the network of fine wrinkles around them and the tiny explosions of blood vessels dotted about her face as if someone had taken a needle and pricked her here and there. Her breath exuded the sweet musty smell of vodka and cigarettes. Again, the profane slithered into his mind. How many times he'd been with women in similar condition. But none as badly off as this one, he didn't think—and lord, he had no scruples about taking full advantage of them.

Carol swayed and put her hand on Howard Johnson's shoulder, looking out over the gray-blue ocean that seemed to recede as if she were looking through the wrong end of a telescope, hastening away from her as all of her life seemed to be at that moment, abruptly finished, vanished, gone, done with.

"Let's go for another swim, Mr. Johnson, farther out this time. We'll hold hands and sink to the bottom, the two of us."

"Enough morbidity. Let's go. We need to get you straightened out, back on track. Come on. You've got a lot to live for, you really do. You're young and beautiful and you've got two beautiful children to take care of and watch grow up into wonderful, strong young men. They need you, don't you know that? You've got a lot to offer this world, Carol." He took her by the elbow and guided her towards the large pink house and the birds shrieked and swooped down at them. She walked slowly and feebly like an old woman and her will seemed to have vanished. He hoped this would continue. Perhaps this wouldn't be so difficult after all. But then just as suddenly as she'd gone slack, she became reanimated.

"Did you say 'back on track?' How priceless! As if I were some bloody railroad car, derailed. Over on my side gasping for air, wheels spinning. All we need to do is get up, brush the sand off a bit and get back on the rails so I can continue on schedule—Massapequa! Massapequa Park! Lindenhurst! Babylon! Mr. Johnson, how dare you!" Carol, suddenly angry, wrenched free from his grasp, took two steps and looked up to see the pink house tipping over on its foundation towards her and the ground spinning up rapidly and she felt a mild, suffocating and not unpleasant blow to her face, reminiscent of a pillow fight— how odd to be struck by a pillow, and in the dark, too!

"Carol!"

She felt a terrible urge to sneeze violently but couldn't. Nothing worse than not being able to sneeze. Her teeth made a horrible crunching noise and she feared they had shattered, their bits rolling around in her mouth like gravel. How could a pillow have shattered her teeth? And who was it that hit her anyway? Damn whoever it was to hit her when she wasn't looking! Why couldn't she move? She seemed to be upside down. Was she dreaming? She hoped that she was. The crunching in her mouth was too disturbing. Slowly the black world gave way to a filtered gray and she was aware of murmuring sounds, as if a crowd had gathered around her. Mixed with the crunchiness was something metallic and sick-tasting. The gray grew to white, with speckles of dark and there were valleys and undulations and a red gemstone sparkled at the bottom of her vision. She made a mental note to pick up the stone—a ruby, probably—when she could. It would be worth something. She needed money, lots of money, for some reason, a reason that gave her an aching sense of being elsewhere, some cherished and lovely place, forever inaccessible—perhaps not, perhaps not. She was down somewhere, in some kind of hole, and though the world was brighter than moments before, at least directly in front of her, there was still the horrible feeling of being in a straightjacket, the peripheral world dim and murmuring. Perhaps this was some sort of limbo, and the light directly in front of her came up through the world from the center, towards which she was going, and the dark murmuring around her was the former world that now seemed but an interlude, or prelude, a fleeting and insubstantial thing, and those she was leaving behind poor victims of ignorance forced to spend their time in restless blinkered agony— poor things! If she could get word to them, somehow—it was all right, it really was! She wanted to tell them about the uselessness of all their struggle and striving, that their time was but a passage from one place to another. It was as if all of them were on hooks and being dipped into hot bubbling fat and they kicked and wailed and screamed with their eyes tightly shut, and what she so desperately wanted to tell them was that they but needed to open their eyes and relax and the hooks and boiling fat would go away, and in the place of these instruments of torture would come the clear, healing liberating light. But these thoughts were followed by a wave of dreadful futility that crushed down on her like a ton of suffocating pillows. There could be no communication, no enlightenment, no salvation. She had been no different than they, after all, and there was no assurance that what she saw in front of her was any kind of light, but rather a milky nothingness that was slowly enveloping her, a kind of sticky porridge in which she was doomed to spend eternity and, in fact, it was those outside who, in spite of their suffering, still breathed the bracing crispness of life and light and it was she who was the blind one, the willfully blind one, now offered a taste of what was to be forever, this mass of pale viscous stuff like liquid plaster slowly hardening, filling her mouth, nose and ears, choked and frozen forever in a cosmic ocean of plaster in God-knew-what absurd position—upside down? spread-eagled? fetal?—a grimace or scream disfiguring her face for eternity, for the endless, countless, unimaginable passage of infinite time where world after world disappeared, came into being, evolved and disappeared again endlessly, on and on, endlessly endless. Did it matter though, that her life was the merest of specks? The tiniest of electrical discharge among an infinite number going off unceasingly? Perhaps if she'd lived better, paid more attention, she might not be frozen in plaster as she was. This might be unpleasant. She'd have to come to some sort of accommodation. Maybe after a while she could just go to sleep and all would be forever dark and quiet, a cold ember drifting in the vastness. No, that was not agreeable because it wasn't tolerable to think of her children ending up like that. There had to be something else. For the children. For the children we all were. The other was too cruel. But if it was the children who died, it was they who became angels, so there was no cold endless drifting. Only for the likes of her, for all the lies and lacking, for all the wasted time and consciousness, absorbed in the most uninteresting and fruitless selfishness. But she'd had her signal of the divine energy. Perhaps there was hope that there really was some sort of purpose and that she was a part of it and in fact had been chosen to impart this understanding to others, now that she understood it herself. No difference existed between the physical and spirit world. All was manifest of the same will or energy. No such thing as nothingness. All was rebirth. All possessed the light, the inextinguishable light, that towards which she headed, that which was within her and without. She felt herself being lifted and the light all around her brighter. There was hope perhaps, after all. No joy but something far stronger. Purpose. And what was that purpose but the sacred opportunity to understand?

The outlines of the water and beach came into view, filtered through a prismatic stroboscopic flashing, as if she were looking through a fan and each interstice contained a different color. A strong force pressed under her arms and it seemed as though she was floating several inches above the ground. The suffocating whiteness relented with the new colorful orientation. The sensation of going up was powerful, lifted by the force at her sides as well as the terrain itself elevating, so that the distant water, now the most extraordinary violet-blue and glistening, as if made of cellophane, was below her level of vision, and she had the oddest feeling of looking down upon it and at the same time understanding that it was the Sea of Galilee she was gazing upon and being lifted over the hills by the extraordinary benign nurturing force of human kindness and Godly power. Over the hills from whence cometh help, and down to the Sea of Galilee, whose plastic glimmering colors restored her to life, so deeply fulfilling a sight, so deeply happy, her ordeal, her descent, her regeneration...

III

On Wednesday Carol awoke at dawn. She wasn't certain how long she'd been at this place. It was East Hill, surely. Where else could it be? Perhaps three days. Cold. She pulled the thin pale green cotton blanket to her chin. Through an opening in the curtains, also green but a deeper shade, she could see the gray sky and the trees moving in the wind. Perhaps there had been rain. Or would be. It seemed as if she'd awakened in a different season than the one she'd just come through. Or a different latitude, or country. A passage of dreams and vivid colors. Aquaplaning in the Red Sea, Paul's slender, naked body, the livid, looming face of her mother, riding to town with the boys in a small three-passenger jet and swerving out over the dunes, climbing thousands of feet above the ocean and far below the enormous storm, tugging at them. She'd been wronged. Taken advantage of. Cause for rage. But she was tired. No more energy. The life spirit.

An hour or so later she managed to get out of bed and look out the window. This seemed like the room she'd been in before. Outside, the sloping lawn, the same dreadful trees, the thing in the distance, a water tower, with the letters ILLE. The drone of a plane overhead, receding. How many times as a child she stood at the window as now, looking out over the fabulous city, a view then that seemed to offer so mysteriously much, and a view now that offered so mysteriously little. ILLE. What did those letters mean? She was ill, yes, and on an isle. An ill isle. Carol looked down at the ridiculous garment that sheathed her. Some sort of laboratory item. Sickly blue. All these washed-out, nightmarish pastels. Near the corner of the room, flung across an armchair beneath a framed reproduction of a Buffet still-life that clashed stupidly with the pale salmon walls, was a familiar item, and her spirit leapt to it: her white terrycloth bathrobe. Carol walked to the chair across the wooden floor, dark from the decades of linseed oil of which it vaguely smelled, cold on her feet (and the pain of the glass still with her), and pulled herself into the garment as she might have snuggled into her father's lap for warmth as a child, had she ever, and beneath the armchair the fluffy comical pink slippers into which, with a rush of joy so sudden that she almost cried, she inserted her chilled feet, happily wiggling her toes while tying the belt of the robe. Partially human now and a moment's sublime comfort.

But only a moment. Terribly thirsty and a craving for sweet. Orange juice. A tall glass of freshly-squeezed orange juice. It took several seconds before the thought of adding vodka to the sweet pulpy drink swam into consciousness. Normally like a bumptious grouper it pushed all other minnowy thoughts aside and filled her head with its gaping mouth and all the little fish swam in and disappeared. The grouper somewhat diminished and late-arriving. Perhaps a hopeful sign. If the bullyfish was tardy and diminished this one time then maybe with a recovery of will some barriers might be constructed and the bullyfish would find it increasingly difficult. To swim in. Then some of the other fish might grow, dazzle the inside of her skull with their colorful iridescence. Well, here she was. Outside the sky was mud and the chill seeped through the window, into her. All the brilliant little fish, fiction. She expected the mournful tolling of church bells, but heard only the sound of the wind and a faint tapping. What was it just a second ago? Yes, hope. That she hadn't thought about alcohol immediately. But all of this was now terrible, the dank room with its hideous salmon walls and green curtains, the dolorous wind, the turbid sky, the tapping noise from somewhere outside. Death's bony finger. From one entrapment to another, suffocating in this medieval dungeon with its collection of wailing souls. And she one of them. Carol thought briefly of escape, but she was on the third floor and had no clothes for the weather. She imagined tying the sheets and blankets together and descending. How droll. But something drained her of the will to resist or even care. She'd been drugged, of course. She felt her sore left arm. The stupid conniving bastards. The sonofabitch Phil. Is that all he can think of? Take me away, lock me up, drug me. Wash his hands of the fucking mess. Ah, but who cares. All I want is some fucking orange juice.

Carol opened the door and stood in a long hallway that stretched in either direction, covered with a worn red carpet. The red-carpet treatment. Was there a kitchen? An eerie quiet. Not even the moaning of the damned. Which way? She studied the carpet, determined to go right, and began walking toward a door at the end, rather liking the combination of red carpet, pink slippers and white robe. A blood-letting from the bottom up. She realized how drugged she was. The effort in getting to the end of the hallway seemed enormous, as if she were staggering like poor Scott towards the South Pole. She was aware of herself as a stock character in a sanatorium nightmare, literally shuffling in the ludicrous pink slippers, her limbs as heavy and dumb as lead. It was damnably difficult just to lift her head, as if humbled and unable to raise her sights to an overarching presence, as if by being in the sanatorium she'd finally admitted her abject unworthiness, with neither the privilege nor the strength to challenge her deserved humiliation. They'd got her. She'd lost. And so what? Here she was protected by those who were obviously more healthy and powerful than she, the agents of normalcy and decorum. After all, they had only her welfare in mind. It was all for the good, for her good. All of the anger, humiliation, claustrophobic fear of being trapped in this Gothic institution was subsumed by the more rational and stronger power that commanded her to relent. This was dully acknowledged, but under a sort of feeble protest. She knew that her once willful self still existed, still attached, as if she were dragging it along behind her far down the hallway, a flayed creature calling out in barely audible tones. If only she could somehow pull it back to her. It was the goddamned drugs. Some small flame ignited momentarily and Carol raised her head to look at the room number she'd just passed. 308. The next was 306. That meant her room was 310. The same as the brownstone on 51st Street. And no different there than here—drugged, circumscribed, simmering with vague wishes, but nothing more. She deserved all of this. And there, like here, she yearned for escape.

Oh, the damned misery and pathos of a wasted life! The self-loathing! Somehow, once and for all, she was going to get out of this. Carol stopped next to 306 and, with her ear next to the door but not quite touching, listened. What manner of poor creature within? She heard a low coughing and something small and hard fell to the floor and rolled, like a marble. Lots of them lost in this place. Eddie went through a little marble phase. Carol moved on slowly, her mouth as dry and dusty as an attic floor, her head filled with a hollow buzzing, a fly trapped on a strand of an enormous web. Others, like her, in their cubicles. Her right leg and left arm throbbed. God, how she wanted orange juice! Tantalizing images of sweet orange juice filled her head, cataracts of foaming nectar, whole tanks of it, fountains, Rube Goldberg machines with their rolling supply of plump citrus. Oh, for a splashing, drinking swim in a sea of sweet orange juice! The trials she'd put herself through. Her body, once so supple, now dulled and deadened. If only, somehow, she could get out of this nightmare. Three days and not a sip of alcohol. Of course, she was drugged. But maybe a slow tapering off. Her Dartmouth bible lay on the dressing table in New York. She would "take up and read," like St. Augustine. Phil could bring it to her and she would read. No more cynicism, no more cowardly arrogance. No more. Jesus, she was low. Maybe this was rock bottom. Maybe, she thought, if I had volunteered to take care of the wounded during the war, like Paul, ministered the bleeding souls and stumps, I wouldn't be such a paltry excuse for a human being. She would read *Confessions*. And Pascal, again. She shuffled down the windowless hallway with her head lowered, as if pushed down by some powerful, punishing hand. I'm being house trained, she thought. Getting my nose shoved in it. A good whacking and the stench of my own mess. With effort she lifted her gaze higher and to her right. Room 304. If I can make it to the end of this hallway, go through the door and to the place where I might quench this crucifying thirst. How amazing that her room number was 310. Was she dreaming? She might pinch herself if she had the energy, but every bit of strength and will that she had was marshaled to attain the goal of getting to the door and beyond. Maybe, achieving the end of the hallway, she'd open the door and step into the airy regions of blue sky and perfumed, fleecy clouds and He Himself there to greet her and take her into his bosom. No, she wanted orange juice. Cleanse the poison in blood and spirit. All that was required was that she reach the end of the hallway, open the door and find her way to the kitchen. A big pitcher of orange juice in the refrigerator.

At room 302 she could make out details of the hallway door despite the shroud that curtained her senses. It was a large metal affair, crudely painted, and white, with a worn, brass key-holed knob. Three big metal hinges. A heavy door. A door that would require some effort to open. Perhaps there would be riddles to answer. And now, only twenty feet away, despite her weariness, she felt a quickening and she heard her heart thump in her ears. Though she'd traveled only the distance of four rooms it seemed like weeks since she'd stepped into the red-carpeted hallway that stretched like an isthmus between a frozen sea of tombs, the great door at the end that she would roll away like the boulder before the Holy Sepulcher and, descending the stairs, discover the kitchen. Restoration and redemption in blessed orange juice. But then she was afraid. Though her room was a kind of cell, a confinement, it was also safety. She was accounted for. Now she was striking out on a quest fraught with uncertainty. What was beyond that massive door? Was she stepping into the labyrinth, like Theseus, to encounter some devouring Minotaur, and without her ball of yarn? The meaning of the labyrinth and Theseus's ball of yarn became clear. Going into the labyrinth was nothing if not a metaphor for any perilous journey, even life itself. To survive this venture one needed one's ball of yarn, a belief system to help navigate the dangers and pitfalls of such a journey. The yarn enabled Theseus to stay on the path. Hansel's and Gretel's stones. What these stories were teaching was that a person was lost without her ball of yarn or pocket-full of stones to find the way back. Life was a series of wanderings into cul-de-sacs where one might be lost forever without a reliable means of orientation. Once she opened the door and began descending the stairs, she'd have no literal or figurative guide to mark her path. Stepping into a howling emptiness with only a stumbling hope and resurrected intentions. The road to perdition. And going down. But not to a subterranean chamber. Only the first floor, presumably. Starting over. How she'd gotten to the third floor without the faintest awareness. Thirty-three years old and not a jot to show except a certain bumbling, passive journey through life, like a pebble thrown into a secluded pond whose ripples succeed only in upsetting something delicate floating on the surface, dimly aware that it was too late to arrest its descent, oblivious of anything that had come before, at this late hour just awakening to its darkening watery surroundings, feeling the enveloping muck beneath, the blackness. What was left? Only one thing, tried and true, escape. And drink. Escape and drink.

Drink and escape. But first she had to get out of this godforsaken dungeon. This would be difficult. She needed clothes and some money. How the hell would she find her clothes? How would she get money? They wouldn't let her out anyway. Things were beyond her control. It was better that way. Maybe if she stayed here longer, stayed off the sauce for a while, got some help, read her bible. But first things first. She needed orange juice. Carol was at the door and placed her hand on the cold brass knob. She hesitated. Perhaps it wasn't such a good idea. They might be upset with her for leaving her room. She had no business on the stairs without permission. She remembered Dr. Campbell's office being on the first floor. Or was it the second? She didn't remember how she used to get there. Certainly not the stairs. An elevator, of course. The big Negro nurse in the elevator. The nurse had a key to operate the elevator. God, she was thirsty! Carol tried the doorknob, first one way, then the other. She tried with both hands, gripping and turning with all her strength. Nothing. Finally, she let her hands fall and she rested her forehead against the cold metal door. So much for escape. She turned around and faced the long narrow corridor and leaned back. The cold from the door seeped through the robe, into her shoulder blades and she shivered, hunching forward, gripping herself. The sonsofbitches. Maybe she would tie her sheets together. Carol reached behind and turned up the robe's collar. Her thirst remained, but as if retreated to a different part of her body, less insistent. She tried to summon some sort of vivid response to her predicament, but could not, shivering and looking blankly at the thin red carpet that tapered to a vanishing point at the other door. She didn't care if it was locked or not. Somewhere in the middle was the inaccessible elevator.

Sometime later Carol was at her window, dimly calculating the distance to the ground and comparing it to the length the sheets and blankets might reach if they were tied together. It would make it. But she wasn't going anywhere. Below, an elderly man and young woman appeared from the left and walked, absorbed in conversation, across her field of view and vanished into the wooded hill. The old man wore a black overcoat and walked with his head down and hands folded behind him. The woman talked animatedly and smoked, tilting her head back with each propulsive exhalation. A section of white bathrobe showed between her brown pullover and blue slacks. A red handkerchief was tied around her head. The father had come to rescue the daughter, leading her off into the woods to an old sod-roofed cabin. Mother home, waiting by the hearth with *kommisbrot* and thick soup. After supper a long sleep on a linen-covered mattress of pine needles, her body warmed under a great down quilt, father and mother talking quietly at the rough wooden table by the fire. But later, while parents slept, the daughter would rise and steal out of the house and go to the city. Her own father was only an hour away, living in a slightly down-at-the heel hotel in midtown Manhattan, estranged from his wife, a bit less so from his daughters, and rather completely disgusted with the world, the war having forever altered his life and certainties.

Carol looked at the Buffet reproduction on the pale salmon wall. A wine bottle and two pears sat on a gray table with a thin vertical window in the background, and through the window some sort of horizon. Various lines intersected, as if holding the objects together lest they float away or collapse. The lines were tremendously irritating, a failed rendering of artifice, the bottle and two pears, the slit of the window, symbols of a lifeless procreation, reinforced by the empty horizon. It suited the place and her temper. She went over to the reproduction and removed it from the wall and placed it behind the green armchair. Then she sat in the chair and waited for someone to come with water. Maybe she could get some orange juice. Carol felt prepared to sit motionless in this way for hours, watching the muted daylight move across the landscape of her bed, an icy land of troubled visions, the barren mountain of her pillow in the distance. It could be that her father was in his hotel room sitting in a corner chair himself, like she, staring at his unmade bed, waiting. She felt connected to him, his drinking, his restlessness, the way the world had gone flat. They'd both had a modicum of glory, hers, young and short-lived, his, more substantial and longer-lasting, if brutally truncated. Perhaps there was no difference. His correspondence had increased in recent years, with barely-disguised concern for her well-being, but there was more in their words than worry. Though affecting a tone meant to reflect a life of contented, civilized activity, his reading, modest professional responsibilities, an occasional round of golf, she sensed how empty he really felt. His anxiety, too, over her ability to survive in the world was discouragingly transparent and conveyed a deeper apprehension that her drinking and youthful impatience masked something profoundly wrong with her character. Carol perceived the subtext of his correspondence, and it served to undermine her confidence. As a child she had assumed that life would naturally reveal its mysteries before her as she stepped, like a pristine ruby-colored carpet unrolling towards a limitless horizon. Things came gracefully and simply then, why not always? She hadn't understood the powerful grip of alcohol, nor did she foresee the penalties to be exacted for her willful, free-spirited youth. It was extraordinary how the golden careless beginnings in the East had foundered and dimmed in the West. Nobody had been there to warn her, to pick her up by the nape of the neck, to give her a good smack on the bottom. In fact, she disliked her father's letters, how-after-the fact they were, completely missing the critical moment of her life, their contents full of anxious, diplomatic didacticism, as if she were still sixteen. Well, she hadn't given him much reason to think she was much beyond that age, flitting about from one thing to the other, drinking like a fool, neglecting her children. It was disabling however that her father was obviously struggling for meaning in his own life, he who had always seemed so capable and full of purpose, the loss of his certainties hastening a further crippling of her own.

Chilled, Carol rose from the armchair and took the green cotton blanket and wrapped it around her, sitting again. She stayed immobile for a while staring at her sheets, a frigid landscape where the wind howled as she doggedly navigated crevasses thousands of feet deep, climbed over ridges and small mountains. The arctic barren then dissolved into something less definable, shifting under her gaze, a silent roiling polar sea that flashed colors and vaguely familiar images. Some sort of chittering rodent seemed to be busy inside her skull operating a magic lantern. She was too lethargic to let it worry her. Let the images come. After all, what was the point in trying to make sense of them? She was merely a spectator now. This effort to understand resulted always in great harm. She would have no part of it. Eventually, this dancing stream of spectral dots would arrange itself into something apprehensible, or not. The pictures were colorful and familiar enough, and the lantern itself, resting on a small three-legged table covered with green felt-like material, was a marvelous brass and bubbling contraption that whirled like a carrousel or muted calliope, and the rodent with its stack of photographic plates under the table removed and inserted them skillfully with its nimble humanoid paws. Occasionally it would stop to re-energize itself and, gripping a small chunk of something in its nervous fingers, flash its yellow incisors. Then there were no images but a black and greenish tumbling that reminded Carol uneasily of the suffocating weight of her abyssal nightmare. But this was tolerable as long as the images eventually resumed, as she knew they would. She had little understanding of where she was or how long she'd been watching—it wasn't "watching," exactly, it was more than that—these parading images—maybe—but—there was something else going on, some "context," or primary situation that enclosed her in a parenthetical existence that was deeply satisfying. The effort to comprehend anything beyond this impossibly steep. Reduced to complete passivity she imagined herself as Gulliver entwined by Lilliputians, not an unpleasant thing. She was aware that her existence somehow now lay in the capable hands of others. A child in the darkened room, afflicted, while hushed shadows glide portentously. The rodent skittered away, knocking over the magic lantern and the screen went very bright and blank, almost immediately populated by shadows the child knew well, with their pointy caps, attenuated arms and legs and menacing teeth, the same shadows mirthfully routed by friendly elephants —or were they merely large ridiculous bouncing beach balls that frightened them away and made the children laugh? The joyous cathartic laughter of children whose nightmares have been comically deflated. And now an articulate sort of droning as the edges of the screen bulged or darkened preparatory to the charge of the elephants or bouncing balls, then a blinding brilliance that caused her to shut her eyes tightly with black, red and green electrical explosions.

"Carol—"

Some other nightmare returning. A world she'd managed to escape for a while. Where was the rodent and his magic lantern? Where were the friendly elephants to chase these intruders away? She'd been caught doing something bad. The grownups were here with their overwhelming authority. Dozens of them, crowding around. If she kept her eyes closed long enough, they might disappear.

"Carol. It's me, Doctor Campbell—"

How grave, this voice. The voice of an undertaker. Am I dead? Dr. Campbell, yes, my tweedy Van Helsing. Why the morbid concern for me? I am not the tiniest bit interesting. This Campbell is no Van Helsing, he's the Count himself. Look what they've done. Sucked the life right out of me and entombed me in this dungeon. Now he's back for his blood. Carol opened her eyes slowly and looked into the doctor's intelligent, serious face, the emerald eyes clear and steady. No, not the eyes of a vampire, but something worse, the gaze of earnest professionalism, somebody paid to care and be responsible, fortified with decades of clinical experience and research. She was certainly a type he was familiar with. Ample justification for a long stay in this dungeon. And the husband with reasonably deep pockets.

"How long do you figure?" said Carol.

"I'm not sure I understand."

"How long do you propose to keep me in this moldy reformatory?"

The doctor responded with a practiced, sympathetic smile. "Well, as long as necessary to get you healthy again. Not terribly long, I'm sure. You know, Carol, you've had a rough time of it. You've not treated yourself very well. Why don't we give it a couple of weeks and see how things are going?"

"A couple of weeks is a long time, doctor. Time for the entire universe to shift on its axis. Time for the souls of the damned to take wings and fly away to a better world. Time—"

"It's completely a relative proposition. And the universe is not going to shift on its axis, I'm reasonably sure of that. As far as the souls of the damned, well, I do believe in the possibility of redemption. And I most certainly believe in the possibility of cure for the ills of body and mind—which is what brings us to you."

"On the contrary, doctor. I was brought to you—forcibly."

"Nobody has forced you to abuse yourself, Carol."

"Absolutely true, doctor. I've done it of my own free will. And what gives anyone the right to impose their will on my behavior? I can damn well destroy myself if I want, and have a bloody good time in the bargain. I've hurt my children though, and for that I'll go straight to hell, no doubt. But as for the rest of them I don't give a damn. Jesus, what a tired world this is. How do you manage, doctor? What keeps you going other than the room and board you collect from these pathetic lodgers of yours? Do you really care? Do you really think you can do any good?" Carol pulled the blanket more tightly around her, shivering. She had no notion of the time. The light through the curtained window was darker. Someone was standing at the door, out of view. She remembered her thirst. "I am dying of thirst, Doctor Campbell. Absolutely dying. Would you be a good doctor and get me some orange juice, please?"

Dr. Campbell turned and instructed the figure at the door to bring some orange juice for Mrs. Heizer. The person left and Dr. Campbell faced Carol, his expression serious. All is artifice, thought Carol. One chooses to play the game or not. I haven't the power to resist. The green eyes bored in and the doctor spoke. "Your drinking is getting to the point where, quite frankly, your life is in danger. Despite your denials, I don't think you really want to turn your back on everything that is important. You have a family, Carol, a family that loves you very much, a family that needs you very much. This latest episode of yours is the worst you've been. I'm sure you don't even remember how you got here." The doctor paused and Carol stared impassively. He went on. "Well, you arrived in a condition of what might be characterized as alcohol-induced dementia. It is a rather advanced stage of deterioration caused by long-term, excessive drinking. I would venture to say that you've had hallucinations." He paused again, receiving no clue from the passive, small-boned, slightly hostile face. "When you arrived, you were agitated and talking about aliens and cosmic energy.

You claimed to have been in contact with people from Venus. In fact, you were quite certain that I was one of them. Under some circumstances I might be flattered, but you were making quite a row. Your husband was the object of considerable abuse."

Carol remembered none of it. "Where are my children? What has happened to my children?"

"They're being cared for by your mother and your sister. There was a Mister Johnson, I believe, who helped. And also, your friend, Simone. Your mother and sister are in Westhampton now with the children. Phil is very anxious about you and wants to see you. Everybody is concerned and upset. You don't realize how important you are to people and how much love there is for you."

"I hardly deserve it."

"It's not a question of deserving. People love you. You've done your damnedest to push everyone away and yet they still love you. You know, you are a rather extraordinary person. You've got so much to offer—and so very young."

"Doctor, please, I appreciate the kind words, but spare me. My life is an insoluble mess. By some lights thirty-three may be young, Doctor Campbell, but my own lights are wretchedly dim. I feel like I've already lived several lifetimes and I still don't know a bloody thing." Carol paused for a moment, remembering the poem in the pompous newspaper: *the present cannot bind me, but, the past, implacable and huge, will hold me fast.*" All I know is that for some reason I feel like a prisoner, a prisoner of the past. And I don't mean my own childhood necessarily, but a past way beyond that."

Dr. Campbell seemed to consider something, then spoke, "Are you speaking of reincarnation? The transmigration of souls?"

"Yes, I suppose I might be."

The doctor's clinically earnest expression altered slightly, his eyebrows raised. She was conscious of his masculinity. The beard was unruly enough to suggest a degree of sensuality. The hands were sensitive and strong-looking. Monsieur Loutrel. What were the secrets of *Herr Doktor*? Dr. Campbell, who had been standing slightly stooped before her, hands clasped together at his waist, sat down at the foot of her bed and leaned forward, elbows on thighs, hands cupped. There was an authenticity about him, Carol decided.

"People in the hard sciences—you know, physics and chemistry and so forth—don't consider psychology a science at all. I am a psychiatrist, of course, which makes me even more suspect. Many find it exceedingly presumptuous that psychiatry makes any claims to understand, much less treat, mental and emotional problems. They think we're charlatans, that it's all just a fad. I admit this sometimes bothers me, but on the other hand it's quite liberating. I'm not sure I would call psychology a science either. How can one quantify what is essentially a mystery? There's a trend developing in my profession, partly born of an inferiority complex, to be more like the other sciences, that is, to understand human nature, consciousness, as a mechanical process and to treat it accordingly. Of course, the human brain is a kind of computer, firing commands around the clock, storing whole libraries of information—but it's the moral, poetic side of human nature that fascinates me, as well as its opposite. How do we have a Gandhi on the one hand and a Hitler on the other? A Mozart and a Henry Ford."

"Or doctor and patient."

"Or doctor and patient. Interesting. Because the doctor, or the psychiatrist, is representative of certain societal norms—not behavioral but societal. We are the new Procrustean enforcers. We view aberrant behavior as something needing molding as to fit more nicely into the acceptable standards of society. At least this is increasingly what's happening. Psychology, psychiatry, is in danger of forgetting one of Freud's greatest insights, that much of what is called aberrant is the direct result of a society that is equally aberrant or repressive, perhaps even more so. We are still Freudians, most of us, I believe, but there is this development that is going quite in the opposite direction—the move to view, as I say, human behavior as strictly mechanical phenomena. Drugs are the coming thing, I'm afraid."

Carol was interested in the doctor's talk. A thoughtful person. One not afraid to be challenged. But, damn him! Wasn't he a hypocrite by the very nature of things? What was he doing here in this morbid place where three-fourths of the "patients" were likely drugged? And the last time she was here she was heavily medicated, as she was now. Yet he was different now in some way. Of course. Last time he had hardly said a word. Now he was talking—in a sincere, self-examining way. It was a technique, of course, to reach her, yet it was, in its clinical way, effective.

"You weren't afraid to drug me when I got here, were you?"

"You needed sedation. And a good rest. You were somewhat out of control. Think of it as a strong soporific."

"Last time I was here you had me drugged the whole time."

"That was to help you sleep—not much different from what we've given you now."

Dr. Campbell appeared uncomfortable and looked down at the floor and then out the window. A small gray woman in a white uniform entered quietly and approached Carol, holding the orange juice in a paper cup.

"Here you are, dear."

Dr. Campbell cleared his throat and waited for Carol. She finished the drink and placed the cup on the floor. A smattering of rain pelted the window, as if someone had thrown a handful of millet. The curtain moved with the wind.

"I'm interested in your view of the past. Reincarnation. Do you feel as though you've had past lives? Any distinct memories?"

So, the doctor was going to take her up on this. Why not.

"I have feelings, recognitions. In the spring we went to the Bahamas and I felt the most incredible, haunted sense of the past. I thought it might be the decay, the old forts, the colonialism, but the feeling was so strong, everything so familiar, I just couldn't shake it. There was a powerful sense of my own death— death by drowning. I felt very strongly that my most recent past life was there and that it was ended by drowning."

"Do you feel that your death there, then, was the result of yet another life before? That this other, previous life was again something unfulfilled, perhaps ended prematurely, somehow? Are there any images or feelings connected with it like there are with the Bahamas?"

"I have no feelings or images specifically. There were times in Paris when I experienced this same sensation, as if I'd been there before. I have—it's hard to say—maybe anyone feels these things when they're around remnants of the past, ruins, old cities, so forth. Maybe it's no big deal. But the feelings I have are very powerful. In Paris I heard voices."

"Voices?"

"Yes, calling my name. At night, in the rain. I also have a problem with claustrophobia, as if things are closing in on me. Somehow, I end up feeling trapped, no matter what the situation. I can hardly breath sometimes. I think this may have something to do with drowning."

"Well, I'm interested in the idea of reincarnation. I think there might be something to it. I believe there is a purpose to life and it's the struggle for self-mastery. There's something compelling about the Hindu idea of liberation. It places a premium on human will, on volition. It's a bit like existentialism in the sense that it places responsibility on the individual. We have choices."

This doctor was skillful, indeed. She was aware of how he was manipulating the conversation, placing things before her in a roundabout way. "Self-mastery." "Choices." It was all right. At least it was interesting and he was not physically repulsive, as so many of them were.

"But Hinduism is a religion, like any other. It speaks of surrender."

"Yes, surrender of the self to God. It seems to be a sort of bargain. One surrenders oneself to God and is granted admittance, at least as a Hindu, to the great continuity, the great stream of being, the cycle of life, death and rebirth. Once you surrender, that is, cease to rebel against the notion that you are really quite a small part of something inexpressibly large, then you are offered a glimpse of peace, a promise."

"The only stream I'm part of is that which flows from bottle to glass. That's my promise of peace."

"Yes, I know. But you know that's a false promise, a destructive promise, one of the countless diversions that takes us away from what is essential. And what is essential, in my view, is a cold appraisal of the individual self, in all its aspects, including what the existentialists call the 'predicament'—something like the claustrophobia you speak of."

"And what is my 'predicament?'"

"Your predicament is no different than anyone else's. It is the self, alone, searching for meaning in what now appears to be an indifferent universe. Few people have the courage to face that sort of universe, yet that is the burr upon which our consciousness rests this day and age."

"But I believe in God, Doctor Campbell—though I'm not sure exactly what that means. It's difficult to express. Some sort of unifying, directive power, I suppose, perhaps even a consciousness. Some people have it, I guess. I don't know how, or why, but they do."

"Do you have any idea what this consciousness is?"

"Vaguely, but I feel like the claustrophobia has defeated me. I'm at the bottom of the ocean. I have dreams of being crushed to the bottom of the ocean. A dark, suffocating mass of water, monstrous, foaming, down at the bottom—and a light, always a light, shining through the water."

"What is that light?"

"I have no idea. Sometimes I think it's rebirth. It's not a bad thing, this light. It's comforting, somehow."

"Yes. A beacon, perhaps. You may very well have died by drowning in a past life. If one carries this a bit further, your drinking can be seen as a symbolic re-enactment of that death. Drowning is a terrible way to die. Now, I'm not necessarily a believer in reincarnation—you can call me an agnostic on the issue—but, like you, I have feelings, strong intimations. Let's play with this a little, shall we? Obviously, and this is also backed up by the teachings on reincarnation, the closer to one's current existence a past life is, the easier it is to recall. It seems also fairly obvious that the more dramatic the life, or traumatic the death, the more vivid, or accessible those memories, or images, are. Now, as you've told me, you started drinking around the age of fifteen. You've also told me that since that time things have gone rather poorly in your life—and I think that's pretty accurate. The drinking has got progressively worse, you find yourself in a sort of crippling bind in terms of establishing, or even choosing, a serious life-role for yourself, you feel you've failed as a parent, your relationships with men you find deeply problematic—" Another smattering of rain softly pelted the window. So, Carol thought, Connie is whispering her impending arrival. How many hundreds of miles away was she? Imagine the winds, the hundred-foot waves, the howling darkness. The storm seemed to be reaching out, calling with a gentle whisper. "—age of fifteen as significant. You say that you felt these intimations most strongly in the Bahamas, well, it could be that that was where this terrible thing happened to you. It could also be that you were quite young when this happened, say, around fifteen. One might fairly assume that a truly horrible death would leave its scars for a long time, perhaps several lifetimes. Being so close to such an event yourself it is understandable that you would be affected. People act in curious ways for all kinds of unfathomable reasons, but sometimes we can discern the connections, the causes."

"So, when I was fifteen somehow the memory, or the unconscious memory, kicked in and I began to drown again. Instead of 'drowning my sorrows' in alcohol I began drowning the memory of something I wasn't even consciously aware of. But all that has done is bring me closer to the event—a re-enactment, as you say. Rather than drowning in a matter of minutes I've been slowly drowning for a lifetime. My whole life has been a slow, painful shadow play, a dumb, futile, ridiculous, drawn-out cosmic theater piece. Nothing more than a wooden-headed marionette, chief idiot in my own tragi-comic farce. Very neat. I like it." Carol found herself longing for a drink. The stuff they'd given her the first time was more than merely something to help her sleep. It was also some sort of suppressant, for she'd never had the desire for alcohol. What they'd given her this time wasn't working. The wind stirred the curtains again and despite the coolness she began to sweat, at the same time shivering and drawing the blanket more tightly around her. She felt the doctor's clinical gaze, but it hardly mattered. All she wanted was to be wrapped in the swaddling clothes of her sweet anodyne. The doctor was talking but she couldn't make it out. Carol felt herself slipping into a sort of woolen tunnel that muted everything but the desire for alcohol, vodka, gin, the clear curative, a craving that came in concentric circles from within, rebounding against the top of her skull and back again. Her skin prickled and she continued to sweat, though she was cold. Carol drew her knees up to her chest. Dr. Campbell's voice, which had faded like a lost radio signal, came back. She fought to regain herself. "—Pythagoras, Plato, the Jewish mystics, all believed in reincarnation. It's not much of a stretch to think of the unconscious as a door to past lives. Colleagues of mine have tried hypnosis. There's been nothing terribly convincing though. Was there any one place in the Bahamas where you felt these sensations particularly strongly?"

Carol strained to focus on the meaning of the doctor's words. They brought forth images of palm trees, a vast azure sky, warm crystalline water, scurrying chameleons. "Well, we were on the island of New Providence. The children and I visited an old fort, badly decayed, falling apart, chameleons everywhere. I remember looking out at the ocean and the sense of being there was so powerful that I almost fainted. It had a rather high tower that was some sort of lookout. Perhaps a kind of lighthouse. Next to the tower were narrow steps that led down to a maze of small cells. The children and I went down there and at one point we were separated and got kind of lost. Mark was frightened and began to cry. We called out and eventually we found each other. It was a very odd experience for all of us. We were quite shaken. Mark kept crying and saying that he'd thought he'd lost me forever. There were moments when we were searching and calling out when I actually felt the same thing—that I was going to lose them there. Irrational, of course, but very powerful. As I recall, that was our second day there. That afternoon we went to the beach and all of us fell asleep and Eddie got badly burned. I don't know why Mark didn't. I think he might have been wearing a T-shirt. Or no, maybe he was with me under a palm shelter. That's right, Eddie was by himself on the beach. Mark was with me.

"I felt the same way, though not as intensely, the whole time we were there, which was about ten days. The airport was another strong experience, arriving and departing. The minute I walked out of the plane I was overwhelmed with a kind of excitement and fear. A strange feeling of coming back to a home I'd never been aware of. And leaving was horribly difficult, horribly complex."

"Complex? How so?"

"I didn't want to leave, even though I felt so haunted the whole time it almost drove me mad. I drank a lot on the island. I was very scared, actually, leaving—torn between feelings of a mysterious past that gripped me and a future that seemed an absolute void."

"And how do you feel now?"

"Exhausted, cold, rather hopeless (and badly needing a drink) —very much as if my life has been a sour joke. Your theories on my life and reincarnation are interesting. I don't discount them. It's more compelling than the usual blather, frankly. I feel sorry for that poor little girl. She must have been caught in a storm or a hurricane. I wonder who she was? What was her name? Was she English? Creole? African? Imagine if I was—if she—was African. How fantastic."

"That little girl is still you. And I suspect that what she—her soul, your soul—would want is for you to remember and understand the tragedy of her life—and not to repeat that tragedy. Karmic law would have it that her terrible death was a penalty for the negative actions of a previous life. Obviously, what she did in that life—or lives—was powerful enough to reach into your incarnation. But you have help, clues. More than she had, probably. You have images and strong intimations. You've lived longer and your age has allowed you to see some of these things. It's as if that negative karma has ahold of your ankle (Carol thought of the glass in her foot) in the form of your drinking, trying to pull you under. But your situation is better than the girl's. She had no choice. She was ruthlessly punished. You have some vision, and some choice."

"Ah, Doctor Campbell, you make it sound so simple, like a very neat story. As if I've been handed a script where the main character, me, has the easy, rather straightforward task of simply penciling in an agreeable ending. I know you're offering me an alternative, another way of understanding my 'predicament,' as you call it. I appreciate it. And whether you believe this alternative or not, it resonates with me. There's no objective reason why I should feel like the world is coming to an end three-quarters of the time. Why, when I try to place myself in the world, I feel like a ghost trapped in somebody else's bad dream. There's no reason why I should feel so unreal all the time, as if I don't have the same substance as other people, but I do. The only thing that gives me reality is drink, and, I suppose, my children. I see my children sometimes and I think yes, that is me, that is my flesh, that's real. But other times they are completely alien and I think it's all a terrible accident, they have nothing to do with me whatsoever, that we're burdens on each other. Burdens and complete strangers.

"I didn't have the classically bad childhood, Doctor Campbell. We've been through this. I grew up with everything, more than most people even dream of. My parents left me alone. Perhaps too much. They had grand parties. I grew up too fast, possibly. I was a bit of the princess. The bored princess. Things came too easily. Then I started to drink. After that, though it took a long time to realize it, my life began this delightful glissade to the bottom of the ocean. But would things be any different had I not started to drink? This is an interesting question. Would I be happy and successful? Somehow, I think not. In any case a life without drink is simply inconceivable. Utterly out of the question. It'll never stop, Doctor Campbell. We both know that."

"I don't know that at all, Carol. We must try. The coupling of your story with the young girl's is, at the very least, symbolic. I don't necessarily believe in reincarnation, but I believe that there is a connection to others who have come before us, whether it's our parents or whomever. Obviously, my profession—and common sense—puts a premium on past conditions, biological inheritance, societal factors. Jung believes in the collective mind, or spirit. So do I. All of who we are is an amalgam of these factors. The wild card in all this is our consciousness, our volition. We have, I think, limited but meaningful choices. Our lives are like a boulder headed downhill. The longer we wait the more difficult it is to nudge it in a different direction."

Carol despaired of the doctor's good common sense. What he was suggesting was nothing less than good old-fashioned Protestant sobriety and hard work. She was going to have to put her nose to the grindstone, hoist herself up by the bootstraps, exercise the kind of Germanic, stubborn singleness of purpose that had always repelled her. She would not! It was so dreary and such a bore. What she wanted was a bolt of lightning. A miraculous transformation of the spirit that might be brought about by say, a visit from extraterrestrials who, with their superiority, would "touch" her and show her the way. Meanwhile, as nothing else of interest or excitement was likely to present itself, she would continue as before. She despaired at the doctor's eminently sensible words because they were lacking. He only got to the surface of things. They didn't touch her down inside, where something indefinable lodged, a constant, luggish companion. This was why she was interested in the doctor's words on reincarnation, and a little saddened when he admitted that, after all, he wasn't really a believer but sought rather to give it a more scientific interpretation, that the idea was interesting as a sort of quaint model but needed some shiny gadgets to make it up to date and valid. Pushing boulders around indeed! How Newtonian, with its depressing associations with mass and inertia. Her life wasn't a goddamned boulder! But more depressing still was that she knew he was right. The boulder simile was apt. She was careening downhill at an accelerating rate and disaster lay not too far ahead. The idea of mustering the will and energy to "nudge" this heavily-rolling, obdurate mass was beyond the pale. It couldn't be done. And yes, the good doctor was there to help, and others might be there to help, yes. Yes—but no. Imagine the time and effort. Imagine all the work that she would have to do. For what? To live a "normal" life? A "healthy" life? To give up drinking? It couldn't be done. Unless there was some sort of revelation that lifted her beyond the dreary mundane, the everyday burden that all the "well-adjusted" people carried around on their backs like some tentacled creature with its beak sunk into their skulls, she couldn't imagine it. It was the horrid secret that no one talked about, this boring, despairing trudge through life. And anyone off the beaten path they wanted to pull back, make them normal so they, too, would carry the burden and shuffle along in fruitless agony. Of course, she carried her own "burden," but it was not the burden of the ordinary nine-to-fiver. She would never be like them.

"You know," Doctor Campbell continued, aware that she was drifting, "I don't—I have my difficulties with the doctrine of reincarnation, particularly in the strict Hindu or Buddhist sense. I can't quite come to terms with the soul as tangible, or sentient, as they would somehow have it, or so it seems to me. But I do believe in karma, cause and effect, the consequences of action. What we have, what I would define as soul, is essence, or power, which derives from action."

"Soul is action."

"Soul is action."

"Then you don't think I, or I should say, my soul, inhabited the body of a fifteen-year-old girl who drowned a hundred years ago in the Bahamas?"

"I have no idea. I wouldn't say it's impossible. Certainly, there are young girls who have drowned in the Bahamas in the past. Some places affect us more strongly than others. Spirit is every-where. The world consists of infinite stories. We've created a story that resonates with you. That's the important thing. What counts is what we learn from these stories. You have, by your own admission, been 'drowning' for eighteen years. Something about the Bahamas was particularly haunting to you. Something about the environment triggered this particular story, perhaps. It's not in the least outlandish or far-fetched. It's a meaningful story. It's your story. That is, you made it up. Now, whether or not the soul that inhabits your corporeal self at the present moment is the very same that inhabited a young girl's who drowned a hundred years ago in the Bahamas is another matter. Like I say, it's not impossible, I just don't know."

"I think you made up that story rather more than I did, Doctor Campbell."

"I provided some details and symbolic parallels. You supplied the matrix. There is some benefit to the doctor-patient relationship, you know," said the doctor, smiling slightly in his clear green eyes. "Providing the doctor isn't a complete idiot."

"Or the patient."

"Of course. It's a partnership. Which illustrates my point about soul. The more effectively, or powerfully, we give, the more far-reaching the consequences. That is action."

"Wouldn't that apply equally to negative actions?"

"Absolutely. Positive and negative have equal force. In my view there is a continual interplay between positive and negative actions. The result of this interplay is what determines the future, as well as the present. We are the products of the past, but agents of the future, and present. And all of this has to do with relationships, the way we relate to others, the natural world, ourselves."

"It all starts with the self, doesn't it, doctor."

"Yes, but without nurturing and a healthy environment the self is handicapped from the start. Handicapped or healthy, one is influenced by the past, by the lives that came before us and their relationships."

"And the self—what part of the 'soul,' as you define it, is that?"

"It is, as you say, a part of the soul, but not the whole thing. Because the powerful and positive soul is one that consciously transcends the 'self.' On the other hand, the very powerful negative souls, like Hitler, are completely corrupted by self, which grows like a cancer, a malignancy. And all of it has to do with one's relationship to death. Thanatos. I'm sure you're familiar with the term. And the obverse is one's relationship with Eros. Love, self-preservation."

"The war between Thanatos and Eros."

"It can be a war, in the confused or unhealthy soul. But in a person who is psychologically clear there is a resolution of this conflict. This conflict can occur in whole societies as well as individuals. In fact, it does, routinely. I think we have such a problem in our own society. It lacks a cohering vision, a soul-vision. It is a collection of selves, each pursuing his or her own end. There is little feeling of responsibility towards something greater than the immediate self, a sense of relationships. Confucius saw these relationships as concentric circles, starting with the family and radiating out to society and on into the cosmos. This vision is dynamic because it continually pulses back and forth so that individual, family, society and cosmos are all contained within each other. Therefore, Thanatos and Eros remain in perspective. There is no conflict."

"Do you see me as someone embroiled in such a conflict? As a 'self' rather than a 'soul?'"

"I see you as one who is still struggling at the beginning. This is why the story of the young girl drowning is so powerful, because you instinctively know that the image of the girl is symbolic of something in your own life."

"I'm a little old to be struggling at the beginning." A wave of hopelessness and fatigue swept over her. She closed her eyes and felt the curtains moving in the wind. Where was Phil in the doctor's blueprint? Beyond her, that was certain, and yet he still seemed a young boy in her eyes, someone completely in thrall to the self, his striving and his success. But wasn't that the measuring stick? What eagerness and singleness of purpose! He was making it. Making what? He seemed to clearly know what he wanted. That counted for something, certainly. She was envious of this. What a zero she was in comparison. Yes, she was still at the beginning. Where did that leave the children? An image of them appeared, dissolving as ghosts and flying out the window. Was there any hope for them? What the doctor was talking about, starting over, finding her "self," or "soul," pushing the boulder in a different direction, was impossible. Then what?

Doctor Campbell put his hands on his knees, hesitated, and pushed himself to a standing position. He retrieved his pipe from his jacket pocket and, holding it by the stem, absently tapped the base of the bowl against the upturned palm of his left hand. "Well, I've blabbed way too much." He looked at his watch. "I hope I haven't thoroughly confused us both with my ramblings. It's three o'clock. Phil will be coming at six to take you to dinner, that is, if you want to go. I know he wants to see you. I'm sure the food will be better than you'd get here." He looked out the window. "We're seeing the first hints of Connie." Still looking out the window, he continued. "I know this all seems rather overwhelming. But I think you have a chance of getting a hold on things." He turned and looked at Carol, whose gaze was fixed at some point beyond the curtains. The small, forlorn features, the scar beneath the cheekbone livid without makeup, a cork bobbing in the midst of giant waves. So many like her. What was the point? Could anyone really be "saved"?

"I'd like to take a bath, if such a thing were possible," said Carol.

In the warm water of the tub Carol lapsed into a kind of dream, a dark room with a musical murmuring and a diffused blue light at one end. The room was the same shape as her thoughts, subterranean, the roots of great trees, clear springs from melting snow, the unceasing, generative activity of every good thing that lived deep in the earth, all of it heavy with nostalgia, existing but at the same time lost and irretrievable. Despite feelings deeper than sadness, feelings that corresponded with both the beginning and end of things, she was peaceful. Everything fit together, parts of a puzzle interlocked in warm concentric circles. Aware of herself in a warm tub in a small bathroom in a place called "East Hill," late afternoon, equally engaged in her subterranean mind and its profoundly consoling message, Carol sank more deeply into the water, a naked aquatic plant spreading its tendrils, opening and closing her legs languidly, the warmth flowing up into her. All was good now, if only, somehow, to be encased in amber and suspended another ten-thousand years, blissful and warm like this. But just outside the bathroom wall was the silent pendular arc of the 15-megaton wrecking ball poised in final, triumphant annihilation. Her mind slowly surfaced, the reverie and overarching observer dissolving. Well, Jesus, not even a moment's bliss. The water was becoming tepid and she flipped the lever to drain some of it and turned on the hot full blast. After a minute or so, better. Nice to have a gin and tonic right about now. And a cigarette. Odd how she wasn't the least bit hungry, though she couldn't remember the last time she'd eaten. So, old Philly-boy was coming to take her to dinner. She'd get him to take her to an expensive restaurant. Maybe there wasn't such a thing around these hickish parts. Maybe that's where she was, Hicksville. In any case she knew she was near Hicksville. Hong Kong to Hicksville. Now there was progress. Let's get ol' Philly to buy me the biggest steak in the house, a porterhouse big enough to feed a football team, sizzling and dripping from the grill. But before that, three rounds of double martinis. The team could eat the steak.

Time was a confusing matter. Even more than usual. Unhinged for years but now completely obliterated. The good doctor had said something about three o'clock some while ago but what bit of a while ago was that? It could have been fifteen minutes or three hours. If it was three hours then Phil would be here because the noble Van Helsing had said six o'clock. Ah, to be floating in a bathtub of gin! She'd lie here until they came with a fresh handful of sedatives and Phil would take her limp hand and lead her to the car, and then to the restaurant where she'd nibble the corner of a Saltine and sip water while the anxious husband appraised her mental condition, relieved that she was under control for the moment. That's all they really want, to have me sedated, under control. No more scenes. Maybe they were planning some electro-shock. She'd met a woman at *Park East* who'd had it and found its after-effects quite pleasurable. Actual peace for weeks. But it always came back, the old cork-screw. She'd begun drinking again and was on Miltown. Everybody she knew drank, and more and more were taking Miltown. Carol had gotten a prescription once but after trying it a few times she flushed the rest down the toilet. They'd made her feel awful. She closed her eyes and pinched her nose, slipping under the warm water at the precise moment the meek little woman who'd gotten the orange juice knocked softly, and hearing no response entered the bathroom. Carol was aware of murmuring and thought she might be slipping back into her dream state but the sound was of a different pitch, not at all musical and soothing, and she surfaced, blinking away the water and meeting the face of the little gray nurse whose round blank eyes and mouth in a surprised circle made her look like Betty Boop's grandmother, oop-oop-ee-doop. Carol managed a smile, hoping to forestall a panicked, emergency response, the silly woman running down the hall yelling for help or some crazy thing. You couldn't blame her, after all, working in the loony bin. Imagine the stuff she'd seen. The smile did the trick.

"Are you okay, dear?"

"Oh, yes, I'm fine." Still supporting the smile, though waning. "Just snorkeling for a minute." She noticed the woman's tiny watch, wondering how she could read it, old as she was. "Do you have the time?"

"Yes, of course. It's—" She held the watch at some distance and looked at it intently. "Why, yes, it's five o'clock."

Good. Another hour that she could spend in the tub, even though she wasn't certain the boopy little nurse had seen her watch clearly. But that wasn't her problem. She'd stay until Philly-boy was here and they had to come get her. He could cool his bon-bons in the lobby while she got ready. She asked most charmingly if she might stay in the tub a bit longer and if, also, she might get another cup of orange juice and the nurse, apparently relieved, answered affirmatively and left the bathroom, returning a few minutes later with a small cup of juice. Carol drank the juice quickly and drained more water while turning the tap on in a scalding plummeting downspout that filled her ears with thunder and echoed in the small bathroom like Niagara. There had been no Niagara honeymoon but rather one in Taxco at the house of an artist friend of Phil's. They spent an agreeable week exploring the tiny, precipitous old-world streets and drinking too much at endless parties. Granted an audience with Spratling, the designer of silver, at his workshop just outside of the town, Phil bought Carol a thick, silver Aztec-looking bracelet with three amethysts, the handsomest of all the elegant pieces on display, they both agreed. Where was the bracelet now? Possibly in the dresser drawer at the pink house. She was a bit careless with it. She closed the drain and allowed the hot water to continue running so that sweat beaded up on her forehead. The level rose a couple of inches beyond the overflow and when she leaned forward to turn the water off, a little of it splashed onto the floor. Then, pinching her nostrils, eyes squeezed shut, she went under, warm and quiet but for the beating of her heart. She surfaced and rubbed her eyes, thinking of poor Harold Rosenberg in New Providence, how she'd tantalized him lying half-naked on her deck next to his cabana. He'd come out in the morning clearing his throat or making some sort of decorous noise so she'd cover herself, which she did, somewhat carelessly. Harold Rosenberg, large, perspiring, vastly better read than she, filled with a jaundiced, weary wisdom that held few remaining enthusiasms. Carol thought he might be a spy whose nerves were shot, inebriated by noon, lying back in the chair with his glass of vodka tonic and lime beaded with condensation and the great expanse of reddening flesh and few strands of graying chest hair, making her laugh with his paeans to plaid thermos bottles and Ed Herlihy imitations excitedly announcing MacArthur's triumph at Inchon, Arcaro riding Hill Gail home to his fifth Kentucky Derby victory, the shameful persecution of Oppenheimer. He became serious and somewhat bitter when discussing what the country had done to Oppenheimer and seemed in some way to identify with him. He discussed the great physicist more than once, staring at the dirt road that snaked in front of their decks and ran off through some bushes and palm trees towards the sea. After a couple of days, more familiar with the place and the water not far away, Carol let the boys go by themselves to play on the beach and she would soon follow. Harold Rosenberg never accompanied them, content to lie in his chair and drink vodka tonics. When she and the children would return several hours later, he'd be in Nassau for afternoons of drinking in a bar he'd discovered. With children Carol couldn't take off like that. But she didn't much feel like it anyway. Besides, there were several bottles of Smirnoff and a case of Schweppes that the owner of the compound had provided for a very reasonable price.

Towards the end of their stay, Phil flew in from Sun Valley where he'd been skiing for five days. She ceased lying on the deck half-naked. The sudden change in altitude and climate enervated him and he lay listless on the deck the first day. His presence irritated her outrageously though she succeeded in suppressing most of her turmoil by drinking constantly and taking the children to the beach and then, after a while, the tension dissipated. Phil and Harold Rosenberg had little to say to each other and Carol dropped the easy informality she had felt with the sportswriter and he quietly slipped away until she rarely saw him, most of his time at the bar in Nassau. She had nothing to say to Phil, as if there now stood a high, substantial wall between them, although they did have their "activities," mostly for the children's sake, chartering a boat for two days of spear fishing and exploring, the second day chased back to port at high throttle by a stiffening wind, monstrous black clouds and silent pulses of lightning on the horizon. They rented a motor scooter and rode around the island and Phil promised to buy her one for Westhampton, which he later did. They filled their days with distractions and Carol drank continuously, though discreetly. The children, while aware of the subtle tensions, remained too absorbed in the mystery and colorful beauty of the island to pay much attention. But the undercurrent was heavy. There was an odd, sad feeling surrounding them, almost a scary feeling. Perhaps it was the island itself. Something was wrong.

Indeed. The air in the bathroom was chilly and she sank into the warm water, her lips submerged, the old craving upon her. It would be quite a coup to get a drink in this place. Well, she could hold out until Phil arrived. She could talk him into buying her a drink at the restaurant. Dr. Campbell was a good egg. Egg drop soup. Dr. Campbell and Howard Johnson. Rather exceptions to the mass-produced dreck associated with these names. America ascendant was quickly becoming a nightmare as far as she could tell. Where would it all end? Thankfully, she would never know. Dr. Campbell was a master of sincerity. Everybody was sincere when it came to her. Sincerely wishing for a lobotomy. Most of all her mother. She'd become, in her mother's eyes, some sort of monstrous aberration. A Moloch devouring her own children, tight-lipped and dissatisfied at the world except for the lush receptivity to booze that changed her from one form of alien to another. After returning from the Bahamas she'd been on something of a rampage, drinking heavily and tearing into everyone around her, especially Phil. She did her best at this time to stay away from the children—some merciful instinct—as even their presence triggered an irrational, often furious, irritation, though fortunately Emma was there to serve as a buffer. But the horrible battles with Phil increased in pitch to the razor's edge of violence. She attacked and harpooned him from point to point so that he had no more room to maneuver and, realizing he was on the verge of physically harming her, packed a suitcase and checked into a single room for $8.50 a day on the twenty-fourth floor of the Beekman Tower at forty-ninth street and First Avenue with a view overlooking the river. He stayed one week. The first few days of his absence there was wild talk on the phone from Carol about divorce and demands for the property, which sent him into apoplectic rages. After a while she shifted to a distracted, relative calm, and by the time he returned she had retreated more deeply into herself.

While Phil was at the hotel, Lottie Sanborn, aware of the crisis that her daughter and grandchildren were in, began spending time at the apartment. Much deeply-rooted enmity had curdled their relationship over the last years with Carol's drinking and what Lottie saw as neglect of the children and, upon her arrival, they proceeded to fight viciously, culminating in a physical struggle one night that erupted when Carol, feverishly abusive with drunkenness, threw the bedroom telephone at her mother and Lottie, a physically powerful woman, retaliated by tying Carol's arms with the cord. They made such fearful noise that upstairs tenants alerted the police, but by the time they came the fight had run its course. Awakened by the struggle, Eddie went into the bedroom to see his mother being overpowered by his grandmother and tied with the phone cord and he cried and punched his grandmother's strong fleshy back with his child's fists, but mother and daughter wrestled until exhausted, finally sitting side by side panting, flushed and wildly disheveled, still hating each other with muttered curses and impotent rage. Eddie cried, hating his grandmother. Despite the commotion Mark had slept. Emma had been sent home for the evening. The police came with a rapping at the door and Eddie let them in. They stayed for an hour and one of them, a tall man with dark hair and a mustache, took Eddie out on the stairwell and talked quietly with him.

A fat fly droned lazily about the steamed room and landed on the edge of the tub, probing the porcelain. It stopped and stayed in one spot for several minutes, its proboscis planted firmly on the surface. Carol watched it, wondering. What possibly could it be about that particular spot to make his buzziness stay so engrossed and enamored? She looked more closely and saw that the fly had dipped its nose, or whatever that thing was, into a small drop of water. So, it was drinking. How marvelous. Anything to stave off the dread desiccation. Even the wretched fly. She supposed a fly could get drunk. Lumpy-loozle-buzzy-boozle. Flip-flop fat fly from the fryer to the fire. All God's chilluns do expire. Soon little miss grayboop will softly tap on the door and stick her vacant myopic head in to inform me that Philly-boy is here pacing, anxiously pacing, his thoughts ricocheting like bb's inside the cannonball head, doing his manly bit and thankful he had the money to do it. Good lord, it must be six o'clock. Where is Miss Mufflehead and her vacuous orbiculars and vaudevillian hook? Poor Carol forsook? April was the cruelest month but August crueler yet. A cruller a collar a six o'clock holler. A holler was some kind of valley, wasn't it? In Appalachia? My counterpart down there in some holler in West Virginia pining in moonshine for sweet dulcimer boy got his head blowed off by Tom McKracken. Say it were an accident but I don't think so. Now he come around all smug and sassy wants to go a courtin', but I just know he done blowed off sweet Hiney-boy's head with that Sears shotgun a his while they's a huntin' turkeys. Says it was an accident but I know better, long with just about everyone else 'cept maybe his wicked ol' pappy and bucky-toothed rickety-legged sister. Uh huh. Jesus! What the hell time was it? Water cooling. More hot? Or up'n at'em out the tub and a brisk toweling with that threadbare, blue rag hanging on yonder wall? The same wall behind which the train sat waiting, its boxcars stuffed with human tatters and tufts of hair. She was getting awfully skinny. Must fatten up there. Fatten down the bitches.

Oh, Philly-boy, where art thou? Wherefore art thou? Take me away from this God-forgotten place and into the land of suckling gin and fizzling pig. What was the use of anything? Can't just sit here and shrivel up, can we? We could. We couldn't. We could. This was it. All the breathing, walking, talking, thinking, fucking, drinking, shitting and pissing of a whole life had ended her up in this cooling tub in this place not knowing whether to get off her misbegotten ass or just sit and shrivel up. She didn't want either. But then, it was too much to drain off some of the tepid water once again and add more hot. How redundant. She'd done it so many times already. Carol sat and watched the fly walking towards her on the ledge, probing with its snout. She placed her hand carefully in its path, hoping it would walk on her, but it flew away with an abruptness that pained her heart and landed on the medicine cabinet mirror, where it stayed in the same spot without moving. Vain little thing. Struck with its own fabulous multifaceted beauty, so narcotized with self-adoration I could sneak up and catch the little buzzler. Ah, my little lovers, little gone lovers, will I ever see them again? They'd be better off though, wouldn't they? At least we had that last ride together into town. That was something. But then it was ruined by what came after, more drunkenness, with Howard Johnson, a stranger, swimming in the ocean as he wept and she so vicious screaming at the children to go away and fat black Emma strong-arming them off the beach. Did they recognize her then as the young Caribbean girl, slipping away, under, forever?

The fly was still on the mirror. Time to get out of the tub. Carol leaned forward and pushed the lever up and the water drained with a faint hollow sucking. She put her hand over the drain for a second, the force pulling against her palm, and she marveled at the indifferent, overwhelming physical world, how this little drain was but a tiny vortex faintly tugging at her palm in the midst of a universe of vortices of different dimensions and purposes, whirling and sucking in every conceivable direction and how one had to navigate this maelstrom, avoiding some, relinquishing to others, and always headed towards the grandest of them all. And what a dreadful, constant, tiresome din, these whirling suck-holes dervishing around one's body, mostly Lilliputian and unseen, but sensed nonetheless, the constant pressure of it, the roaring and howling always in one's ears, pulling everywhich goddamned way, never a moment's relief unless one had one's good glass of vodkaginrye tucked neatly between the lips and guzzling happily. She shivered in the cold and dripped water on the tiled floor that had no bath mat and thousands of tiny blue goosebumps sprouted, altering the topography of her body, the ever-onward bodily responses, the monstrous, willful flesh. She yanked the raspy towel from the rack and briskly rubbed herself from head to foot, the whole time watching the unmoving fly on the mirror, and then removed her terrycloth robe from a hook and put it on. Fat fly still making like Narcissus. Carol moved slowly closer to the fly and still it did not move until her nose touched the creature and it launched itself away with a frightened, explosive buzz, flying around the bathroom in looping, bumpy circles, then left with her own naked image staring blankly back, the pale skin despite summertime, the hazel eyes bloodshot and hollow and dark below, transmitting a huge nothing that almost took her breath away, the jagged scar beneath the cheekbone extra raw as if she might with her fingertips on either side of the wound pull it apart as it was that drunken night in Berkeley, twelve, thirteen years ago. How suddenly the car did stop, running into the telephone pole springing up out of nowhere. Nowhere! And then she somehow walking away from the wreck vaguely aware that she might be hurt and thinking that the farther away she walked the less severe her injuries might be, completely forgetting the male companion slumped unconscious in the front seat with a fractured skull. Dean Williams, sweater-wearing fraternity boy and fellow tippler, who recovered finally but never spoke to her again. That was the abrupt end to the Berkeley career, the fledgling drama major scuttling it all in minor theatrics, leaving the place in stitches—thirteen, to be exact.

As Carol dried herself in the small, cold-tiled bathroom, shivering slightly and thinking of the boy with the fractured skull (Where was Dean Williams now? He was the sort of boy a crack on the head would send straight to daddy's business, no more monkeyshines for him. She'd done him a grand favor then, after all. A nice home in Palo Alto with a swimming pool, fifty-thousand a year, blond wife and two shining kids. Still drinking though, along with the pills, for the headaches. She'd left a lasting impression), Phil was pulling into the newly-paved, oversized parking lot of the East Hill Sanatorium. There a dozen or so cars, older, plainer models that he guessed belonged mainly to the staff, were parked in orderly fashion perpendicular to the building. The lot was disproportionately large, its vast emptiness along with the weather and his own state of mind accentuating the forsaken atmosphere of the place. He supposed he might be the only visitor and he wished that he were not there at all. The rain fell in a soft gloomy whisper and the wind, while not strong, had a stubborn, insistent quality. It was exactly six p.m. At that moment Hurricane Connie was two hundred-twenty-five miles east of Charleston, churning the sea into a tumult of huge waves, its winds more than one hundred miles per hour. Phil had been following the reports on the hurricane in the paper. No one could say when or if it would hit the mainland. Of course, his concern was that it would hit Westhampton. One could certainly expect high seas, wind and rain. The dunes were not anywhere good enough, especially after last year's hurricane. The Goldens' house was larger than theirs and not a bit was left.

Phil waited a half an hour in the visitors' lounge before Carol finally appeared. It was the sort of room he dreaded, dim, with oversized, soft leather easy chairs into which one sank as if falling backwards into quicksand. It was the furniture equivalent of being drugged. Several reproductions of clipper ships arrowing through choppy seas hung on the paneled walls. It seemed to Phil they might all be the same painting. When he'd entered, the overweight blond receptionist in her starched white uniform dourly informed him of the need to bring his wife back by eight o'clock. Then she buzzed someone on an intercom. He felt uncomfortable and guilty, as if the whole sordid business was his fault. The receptionist had treated him as if this were indeed the case. To hell with her and everybody else. Falling back into one of the nightmarish chairs he angrily pulled himself forward and sat on the edge, his elbows resting on his thighs, hands folded, the balls of his feet touching the floor, ready to spring to the middle of the carpet as if it were one of the boxing rings of his youth. He was angry, yes, angry with Carol for the weakness and dead weight of her existence, angry with himself for falling into this trap, angry with fate and its mocking irony. To be free of this! If only he could just get up and walk out the door, washing his hands of the whole thing. And damn Carol! Making him sit here for so long! She was doing it on purpose. There was a small hope that perhaps she wouldn't come down at all. A sudden change of mind or mood, an incapacitation. This was beyond him, as, he suspected, it was beyond everyone. The good *herr doktor*. What the hell was he going to do other than take Phil's goddamned money? But they each played their roles. These things had their own dynamic. Either Carol would pull through or she wouldn't. He would play his part, the doctor his own, and so forth. This was to be expected. In truth he had already given up on his wife. There was a strong possibility, at this rate, that she would kill herself one way or another. He found himself increasingly wishing for that and feeling less guilty about it. Hell, all people had these thoughts. More than likely the thing would end in divorce. He'd been adjusting to the idea over the last months, though he knew it would be difficult. In all likelihood her instability and alcoholism would work against any serious claims she might make on his possessions. Alimony he could deal with. As the responsible parent Phil would keep the children. He had the money to see that they were cared for. Neither he nor Carol were much in the way of parents. But kids were tough. Hell, look at his own childhood. If he could make it, anybody could. They had much more than he ever had, and besides, the country was booming. There wasn't the struggle like there was when he was growing up. They had every natural advantage. There wasn't a thing to feel guilty about.

Carol came through the door accompanied by a small graying nurse who wore a startled expression and gripped his wife by the elbow as if afraid her patient might not be able to navigate on her own. When they stepped onto the carpet Carol stared straight ahead and the little nurse smiled at Phil in a self-conscious, apologetic manner. Phil bounced to his feet and strode aggressively to his wife and took her by the opposite elbow as the nurse backed away. He looked into Carol's impassive face and forced a smile, half hating her. She continued to stare straight ahead, clearly ignoring him, a subtle malicious gleam in her eye. She was under medication but obviously conscious of what she was doing. He thought she looked terrible, her eyes bloodshot and darkly circled, the small face pale and drawn, makeup plastered carelessly over the scar beneath the cheekbone. This was a wife he wanted no part of. He was here only because obliged, wanting nothing more than to do an about-face and deliver her back into the hands of the trepid little nurse who had already disappeared. As the door shut behind them and they walked to the car, Phil's impatience and anger surfaced. "What have they got you on? Are you as out of it as you seem? Are you sure you want to go out to dinner? Why don't you say anything, Carol?" She continued to ignore him and Phil, dreading an absurd, demeaning evening in a public setting with a woman who seemed to be playing games with him, afraid of the twists his wife's erratic behavior might take, and his own angry responses, was sorely tempted to turn around and march her back to the sanatorium. Damned and double-damned. So, one went through with it.

The absurdities. He'd lost his strength to this woman! He was being controlled by her as surely as he controlled the models he photographed: *Chin up! A little to the left! Hold that! Very nice!* If mental illness or alcoholism was a cry for help it was also a way to control the people around you, immobilize them in the force field of your behavior, except for the very crazy, who truly had no idea what they were doing. Carol was far from very crazy. She wasn't in fact crazy at all. But the alcohol had eroded something essential and what was left was perhaps a little crazy because of it. It wasn't crazy so much as it was a loss of something that kept things solid and under control. She was slipping away, losing her will to live and govern her thoughts and impulses. It was the kind of abdication that Phil detested, and while he knew it wasn't completely her fault, he nevertheless blamed her for it, resentful that this profound slackness of spirit was dictating so much of his existence. And here she was, playing him for a fool, ignoring him as if he didn't exist, he who had cut short an afternoon's work and driven through rush-hour traffic to spend time with her and take her to dinner, not to mention the ungodly sum he'd end up paying to keep her in this place. It was too much. "Listen to me, Carol." He stopped somewhat theatrically about ten yards from the car, expecting, hoping, Carol would follow suit. She did not. "Dammit, listen to me! Why are you behaving this way? Don't you appreciate the fact that I've come to see you? I know you're not as doped-up as you're acting. This is completely unfair and childish on your part and if you don't stop it we can forget about dinner and I'll take you right back and you can go to your room. Is that what you want?"

What she wanted was something to drink. "Oh, Phil, for God's sake calm down. You're overreacting. I'm just a little preoccupied. You have no idea what it's like to spend time in that place. And please, don't threaten to send me to my room as if I were a child. How ridiculous you sound."

"What the hell am I supposed to do, Carol? Really. Every day I break my ass for you and the children. It's costing me a fortune to have you here. But that's all right. You need help. I just don't think you have any idea of the responsibilities I have and how hard I work. Do you even know where the children are? Who's taking care of them? How they're managing to eat three meals a day? That doesn't even enter your mind, does it? No, everything is Carol, Carol, Carol. Poor Carol. There's a whole universe out there beyond your immediate concerns. Please get in the car." He had walked to the passenger side and was holding the door open for her. With deliberate steps, her head down, Carol moved in an arc around the front of the car, behind her husband, and ducked carefully into the seat. Phil made sure she was safely inside and shut the door. There was a tavern, *The Brown Steer*, several blocks from East Hill, that advertised the "finest steaks east of Kansas City." What appealed was its darkness and the fact that it was early, so there would be few diners. If this dinner proved difficult at least there wouldn't be too many to witness it.

Standing at the passenger door, Phil took a deep breath and made a conscious effort to relax. He saw his life in its entirety, the mean, struggling years of his youth, the hard work and triumphs, the flowering of his career, the discordant sadness, the failure of his own attempts at family and parenting, the certainty of aging and death. Here was this unfortunate woman, part of the flawed facet of his existence, mired hopelessly in the tar pit of her own turbulent, misguided passage, and the remarkable thing, the true mystery, was that somehow they were conjoined, perhaps briefly but without question profoundly, if for no other reason than the children, and would, until they died and even beyond, remain a part of each other. Phil understood again that he, like most people, rushed through life as if caught in a whirlwind, the powerful, churning engine of survival, responsibility, occasional moments of pleasure, the never-ending vigilance for the twin-headed demons of catastrophe and pain and the ironic, almost terrifying consequence of these preoccupations—the ordinary business of being human—was that in a flash one's life was over without truly understanding what was important and what was not. Indeed, it was possible that one would hardly remember a thing. It occurred to him then that what was perhaps really important in his life was this sad, irksome human being sitting before him at this very moment, that instead of wanting to be rid of her his life would be better served by turning towards her, embracing her turmoil. Indeed, if she were to be saved his role was essential. He'd always strongly believed that the success or failure of one's life was firmly planted in one's own hands—he still believed it—but he was willing to acknowledge that there were cases when a person needed help, and that this help was of its truest, most effective nature when it came from the deep and sacrificing heart. It was the only sort of help that could be salvational. Well, he wasn't anybody's goddamned savior, that's all there was to it. It just wasn't who he was. He felt sorry for Carol, and perhaps, yes, he would do more, maybe a lot more, but the truth was that he didn't love her any longer (did he love anybody?), and that being the case he doubted the sort of effort he'd be able to summon would come from as deep a place as necessary. So, what could he do? In truth, not much more than what he was already doing. He might call her more often when she was at the sanatorium, come for more visits, maybe even write some letters. But she wasn't going to be in this place forever, and then it would be more of the same, her addiction, her pathetic, underdeveloped sense of identity, the restlessness and dissatisfaction, his constant anxiety over what was going on with her. No, it was too much. He wasn't a saint or a savior. And though it seemed she'd never make it on her own, that is, without the deep and selfless nurturing she needed from another human being, it still wasn't enough to pull him towards her. Sad but true. Perhaps he was a selfish person, but these were the realities. Yet one didn't abandon a person in such condition. His wife. The mother of his children. It wouldn't be an abandonment though, would it? He would still see to it that she was cared for. He had the money. This was the great blessing of the stuff. It covered a multitude of sins. One could afford a certain laxity at times. The money covered your tracks. That would be it then. He couldn't raise himself to the level of saint. He didn't love her. But he would not abandon her completely, though of course if they divorced, which he now felt was a certainty, the legalities would see to it that she was well provided for. There was no such thing as a complete separation from someone you had children with. It was a kind of trap. Again, the money. Pity the ones who had little of it.

These thoughts passed through Phil's mind as he stood beside the passenger door. He would divorce her. He'd talk to Goldstein, his lawyer, tomorrow. Finished. Things would be worked out. He walked around the front of the car feeling already as if he were a thousand miles away from her, though he could feel the confused jumble of her psyche like some mass of wires crammed into a space too small with the lid tightly shut. She was probably not going to make it, but that could no longer be a primary concern of his. Life was a rough business. It was as if she'd fallen overboard in seas too stormy for rescue and he'd resigned himself to watching her recede in the distance from the deck of his boat headed towards destinations still full of promise. Soon he would have to turn his back and put his mind elsewhere. One did that for survival's sake. He opened the door and slid in next to her. Having made the decision to divorce her, he felt less tension. He watched her impassive face as he started the car's powerful engine. She wouldn't do very well with a divorce. There would be a hellacious cash settlement. He'd have to sell some of his property, probably the beach house. One never got out unscathed. "Are you hungry?" he asked.

"As a matter of fact, I'm famished," lied Carol, whose only interest was drink. She hoped she could talk him into it. Poor Phil. She did know how hard he worked. She hadn't offered a compelling case for him to do much else. He was a selfish, somewhat limited man, but talented, and serious about meeting his responsibilities. She still found him attractive, though desire for intimacy had abandoned her long ago. What would life have been like with Paul? With his religion probably a disaster. It might be possible to save her marriage with Phil. He didn't have the depth of Paul but it wasn't as if he were insubstantial. As self-absorbed as he was, he still had warmth, though she was quite certain that he didn't love her any more. Perhaps it was possible to rekindle those feelings in both of them. More likely not. What was Phil thinking? "I haven't really had anything to eat in a couple of days. God, I've been out of commission. You're right, I am a bit doped-up. They've put me on some sort of sedative, though I haven't had anything today. I feel like I've been living in a cave for a month and the circus is beginning to move in. It's been very interesting, though I wouldn't necessarily recommend it. Your doctor is an amusing man. Kind of handsome, I think. We had quite an interesting discussion this afternoon, at least I think it was this afternoon. He almost believes in reincarnation and thinks it possible I might have drowned in the Caribbean a hundred years ago. It seems quite likely to me. That would explain my nightmares of being swallowed up by the sea and going straight to the bottom like a lead rocking horse. Am I dressed for where we're going? Where are we going? Oh, it doesn't really matter, as long as they mix a good martini." There. She'd said it. Carol looked at Phil, who had no visible reaction as he steered the car out of the parking lot. "You don't suppose a martini would hurt, do you?"

"No, I suppose one wouldn't hurt."

If one wouldn't hurt then two couldn't be much worse. She was a bit surprised, thinking Phil would make a stink. All right then, I'll drink a dozen, since he doesn't seem to care one way or another. There was something about his manner that was a bit too relaxed. He'd been agitated enough when he'd arrived. What had changed? "You're acting much too calm, Philly-boy, what's the deal? Are you taking your wife to the river? Getting rid of ol' Carol-o, are we?"

"What kind of nonsense is that?"

She'd gotten a rise out of him. Things weren't so strange after all. "I don't know. There's a certain peaceful resolve about you, like you've decided to get rid of me. Have you decided to get rid of me, Phil?"

"Cut the crap, Carol. We're going to have dinner and then I'm taking you back to East Hill."

"No need to get excited, Philip. You're always so touchy about answering simple questions. I just thought you might be thinking about drowning me, that's all. I wouldn't blame you, my God, I'm nothing but a burden on everyone. The truth is, I'll be drowning myself one of these days." She glanced at Phil and saw that he was becoming considerably less relaxed. "Our good doctor thinks that I've been drowning myself symbolically in alcohol for eighteen years, that in another life I drowned at the age of fifteen somewhere in the Bahamas, and the recollection of that catastrophe triggered my drinking—at the precise age I drowned in the previous life. I don't tell you these things usually, Phil, because I know how little you believe in them. For you it's blood, sweat and sirloin steaks, isn't it? I don't think I've met a more materialistic person in my whole life. I've never heard you talk about anything remotely spiritual. Why is that? I know you think it's dog-eat-dog, but don't you ever reflect on anything else? Don't you think there's more to life than just struggling to survive?"

"I haven't noticed any revulsion on your part to these things. You've certainly taken advantage of my hard work and success, haven't you? Don't you think it's a little hypocritical to be talking this way? Your inebriated spirituality is a luxury I can't afford, quite frankly. And do you ever think about the children? Do you know where they are now? What they're doing? Who's taking care of them? If they're getting enough food to eat? Have you ever really thought about the children, or has it been about Carol all the time? You've got a helluva nerve asking me about my spiritual beliefs when your life has been wrapped around a bottle all these years. Have you ever thought about the effects your drinking and irresponsibility is having on the kids? And since when have you been such a spiritual person, anyway? Dammit, don't talk to me about spirituality, Carol. I've sweat more spirit taking care of you and the kids than fourteen bibles put together. Spirituality my ass."

"You're right Phil, I'm a failure as a parent. I haven't contributed a thing except anxiety and pain. I can only hope there's something good about me that I've passed along, genetically at least. It's not fair of me to put you on the spot about spirituality. How ridiculous. Who cares if you're spiritual or not? You do your duty as a parent. You meet your responsibilities—"

"The fact of the matter is, Carol, we could both do better as parents. But don't feel too sorry for the children. They're well provided for. A lot of children don't have anything near what they have. I had nothing of what they have. You're right, Carol, I'm not a spiritual person. I don't even know what it means. There's not much secret about who I am. I've known nothing but struggle and hard work my whole life. My station in life is to work hard and to provide for myself and my family. I'm a fucking peasant, is what I am, not a goddamned mystic or rabbi. My father was a much better man than me. He worked the bones right out of his back and he still had time to think and study the Talmud. I don't believe in God, Carol. How could anybody believe in God after what happened to the Jews? But I've never believed in God. I believe in myself and the rewards one gets right here on this good earth."

They came to a stop sign. *The Brown Steer* was several blocks away. The rain had let up a bit but the wind was stronger. Through the window Carol could hear the muffled, oceanic sound of the highway almost a mile away, like some merciless beast continually unfolding. It frightened her, this beast. It was the sort of mindless, massive expenditure of pointless energy that typified the country, the opposite of the God-energy that she sought. If there was a constant field of energy in the universe—which of course was God—then a person needed to understand its source and align oneself with it, that which gave form and essence to everything, that which had its own laws and demands and made pitiable much of what mankind attempted, its machines and bombs, its hideous striving after meaningless "success." Pity them. Pity Phil. How could they know? But, dammit, didn't they have any idea? How could it be that humans, the supposed pinnacle of creation, had the least notion of any of God's creatures of what it meant to adapt one's energy to the God-energy of all that was? The Greeks were right, after all. It was hubris. It didn't bother her that Phil wasn't spiritual. As he had said, what was spirituality anyway? She certainly wasn't spiritual in any conventional, church-going sense, and yet she considered herself a spiritual person, had always, in some sense, considered herself as such. What bothered her about Phil was that he gave such little evidence of—he'd just now admitted it—even thinking about these things. Spirit, for Phil, if it existed, was the thrilling, propulsive spectacle of the culture, a culture that unselfconsciously proclaimed itself the apotheosis of a new order of existence. And Phil was a prime, unselfconscious example of this new order of being. Everything old was, if not forgotten, packed away in a steamer trunk in the attic of one's psyche, its usefulness relegated to a time when none of the present miracles existed. His father's faith was one of those things tucked away. Phil might not be aware, Carol thought, of the importance of that particular item, the deep tradition that served to quietly hold the family together in the dark and difficult times so that he, one of the country's "new men," might be catapulted into the glittering future. She thought he might be a little ashamed of his past and the reticent, pious tailor, or, perhaps, so strong was his desire to escape these beginnings that to think or speak much about them was simply too painful and perhaps a little frightening. Was Phil aware that he was connected to a larger ultimate energy? And that the energy of the culture that had captured him, of which he was so enamored, was a kind of maniacal, compulsive behemoth madly in the process of devouring itself? How overpowering was the engine of this conflagrant, aberrant force! How blinding its dazzling allurements! He appeared to her, looking this way and that for oncoming traffic as his powerful car rumbled at the stop sign, as some kind of idiot, a pathetic, unreflective pellet of fuel whose purpose, ultimately, was to be used up by the monstrous machine of which he and she and everyone was a part, whether willing or not, knowing or unknowing. This machine would destroy all of them sooner or later, herself sooner than Phil, but him as surely as he gripped the wheel of his beloved automobile. It was a society that claimed to offer more than any that had come before greater recompense for the pound of flesh it would extract. Apparently, it was true. The kingdom of riches right here on earth. What could be more intoxicating, more fulfilling, than that?

Phil was riding the big energy, that was certain. But it seemed clear to Carol that this big galloping miscreation was going off in the wrong direction. They were all bull riders, these new cowboys, on an exhilarating adventure holding on for dear life. It didn't matter where they were going. The thrill, the danger, the speed was enough. Nowhere on earth was there energy like this. At no time in history had there been energy like this. She had been captivated by it herself. Who wouldn't be? The whole world was fascinated by America.

"Which way to the ranch, partner?" She looked at Phil with some affection. He was, after all, human. And a better man than most. A person was a product of his time. If he wasn't the reflective sort, what of it? Who got closer to the essence of things anyway, the one who rode the bull or the one who contemplated the meaning of the ride?

"There's a place I saw up here to the left. *The Brown Steer.* I hope it's not the bum steer." He looked at his wife and saw that she was clear and observing him with warmth. He forced a smile and she turned away. It had always seemed to Phil that their moods or responses to a moment were out of harmony with one another. It apparently was a matter of principle with her. A very childish principle, he felt. Part of being adult was that one made an effort to respond to the feelings of the other and that both shared a responsibility to try to lighten the burden of a life that was difficult enough. A little happiness, for Christ's sake! But not Carol. Or maybe it was something about his personality that just irritated her. Maybe she just didn't like him. "For God's sake smile once in a while, Carol! Life doesn't have to be so grim all the time, does it? What is it about me that irritates you so much?" He hadn't meant to say this but it slipped out. "Never mind, forget it. We're all under a lot of strain."

"What irritates me is that it's all about form, like the smile you just gave me. You can't force people to smile as if they were machines you just turned on and off. I've always been something of an adjunct to your life. The little wife and the little kids. The big houses and the big car. What meaning does any of it have for you? I don't think you really care that much about us, Phil. It's all the photographs and the accoutrements, isn't it? You accuse me of not being aware of the children, what about you? You never do anything with them, you hardly know a thing about them. They're just there, like a couple of pieces in your art collection. I'm beyond this mother business, Phil. I'm beyond anything expected of me. It's too late. My life is finished. I'm either going to die or end up cohabitating with aliens. I'm quite serious. Somehow, it's never worked out, so now what's left for me is to do something very different. I give you the kids. They're yours. Congratulations. I love them more than you ever will but you're much better equipped to care for them than I am. I'm a miserable failure, I know. Therefore, I need to look elsewhere. Maybe I can salvage something. Even death would be a kind of salvation. I want to fly, Phil, away from here. I want to buy a plane and fly around the world. I want to get into a flying saucer and go to Venus. The love planet. There is no love on this planet except love of one's own precious self. I'm pulling out, Philly-boy. I don't want to be a part of your game anymore. I don't want to be a part of my own game anymore. Our good doctor says that I need to work very hard to save my life, that I have so much to offer, all that divine garbage. But working hard is a bore. I will not work hard. Either it's going to come to me or it's not. Meanwhile I'll be like St. Augustine and drink as much orange juice as possible and cultivate the light within. But tonight a good steak and martini would be divine."

"I think you might be advised to listen to Dr. Campbell, Carol. I think he knows what he's talking about. It's not a sign of weakness to admit that you don't have all the answers, that you might need help."

"Oh, I don't deny that at all. I know I need help. I know I don't have all the answers. I'm simply *muy contento* to be just as I am. And what that is is continually unfolding into new and astonishing dimensions. Actually, I'm rather serious. I've learned more about life and myself in these last few days than I ever thought possible. And your good doctor has helped. I rather like him. He's got a head on his shoulders. Quite unusual for the breed. Your money is well spent, Philip. Fret not, I am unfolding in new and astonishing ways."

"The most astonishing thing would be for you to give up drinking." After a wrong turn Phil had located *The Brown Steer.* The parking lot was still relatively empty, a welcome sight. The few cars parked in front were recent, expensive models, another good sign. This was a tavern noted for its food, hopefully, rather than as a place to drink after work. Nothing like the *Black Angus* or *La Cave Henri IV*, of course, but it would probably do. He wasn't hungry anyway. What he wanted was a dark corner and few prying eyes. Carol would have her martini and glass of wine, nibble on her steak and talk whatever nonsense she wanted and he would ride it out. The best he could do under the circumstances. He felt a little guilty for acquiescing to her desire for drink, but it was easier than battling. A couple wouldn't hurt. She was good after a couple but trouble beyond that. She sensed his difference. Amazing. Getting rid of ol' Carol-o. She was as perceptive as a she-devil. Women were like that, damn them. Well, she had apparently reached some sort of determination herself. Getting rid of him. Or some kind of big change in her life. But what? How could she do anything, the way she was? Was she contemplating suicide?

***

For dinner they had hamburgers, French fries and string beans. Eddie wasn't very hungry, but Mark finished his plate quickly and asked for more French fries. Eddie asked his aunt Deborah and grandmother if he could be excused from the table and he went downstairs to look at his baseball cards. Deborah served Mark more fries and sat down next to him. The three of them, Mark, Deborah and Lottie, sat at the kitchen table eating their food. Over the course of the day the wind had picked up and late in the afternoon it had begun to rain lightly. The ocean, increasingly agitated, produced larger swells that pushed shoreward with pugnacious insistence. The usual midweek's number of people walked the beach despite the weather and there were more swimmers than in previous days, the strong waves providing sport for bodysurfers and divers testing their small, innocent strength against the ocean's power. The feel of the air, the wind, the bullish waves, foretold the fury of the storm headed towards them. The early evening temperature was not disagreeable and they plunged into the water and rode the waves to shore, tumbling like sacks of bones, gathering themselves and plunging in again, exhilarated. In a matter of time the she-bear cuffing and tumbling her cubs in rough, benignant play would be roaring in the full aspect of her rage. But now was the time for innocent thrills, to flirt with the power that with the smallest shrug of the slightest part of its vast liquid body would crush their bones to the bottom or fling them to the ends of the world.

Eddie soon tired of looking at his cards and listened to the ocean. He'd been aware of its gradually-building agitation, but suddenly he was filled with the peculiar excitement and fear that such rough conditions always brought. He now heard the crashing waves and hissing water as if no other sound existed, and he pushed the pile of cards away, left his room and exited the screen door at the back of the house, going up the stairs to the deck and then down to the beach. Eddie liked to play at the edges of the rough ocean, a little frightened, but filled with its wildness and power. He'd been caught many times in its muscular currents and swept down the beach, or pounded rudely to the bottom by the heavy, sumo-like waves.

It was not terribly big or angry, but strong enough to make him pause a moment and wonder if he'd dare go in a little bit, not as far as the grownups but far enough to feel its force, to battle the smaller waves, knocked off his feet, tumbled, rolled under, close enough to shore but not far from the real power and depths so that always there was the edge of danger inside him. He'd seen more turbulent seas, the worst last year when they'd had to evacuate and go inland. Then the ocean was a swollen, dirty mass that seemed close enough to be in their dining room and which, indeed, a short time later, was. That was an ocean of a different order. There would be no thought in his or any grownup's mind about a thrilling test of skill or strength in that water. It was a surging primal force in whose face no sane person could remain without turning to flee in terror. As it was, they'd stayed too long, having been told to evacuate the night before. Eddie remembered vividly the howling, nightmare wind that came close to knocking him off his feet and how they'd all struggled to close the garage door and failed, and then piled into the car as if suddenly realizing the peril in which they'd found themselves. They drove off the beach, his parents tense. It seemed they were the only ones left. Parts of the road were flooded and the wind blew the rain so hard against the windshield that his father cursed and strained to see. When they were about halfway to the bridge a police car appeared and pulled them over, the officer in his yellow rain slicker coming to the window and yelling at his father over the wind. He was clearly upset that they were still on the beach. It was embarrassing to see his father scolded but everyone became more nervous and, driving off, it was soon forgotten. There was one stretch in front of the Swordfish Club that was deeply flooded and the car went slowly through it and then they were on the bridge and away from the danger of the ocean.

Eddie walked towards the turbulent ocean, the memory of the year before inhibiting him slightly, the image of the turgid, pushing mountains of gray water still fresh in his mind, a nightmare. He realized with a blunt fear in his stomach that this ocean could rise up and take him away forever, as if he were the merest piece of driftwood, and it could do the same to anyone, including his own mother or father. That they were no more substantial than he compared to the power of the ocean brought him back to the extraordinary recognition he'd had a few days earlier when his mother had started the fire in the living room: people disappeared. He thought that someday the ocean might swallow him up and he would disappear forever, taking him from his family and friends and everything he knew. The thought saddened and frightened him. He didn't want this to happen. It didn't seem possible that he would ever die but if he did he didn't want it to be in the vastness of the ocean in the midst of towering waves and the terrifying wind. But this ocean today wasn't so bad. He could go into it a little way and it could do nothing to him if he was careful. He could be strong enough and careful enough so that this power would not be able to master him and, in this way, he could reassure himself that he was not going to disappear and that in a certain way he was, if not its equal, its respectful confederate.

Carol had decided at the last moment on rye and soda. Perhaps it was the way the place made her feel, with its darkness and hushed, murmuring voices. Heads had turned when they'd entered and she was certain they knew she was from the loony bin. The loafers, gray flannel slacks, white blouse and thin blue sweater she wore seemed a dead giveaway. She might as well have been wearing her pajamas. When the men sitting at the bar turned around on their stools and stared, she could feel Phil's tension and hostility rising, always a given in situations like this. An older couple sat at a table near the wall in the dining room cutting their steaks. The bartender, who looked like an actor whose name she couldn't remember, filled his containers with ice. A waitress with a wide, tragic country face looked into Carol's eyes and led them to a table in a corner away from the older couple. She and Phil ordered their drinks immediately, Phil his usual scotch. They sat for a moment avoiding each other's eyes, looking around the place uninterestedly. Phil cleared his throat.

"Well, it must be good to get out—"

Carol continued looking around the tavern. Sepulchral. Everybody in the joint waiting for Charon to ferry them across the Styx to Hades. The river out back, hidden from view by the oak trees.

"I had an enjoyable circus this morning in my hotel room. An actual magic lantern show. Thanks so much for bringing me here, Phil. This feels like the penultimate stop. I can't wait for my rye and soda. There are two things in this wretched world I care about, my bottle and my babies. Harsh but true. I don't mean to offend you, Phil. You're a good man. But what is the point of all this fuming and mad running about? Have a drink and relax, Philly. You're going to divorce me, aren't you?"

"This isn't the time to talk about things like that, for God's sake. No, I'm not going to divorce you."

"You're not a convincing liar, Philip."

The waitress brought their drinks. She was tall and large-boned, about Carol's age. There was something hauntingly familiar about the waitress' sad intense gaze that focused on Carol to the virtual exclusion of her husband. *She recognizes something in me. A hundred years ago in the Bahamas? No, too Dorothea Lange. Dust Bowl mystic.* Carol returned the woman's intimate look. The waitress took their orders, sirloins, rare, salad, baked potatoes, two glasses of Burgundy. No appetizers. Carol ordered another drink.

"That was strange," said Phil. "What the hell was that all about?"

"I think it's a fellow Venusian. A Venusian sister." Carol finished her drink in three long swallows, closed her eyes and entered a soft green chamber. *Better.* She opened her eyes and smiled at Phil. "What transpired was an exchange of sympathetic energies. One has to be receptive to these things. I am only very recently becoming receptive, I'm afraid. My God, Phil, what are you doing with your life? Don't you see that you're being devoured by this horrendous, aberrant force? Perhaps you should drink more, like me. Can't you see yourself staggering around, belligerent as hell, punching everybody in the nose? We could be co-belligerents. A great team of battling booboisie-busters. You need to fall, Phil, get down to my level. Then you might save yourself. That woman, whoever she is, is right down there with me. Way beyond me, in fact, I'm sure. Join us, Phil. Join us—"

"Carol, for God's sake."

"Please, Phil, let me talk. I've never talked enough to you. It's my own fault. I'm such a terrific snob, really. Who the hell do I think I am? I've been so wrong, so ridiculous, it's embarrassing. To think, people live their whole lives like this, sleeping, in a dream, thinking that the world in front of their nose is the only world that exists. I—there's no hope, I know, for me, but you still might have a chance. Get out of it, Phil, before it's too late."

"Honestly, Carol, I have no idea what you're talking about. I'm doing what I want to do. I'm happy with my life. I work hard. It's you who needs to get out of it, the drinking, this morbidity, all this crazy talk. You're at a crossroads here, Carol. You need to understand that."

"I'm surprised at the Christian imagery, Phil. You, of all people. How touching, really. What would be the Jewish equivalent of a crossroads? Do you see me standing alone, casting a long portentous shadow? Trembling with indecision? Possibilities? At the brink of despair? Annihilation? Just how do you see me, Phil? In fact, I don't think you see me at all. I'm a tremendous irritant, a festering splinter you can't remove. Isn't that right? This is not at all what you imagined, is it? God knows what I imagined. Nothing, I suppose. I can't even remember. All I can remember is how glorious you were, all that marvelous energy, those dazzling blue eyes, your beautiful legs. I suppose you wanted me as badly as I wanted you. How do you feel now? Not a fair question. I'm sorry. How would anyone feel? Well, I guess there are some—what a pathetic joke. But I was something once, wasn't I? But you're right, I am at a crossroads, or maybe some sort of bizarre chrysalis that's been marinating in alcohol for decades and now finally beginning to stir. But God knows what sort of distorted form will emerge. Probably still-born. Nothing ordinary, that's for certain. A mutation. Only it's too late. But you have lots of good years left, lots of fun and excitement. Ah! Our salads—and my drink."

The waitress balanced a basket of dinner rolls, two salad plates, and Carol's drink on a black tray. Again, she directed her attention at Carol, smiling in her sad, otherworldly manner.

"What is your name?" asked Carol.

"Rachel, Ma'am."

"A biblical name, is it not?"

"Yes, Ma'am." The woman seemed a bit uncomfortable and stood holding the tray against her like a shield. Phil glared at Carol.

"Do you have any children?"

"No, Ma'am. I was married once, a long time ago, but we didn't have any children." Her expression became distant. "Will there be anything else?" She looked at Phil for the first time. "For you, sir?"

"No thank you," he said.

"Ma'am?"

"No thank you," said Carol.

The waitress looked at Phil again and then at Carol, seemed on the verge of saying something, thought better of it, and instead offered the same dolorous smile.

"Your steaks will be out in a minute."

Carol took a long deep swallow of her drink and Phil reached for a roll, tore off a piece and buttered it from a stick in a glass dish resting in a bowl of ice. The older couple across the room had been staring at them indiscreetly. They had finished their steaks and were both eating cherry pie and sipping coffee. Phil caught the woman's glance and looked at her icily, wanting to cross the room and smash the piece of pie into her silver, tightly-coifed hair. They were both overweight. After he squashed the pie into her hair he'd turn and catch the husband with a left hook as he was rising from his chair, knocking him backwards over the table behind. The bartender would come running into the dining room and Phil would coldcock him too. Agitated with these thoughts, but satisfied, Phil turned to Carol and saw that she had already finished her drink and was motioning with the empty glass to the waitress for another.

"Carol, really, that's enough."

"Oh, come on, one more won't hurt. I'm just starting to calm down a little. Don't you want a calm little Carol? Or would you rather have me shivering and watching little brown bugs crawl across the ceiling? They're there, you know. Most people just can't see them." The waitress appeared.

"Would you like another?" she asked Carol, glancing at Phil.

"Yes please," said Carol.

"And you, sir, would you like another?"

"Yes, all right, another scotch on the rocks, please. Thank you." It was, Phil decided, too much to fight. Anyway, she was right. One more would calm her down, not that she seemed especially agitated. It would certainly calm him down. The woman was strange. A Christian, religious type. Some kind of Baptist. Just what the hell was a Baptist, anyway? But there was something about her. Carol was right. She had a kind of power, some odd quality. Probably just a nut. The waitress took their glasses with what seemed like reluctance, avoiding their eyes, glanced at the basket of rolls, and walked away. Phil looked from the waitress to Carol, who was watching him with amusement.

"If you can't beat 'em, join 'em, eh? I'm worried about you, Phil. I expected more of a fight. This is a bad sign. You really have given up on me, haven't you? Old Carol going under and the ship with no more life preservers. Might as well contemplate the thing with a drink, I suppose. No use jumping in and running the risk of drowning oneself. I don't blame you. That's an interesting girl, isn't she? What do you suppose she thinks of us? She seems prescient, somehow. As if she knows us terribly well and can see what is going to happen. Should we ask her? She's an oracle, or soothsayer of some sort, I'm certain. Isn't she marvelous? I do believe she's the most extraordinary person I've come across in years. But I don't think we need a soothsayer to tell us what's going to happen, do we? I think Odysseus has returned to find his Penelope beyond hope, besotted and gone to wrack. Cruel recompense for years of struggle, constancy and heroism, though we did have a little time out with Circe, didn't we? We do have a Circe out there somewhere, don't we, my Odysseus?"

"Would you please stop this nonsense—"

"Nonsense? What is nonsense? Certainly not Phil Heizer's own peculiar corner of the world with its atomic-powered commuter ride into the next century and beyond. Granted, you don't ride the train, and you don't wear a gray flannel suit, thank God, but you are so very sure of yourself and this culture you inhabit, so much so that everything else becomes 'nonsense.'"

"You're a helluva one to talk, goddammit." Phil spoke in a low angry whisper, squinting his blue eyes. "Once again it's the golden princess on her feathered perch passing commentary on the stupidity and falseness of the ordinary human world, as if you were so much better than anyone else. When's the last time you did a goddamned piece of honest, ordinary work in this foolish 'culture' you're so disdainful of? When's the last time you wiped your brow from effort instead of the alcoholic sweats? What's so shallow and middle-class about being an ordinary mother to your own children? Or is that part of the 'atomic-powered commuter ride' you despise so much? Who the hell is paying the bills so you can pontificate in your drunken slop about this pathetic 'culture' we live in? Don't you think you're one of the biggest hypocrites that ever pissed down a pant leg? It's galling, this bullshit of yours. I work my ass off to support you in your supposed style when in fact you're nothing more than a spoiled, alcoholic little girl. I've had it up to here with this crap, Carol, believe me." Phil glared at the couple across the room. If they were staring, he was ready to walk over to them. They were both sipping their coffee with their heads down.

"You don't see my point, Phil. You never will." Carol was a bit shaken by the vehemence of Phil's attack, but it was more a feeling of being beaten soundly about the head in a pillow fight. A buffeting, to be sure, but nothing too damaging. Phil was absolutely right. This was nothing new, nothing she'd not lacerated herself with hundreds of times. There was no question that she was essentially worthless and horribly spoiled. This was universally agreed upon. Her little drama had played out and all that remained was the afterword, to be written by someone else. It wouldn't be a pleasant commentary. Phil was far from being a stupid man but he lacked the whatever-it-was to get much beyond the absolutes of his own existence. Of course, he understood that other people had different "realities" than he and would probably acknowledge the possibility of realities other than those offered up to the five senses, but ultimately these things didn't matter. It was his own substance, his own meat, that had the greatest gravitational pull, commonly enough, and those within his orbit were expected to conform to the physical laws and peculiar customs of his system.

"Everything you say about me, almost, is right. I am a spoiled alcoholic little girl. But you're no less addicted than I am. Addicted to your work, your success. The difference is that what you do is normal and accredited and what I do is anathematized. I agree, my contribution is nil. I can't deny the validity of your hard work and the way you admirably uphold your responsibilities. You also add to the quality of the world with your talent. I'll never deny that. All would agree that you are an exemplary fellow. But I, critical, nasty, boozy little bitch, am not satisfied, with you, with the world, nor with myself. Yes, you are an exemplary fellow, along with millions of other exemplary fellows, all doing the exemplary things, those things I've tried rather half-heartedly to do but for some reason or other have never been able to generate the required seriousness. Something's missing with me, Phil, something's always been missing. I don't quite know what it is. But lately I've been getting feelings about it. Feelings that frighten you so much because they're strange and not part of the imperial reality. I can't blame you for being frightened. My God, I'm your wife, the mother of your children. The whole gleaming applecart bursting with fruit—the fruits of your labor—is veering wildly off course and about to crash because of a crazy, alcoholic miscalculation. I'm used to it, of course, being a miscalculation. I've been miscalculating all of my life. Just call me Little Miss Calculate, wandering down blind alleys and into dead-ends in a perpetual fog, absurdly thinking that I've been the master of my own vessel, so superior to the common ruck, knowing all the while that really, if someone with any sense and concern had the guts to sit me down and slap the silliness out of me I could have been told in no uncertain terms that I was an idiot, a drunken foolish idiot, and that I'd better wake up before it was too late. Well, it is too late. Paul tried to warn me but I wouldn't listen. I thought he was a fool. I thought he'd gone off the deep end. Catholicism. How I looked down my nose at him. How I pitied him. *I*, pity *him*! Imagine! And now all I can think about is St. Augustine and the glorious glowing light within. Pascal and his faith, his divine calculations. I read Pascal in high school. I loved him and forgot about him. Until now. Too late."

"You keep saying it's too late. Why is it too late?"

"Because it is. One knows these things. Someone like you finds this impossible to believe. I'm not criticizing you. You are a man operating successfully and beautifully in a man's world. Every doubt, every insecurity, has been conquered by will and manly effort. You've proven yourself over and over again—and you'll continue to prove yourself. You battle and you fight and you win. You know what it's like to knock someone down. You know the taste of blood and you like it. It redeems and fortifies you. I'm not being critical. This is the way of the world. If one succeeds one can't imagine how others cannot. All it takes is will and effort, you think. You secretly have contempt for me just as

I had at one time for Paul. I thought he was weak and foolish, but most of all I thought he was a little crazy. Maybe more than a little. How could someone so rational suddenly give himself over to religion? To faith? It was inconceivable to me, just as it's inconceivable to you that a person, that I, cannot simply decide to throw away my crutches and start walking just like everybody else. After all, you did it. You came from poverty and a horrible childhood—"

"It wasn't so horrible."

"Well, it was very difficult. I know it was. You overcame a lot. You struggled and you fought. You beat the hell out of everybody and you ran like mad, never looking back. You're still running like mad. Someone running as hard and as fast as you doesn't have the time or the inclination or even the ability to pause for a moment to try to understand how someone like me could be floundering so—could be so pathetic and helpless. This is what I mean when I talk about different realities. You are *le grand lion*, the great Leo. There is no other reality than yours. You've roared grandly and beautifully and devoured everything in your path. The self-made man in the self-made culture. It's a beautiful fit."

"You speak so critically of this 'culture,' as you call it," said Phil bitterly. "But it seems to me that it's done pretty well by you. You've never turned your back on any of the material rewards, which for the most part other people have provided. You criticize and complain, but you never do a thing about it. But I suppose what you're trying to tell me is that your reality, so unfathomable to me, for whatever reason prevents you from functioning in this horrible 'culture' you speak of. Well, somehow, I'm not buying it. Frankly, Carol, your reality consists of a bottle of booze. You've had every advantage in the world and you've squandered it completely. Are you trying to tell me that your sensibility is so much finer than mine or anyone else's? What a bunch of crap. Poor, misunderstood Carol. Empty the bottle in the toilet and get off your self-pitying ass, Carol. That's reality."

"Robert Ryan."

"What?"

"That's who the bartender looks like. Such a rugged, mean-looking type. But you could knock him down, couldn't you, Phil? I'll bet that's the first thing you thought of when you saw him—that you could knock him down. That's what males do, I suppose. I can't refute a thing you say. But the point is, I don't care anymore. Somehow this all seems preordained and I'm one of the ones washed overboard. It's true, I've never made much of an effort. I think it may be because I've known all about this hopelessness from the start. It all ends so dismally anyway. Why bother? What is the point of all your manful striving? Where does it get you? What is the purpose of your life, Phil?"

"You're asking me what the hell my purpose in life is, eh?" Phil glanced at the couple, discreetly sipping their coffee. "Well, obviously one of my purposes is to work my tail off so I can keep my family alive. You and your goddamned philosophical questions. I guess that's another one of my purposes—to keep you supplied with liquor so you can ask all these deep questions. It's beyond me, honestly, how you can be so blind. Here you are drinking rye and sodas and about to eat a steak dinner that I'm paying for and you have the nerve to ask me about my purpose in life. It seems like everyone you've come in contact with has the purpose of keeping you alive. I'd say that's a pretty noble purpose, wouldn't you?"

"Do you know what I just remembered? How when I was a child in Hong Kong coolies used to carry me to the Peak School in a sedan chair. Can you imagine that? It never occurred to me that it was the least bit unusual. The coolies were old men—or they seemed old to me—and I remembered how they grunted, like pigs. I wonder if they thought their purpose was noble. I don't suppose they did. But it was great fun to ride in the chair. I loved it—such an adventure, bouncing along looking out over the harbor, all the wonderful boats. We used to go on this marvelous two-masted ship, the HMS *Tamar*, once a year for an open house for children. Deborah and I went. Lots of silly games with all those British sailors looking on, so smartly dressed in their clean uniforms. They gave us chocolate-filled gold coins. How I loved them. I still do. That's where I developed my addiction to chocolate. If it were only chocolate, eh, Phil? Those coolies never said very much but they were nice to me. I suppose I did feel a bit superior. A birthright, you know. We were white, after all, Americans, the Empire's little brother. There was a sense, even then, somehow, I was aware of it, maybe it was the Standard-Vacuum talk—that little brother was one day going to grow up to be very big indeed. And while I was being carried around in a sedan chair by grunting coolies, you were in Hell's Kitchen fighting neighborhood kids ganging up on the Jew. You rode the subways and walked while I took the Peak Tram and the *Star Ferry* to Kowloon and the Shanghai American School. Realities. These are realities. A privileged wonderland for me and a grim battleground for you. When I was one year old, or so the story goes, I sat on the Prince of Wales' knee. He was touring the Empire. He had ridiculously long legs, you know, the Prince. Not that I remember. I've told you all this before. You probably don't remember. Oh, Phil, one more drink, please? I'm fine, really, I am." The waitress, with her raw, grim visage, approached carrying their food stacked up on a large tray. She no longer smiled sadly, her aspect now somewhat forbidding. Phil decided that she was a nut. They cleared their spaces for the food and wine, both looking at her curiously, Phil with some hostility and condescension. The waitress transferred the items from her tray to the table with professional alacrity, conveying an attitude that had shifted from what had been a heavy, almost morbid sympathy to a kind of stern disapproval. She stood stiffly, looking impassively from one to the other.

"Will there be anything else?"

Phil noticed the couple across the room getting up to leave, both staring. He glared menacingly and they looked away.

"Yes," Carol answered quickly, "I'd like another drink." Phil turned his threatening gaze from the intrusive couple to his wife, but said nothing. Carol smiled sweetly.

"Sir?"

"No. Nothing for me. Thank you."

"I'll be back in a minute with your drink, Ma'am." She walked away.

"Carol, goddammit—"

"Oh, Phil, relax. I'm completely sober." She took a deep swallow of her Burgundy. "This is just what I needed to get me right. That couple was awfully rude. Did you see them stare? Of course you did. I thought you were going to go over there and beat them up. Wouldn't that have been a hoot. Here I'm the one from the loony bin and you're getting violent. Now, did they give us rare steaks? Let's see." Carol took her knife, a stiletto-looking implement with a bone-white, plastic handle, and cut into the middle of her slab. The meat opened in a small canyon, red and flowing. "Excellent. Just the way we like it. Five minutes from the slaughterhouse and once over with a blowtorch. We're such barbarians, aren't we, Phil?"

The waitress appeared next to Carol with her drink. "Here you are, Ma'am," she said in a flat voice, placing the glass next to Carol and picking up the empties. As she leaned over the table she said, "We will all be changed, in a moment, in a twinkling of an eye."

Carol and Phil stared at the strange, haunted woman and then looked at each other. The waitress, the biblical Rachel, disappeared as suddenly and as silently as she had appeared. Well then, thought Carol. Extraordinary. Phil took a sip of his wine and commenced cutting into his steak. He looked up abruptly at Carol and saw the thoughtful, inward expression on her face. "The woman's a kook, that's all there is to it," he said. Carol looked at Phil as if he were a salesman she'd just met in a diner. She lifted the rye and soda slowly, looking at Phil, and took a long, deep drink. It was much stronger, almost straight whiskey. Wonderful. The liquid laid a smooth ameliorating track down her throat. She was beginning to feel it. The room became less tomb-like. The murmuring people at the bar bent over their drinks seemed a prehistoric gathering of cave dwellers sipping some relaxing concoction. Her husband, digging at his steak, the brow of his bald head furrowed in preoccupation, was an inarticulate, formidable brute. Safe from the elements, the people in the tavern treated themselves to these small pleasures of drink and quiet talk, each with his own sack-load of troubles, on some weighing more heavily than others. It was a place to find a moment's respite, to let food, drink and companionship work their soothing properties. But as she looked at her husband a feeling of pity came over her. He was not finding any comfort in this place or in the partaking of its sacraments. Of course, it was the circumstances, and maybe his Jewishness, his embattled background. There was a combativeness about him that she did not possess. Again, a good cultural fit. All these poor males out there cruising like potent little gunships guarding their hard-won patches of water. This was the essence of the place, each one suspicious, battle-ready, forming small shaky alliances here and there with similar types. To Phil, everyone in the tavern was a potential enemy, though, with his basic decency, he would treat them all courteously. Should anyone display even a hint of perceived disrespect however, his defenses would slide into place like imbricate segments of tempered steel, his red flags snapping smartly in the threatening wind.

Carol had no appetite but sliced a small piece from the corner of her steak and chewed lethargically. She washed it down her throat with a swallow of wine, watching the top of Phil's bald head, the scalp impervious to the brow's activity, the muscles of the face and jaw working mechanically on the warm meat. The small moles and blemishes she knew so well, fixtures of a landscape at once barren and sensual—his baldness had attracted her —moved in concert with the larger surface to which they were attached, as if mountains or plateaus on an erratically moving globe. Inside that globe was an animating, survivalist force that navigated its known galaxy, fighting, consuming, achieving. The head she stared at was an obdurate bludgeoning instrument alive with a complex survivalist's intelligence. There was something awesome about it. It overwhelmed her with an absurd giddiness that wickedly prodded her to reach out and touch it with the fork that she held in her left hand, and she moved it slowly in the direction of her husband's glabrous dome. The head was down, concentrating on the meat. The fork hesitated in its path and then retreated to a spot just in front of her left eye, and she looked at him through its tines, the other eye closed, as through the bars of a cell. Phil looked up momentarily and regarded her coldly, taking a sip of his wine and recommencing on his steak. There was nothing left but to get through this and see her back to the sanatorium as quickly and cleanly as possible. The less talk the better. She'd had way more to drink than he'd figured on allowing and now the frayed bridge upon which they'd been carefully walking threatened to break and drop them into the gorge below. Carol understood that Phil was all business now and wanted nothing but to get rid of her. It infuriated her briefly but then she found it amusing. This helpless man before her, this utter stranger determinedly chewing his meat like some kind of farm machine that ground up corncobs and expelled them as fertilizer or some such thing hadn't a clue about what to do than immediately and forcibly, if necessary, transport the alien, inebriated—yes, she was definitely feeling it now—female back to the place that would insure his own comfort and peace of mind. She stared at his skull and saw it filled with a few ill-fitting gears that needed oiling. This farm machine was clanking and stoically foraging its way through the last acre of stubble, hoping to get home before nightfall. She watched the pumping jaws grind its fuel, a bit of pinkish juice forming at one of the corners of the lips, angry eyes averted, conscious of her attention and mockery. She recognized the danger signs and looked away from her husband and drained the glass of Burgundy. He wasn't far from exploding, a potentially compelling drama that would pay no heed to the formality of the setting or its occupants. Phil could make quite a spectacle if pushed far enough, and they were both aware that she was doing it, digging, prodding, quietly taunting, ridiculing his mannerisms, his very being. How much could the picador stick the bull before it would erupt in a flaming red fury? She might do it for the hell of it, have him disgrace himself in front of everybody, storm out of the restaurant, get in his car and spin his tragic, smoking tires out of the parking lot while the good people inside peered out the windows. But then he would have to come back, having left a patient from the sanatorium alone in the tavern, quite helpless and somewhat drunk. His wife. The mother of his children. She cut a small piece from her steak and for a moment contemplated laying it delicately on the edge of his plate as a kind of absurd, goading gesture to see what sort of response it would elicit. But she felt a cold determination in him, complementing his seething anger. She was defeated. Carol pushed the piece off her fork with the knife, onto the top of her steak. She finished the rye and soda and cleared her throat.

"I guess I'm not very hungry." What was the use in tormenting him? All these poor people in the tavern, quietly in refuge from the scissoring, slicing blades of everyday life, diminishing them piece-by-piece. What was the point in disturbing their few moments of comfort and escape? Escape. She wondered.

"Do you still have those pictures of the children in your wallet?

"Yes, I do. Why?"

"I'd like to see them if I may. I miss them very much. Please let me see the pictures."

Phil put down his knife and fork and, without looking at her, rising slightly out of his seat, solemnly reached into his back pocket and handed the warm, comfortable object to Carol. She opened the wallet below the level of the table where he could not see, and carefully removed three twenty-dollar bills—Phil always carried plenty of cash—leaving in place several of the same denomination, at least two hundreds and a few singles. Carol slid the bills under the napkin on her lap and located the compartment that held the requested items, withdrawing the pictures and placing them on the table to the right of her plate. Then she folded the wallet and handed it back to her husband. Phil, eyeing Carol suspiciously, tilted his haunches forward again and inserted the slightly less substantial billfold into his rump pocket.

"My little darlings," said Carol, as she crumpled the bills in her left hand while with her right hand neatly arranging the pictures side by side. "So innocent, so sweet, so sad."

She slowly moved the wad into the pocket of her slacks, and then withdrew her sweating hand. She must not move hastily.

"Oh, for God's sake, they're not sad at all. There's no need to project your morbidity onto them."

Carol's heart beat rapidly. "Oh, right you are, *El Capitan. Pardonne-moi.* It is indeed my own sadness that I am projecting." Carol bent over the pictures. "But look at them, Phil, maybe not sad, but serious. Little Mark—what a little man! What a little, wise, grown-up face! He looks like you, Phil. That's your boy right there. And Eddie. Do you suppose anyone will ever touch him? He's so distant already. He's in his own world, isn't he, Phil. Our baseball boy." And then unexpectedly her eyes filled with tears, but she did not cry. She took the napkin and pressed it tightly to her eyes. Would she ever see the children again? It seemed that she would not. Better to leave them as is. Not to cause any more damage.

"Carol, please get ahold of yourself. The children are fine, really, they are. You'll be out of this place soon enough and see them again. Things can change, we both know that. Yours is not a helpless situation. Carol, please look at me." She shook her head almost imperceptibly, indicating that no, she would not look at her husband. She would see the children again, at least once more. Carol removed the napkin from her face and looked at Phil, who appraised her with his blue eyes. This was his engineering, or nautical look, she thought. He's in the pilot-house reckoning the dimensions of a channel, or calculating the torsional demands on a suspension bridge. He's wondering how serious this latest episode is. Will there be more to follow, causing a scene? He can see that I'm not eating my steak and he certainly will not buy me another drink. He's wondering if I'm suicidal and if I might try something at the sanatorium. He's figuring how he can get me out of this place and back to the loony bin as quickly and as unobtrusively as possible. He's at a loss as to just what exactly is going to happen with the children. He thinks I am a lost cause. He doesn't give a damn about me. He's burning his bridges.

Carol forced a smile. "My little babies. I'll never see them again, will I, Phil?"

"Don't be ridiculous. Of course you will. It's just a matter of time, that's all. You'll stay as long as necessary and this time you'll make yourself better. You have to want to, though. That's the thing. I have doubts if you really want to make yourself better, Carol, I really do. But if you want to see the kids again then you'll do it. It's that simple. You mocked my 'Christian imagery,' as you called it, but you really are at a crossroads, Carol. I think this is it, I really mean it."

"Yes, of course you 'really mean it,'" said Carol, angered at Phil's platitudinizing. "You 'really mean' everything you say, don't you, Phil? You're a scrupulously honest man, aren't you? You are an honorable man, Phil, I'll give you that. You do your duty, your marvelous duty. You reach into your marvelous pants and pull out your marvelous wallet and sow beneficence all over the world. You spill it over everyone you care for, or are supposed to care for. That's your way. Your life is a bit too important to open up other things, but your wallet is always available. It's better than nothing, I suppose."

Carol could see the deep hurt these words caused, followed by an instant, incinerating fury. Phil's face reddened and he quivered. His eyes, startlingly, glacially blue, bulged with the pressure of a barely restrained violent eruption. She met his hostile gaze with her own. He breathed deeply, looked down at his plate, picked up the knife and fork and began cutting into the cooling piece of livid, red steak that remained. "As you wish," he said, his voice thick with hurt and outrage.

"If only as I wish. I wish, I wish. The luck of the Iwish, eh, Phil? One more usquebaugh for your old Carol? I know what you think. The woman has completely lost her self-respect. At the very bottom, she is, swimming with the flounders and eels. A starfish once, cartwheeling across the heavens, an incandescent, glorious streak. If you hadn't been looking you would have missed it. I hurt you a second ago, Phil. I'm sorry. You're a good man, don't you forget it. We do what we can with what we've got. You've done way better than I. Everything about me is a dismal disaster. Please forgive me, Phil. And now I need to use the bathroom."

They looked at each other, Phil with his appraising gaze, and Carol, her eyes still moist, with grave solemnity and a reservoir of affection, if not love. The bathroom was around the corner next to the bar. Carol left her husband, turned the corner and stopped, out of Phil's view, and motioned to the Robert Ryan look-alike. She ordered a double rye and soda, paying the mean-looking fellow with one of the crumpled twenties. He returned quickly with the change, his face impassive. The men at the bar stared at her, some leeringly, a few with curiosity. She ignored them and took two deep swallows, draining the drink. Then she held her breath and peeked around the corner at Phil. He sat leaning slightly forward, alone and serious, cutting the last of his steak. She saw the top of his tanned bald head, the forehead, the strong fleshy nose, the mustache. And then, aware that a couple of the men at the bar were tittering, she placed the empty glass on the bar, turned, and went into the ladies' room and locked the door, hoping that she would find what she was looking for.

The room was dank, dark and small and smelled of effluent. A bare bulb and pull chain hung from the ceiling. A submariner's quarters. A small sink with rust stains under the taps stood beneath an ancient dull mirror that reflected her image as if a fading, sepia-toned photograph. But this was not what she saw at first or indeed what she had been looking for. On the far wall between the toilet and the sink was a double-hung window with the bottom sash open and behind that a screen, hooked at the base, that she disconnected and pushed outward so that she determined there was ample room for her to squeeze through and drop to the grassy, rank growth behind the restaurant. After that there was no definite plan other than to see her children and to drink, to keep on drinking. She would need to get back to Westhampton but had no real idea of how to get there. She'd do it on the hoof and already a scheme was forming as she stood, her heart drumming and full of a kind of dark excitement, one hand gripping her neck, looking at the haggard visage in the smoky mirror—not her, not anyone she recognized.

***

As Carol's feet touched the ground in the back of *The Brown Steer* somewhere around seven-fifteen, Wednesday evening, people of the metropolitan area and Long Island were making preparations for the hurricane. Large numbers of boats had already been pulled from the water and the owners of those that would stay moored threw in more anchorage and hoped for the best. Shopkeepers and homeowners made ready their pieces of plywood to protect large windows from the atomic winds of the storm. In supermarkets and grocery stores people bought candles, matches, Sterno, canned goods and batteries, rolling their carts purposefully, thinking of things they might need. Were there bandages? How full was the bottle of Mercurochrome in the medicine cabinet? What about the aspirin? They bought themselves extra treats should they be stranded longer than anticipated—packages of Oreos, cigarettes, liquor, potato chips, olives. At gas stations they filled their gallon-cans of kerosene and their cars. Batteries and tires were checked and radiators topped-off. Fuses, hammers, saws, nails, lanterns, galvanized buckets, electrician's tape, sponges, flares and more were purchased at hardware stores. Lumberyards did a spirited business. People listened to their radios for reports on the storm's progress and for instructions on how to prepare. There was apprehension and fear, but also excitement, especially among the young, the adventurous, the anarchistic. Those with property near the water were anxious. The weather service was predicting the storm possibly to hit the following day, with exceptionally high tides, winds and torrential rains. Storm warnings were posted as far as Block Island. The forecast in the papers conservatively called for easterly winds, afternoon clouds and rain.

Carol walked quickly into the woods behind the tavern, soaking her slacks to the knees in the wet underbrush, the branches whipping her face. She was gripped by a nervous, giddy excitement, alternately laughing at and feeling sorry for Phil, sitting at his table waiting for her. The growth was thick, she had no idea where she was going, but it was certain to lead to a place where she could compose herself and walk about like an ordinary citizen. Must make sure that Phil, who would be searching, did not spot her. Carol had a vague notion of calling a cab to take her to the train station and then out to Westhampton. She had money enough for both. Within a matter of moments, she found herself completely surrounded by damp and dense forest. She might have been somewhere in Maine or New Hampshire under a canopy of dripping maples and oaks, the waning light of early evening, already dimmed by the overcast sky, offering scant illumination. All was hushed, even the steady wash of noise from the highway barely audible, as if it belonged to another dimension or reality, slowly slipping away. Carol stopped and put her hand on a red maple and looked up at the gray evening sky. A few branches above, a robin sat eyeing her, its throat silently pulsing. A large drop of water landed heavily in the middle of her forehead and she closed her eyes and let the water run down her face. Another drop landed in her hair. All around her feet lay an unruly growth of sodden shrubs, rhododendron, mountain laurel, a kind of wild rose with small thorns, much poison ivy. Wild grass swayed in the wind that wended its way into the bush. Scattered about in the gloomy light was a plant that looked like Solomon's-seal, with clusters of white, star-like flowers. Ahead the woods lay dense and dark, a bit forbiddingly. Behind her was the tavern and Phil. It would be about now that Phil would bestir himself in agitation and anxiety. They would naturally be out back, looking for her. Maybe they'd broken the door open. Carol expected to hear her name called at any moment. He might even charge into the thicket like a large distressed animal, a bear or water buffalo, to find her. With a start she moved quickly and more deeply into the trees, suddenly terrified lest she be caught. This was it. She was getting away, perhaps for good. Where she was going or what was going to happen, she hadn't the slightest idea, only that she wanted badly to see her children at least one more time. Here was the opposite of Hansel and Gretel, she thought. It is the parent going off into the dark, haunted forest instead of the children in a kind of wild, hopeless exhilaration and at the same time stricken with as deep a sadness as she felt one could possibly endure. The spirits of her children were with her in the woods, ghostly, flitting behind the trees, just beyond the power of her vision. She moved forward rapidly, a bit fearful. She pictured Phil crashing through the brush. He might be accompanied by a contingent of orderlies from the sanatorium in their ghastly white coats, lurid like grave robbers in the murky, drizzling forest. She was afraid that if she did get caught they might not let her out ever again, everyone now convinced that she really had lost her mind. Perhaps they were right. In this evening's wood with the wind a messenger from a baleful region and the skies steadily weeping, it seemed entirely possible that she'd entered another realm. It may be that she'd never get out of the forest, that she'd entered a tract that covered thousands of acres and she'd be lost forever. Impossible of course, this was Long Island, 1955. But such was her state of mind that even passing thoughts had the power of a superseding reality. This forest might well be some vast Canadian wilderness, taking the first few steps, moving deeper into an odyssey that would consume the rest of her days. Phil and his posse would venture in for a short distance and give up, frustrated, ruefully understanding that this was as far as they might safely venture, that they might never see her again. Eventually, after traveling hundreds, perhaps thousands, of miles, subsisting on wild berries and sleeping under leaves and pine needles, she would find herself at the edge of the forest, and stretching before her in a brilliant, awesome whiteness would be the true far northern country of ice and broken blue water with whales spouting their mists that turned to crystal in the freezing air refracting spectral colors, above which white birds with enormous wings glided, and on the great ice floes seals and walruses by the thousands herded together in a great nation of families, squabbling, sleeping in the precious hyperborean sun, tending their young, making love. She would eventually be taken in by an Inuit family and travel from one place of sustenance to another, following the seals or caribou, bundled stiffly in skins, packed tightly together with the rest of her adopted family on a bone sled lashed together with sinew and pulled by exuberant huskies as large as small bears. She would sleep in igloos in communal warmth and eventually the clan would decide that she become one of the wives of its leader, a great hunter and skilled carver of ivory. She would have three fat Inuit babies, her breasts heavy with milk that tasted of seal. Her husband would die in a hunting accident and she would wrap his body in walrus skins, place it in a kayak and lie down next to him as one of their children pushed them out into the blue, open water where she would quietly expire, their spirits eternally to ride the backs of killer whales, their names passed along through generations.

It was growing darker and the forest stretched before her with no end in sight, but her eyes were acclimated to the surroundings and she felt more relaxed. Carol could not hear the highway. Rush hour was past and the wind superseded or merged with its sound. No voices called her name. The drizzling rain continued to fall, but blocked by the trees little of it reached the ground. Only the random pattering of drops falling from laden branches and leaves. She heard an occasional rustling but saw no animals, and no birds save for the one robin that had eyed her and whose throat pulsed as if in sympathetic reverberation with her heart. She stayed for a moment, as still as a wild animal, and then began moving forward slowly, hoping that she was navigating a relatively straight path. Carol's shoes and socks were soaked as were her slacks to just below the knees. She was not cold. Her sweater, while damp at the surface, still kept her warm and dry. Wouldn't it be nice if there really were ice floes and Inuits at the forest's end, and rather than walking thousands of miles it were only a matter of a few? Instead, there would be sidewalks, driveways, framed houses and ultra-green fertilized lawns soaking up the rain. Inside the houses would be yellowish lights and families at dinner tables eating their potatoes, meat and frozen vegetables, mom and dad already three sheets to the wind. Carol felt wild and free—marvelously exhilarated—to think of herself drenched to the knees in the dusky woods and only a stone's throw, probably, from the very heart of middle-class America. Maybe that's what she would become, the mad stone thrower, living in the forest and launching missiles at the plywood houses. Eddie liked to throw stones, sometimes for hours, into the bay or ocean. He was getting good at skipping them. She thought of him and Mark with their fire on the beach, like aboriginal children, infinitely wise, profoundly wild, while in the background gulls crashed into the ocean for fish.

Her heart raced with the wildness of it. Extraordinary how she hadn't thought of it before, the wildness. This was one of the missing things. A big missing thing. Inside her this force, constricted by all sorts of notions and conventions, crippled by the choices she'd made, drowning in booze, struggling with beak and talons to rip its way free and fiercely work its atrophied wings. Her fascination with flying. It wasn't merely escape. She viewed her life with an irony so sour she could almost taste it. The young supercilious sophisticate with her money, glamour and eternal dissatisfaction. Once again, Paul's admonitory words, "*...be a real personality Carol and go after the things that really count...live deeply and leave the froth to those who want nothing else and having nothing else to offer...*" He had pleaded that she settle down and raise a family, become a solid, serious wife and mother, filling her life with love and responsibility. It was more than the Catholicism speaking. The Egglestons were a comparatively sound unit. It was where Paul had come from as much as his newfound faith. One always returned. Now she was in the wilderness. Figuratively and literally. Was she possibly an aberration? One of the few born with no preordained place in the world, who either ripped apart convention and expectation and forged a singular courageous identity or, having failed this, end up in frustrated, dissolute ruin? Not with a bang but a whimper? After all this Carol still had no idea. She was fairly certain though—and she would flay herself unto eternity for this—that she was not meant to be a parent, as much as she loved her children. It was certainly well past the moment for striking out for a "singular courageous identity." Running away from Phil— and Dr. Campbell's loonitarium—in these dark, silent woods, had revealed, however, almost as an epiphany, something about herself that she had only been aware of in the dimmest way. The wind passed through the trees with its occult whispering and she recalled the waitress' mysterious words, *we will all be changed...* Were those words directed at her? They could have been directed at anyone. Who really knew where one's life had come from or where it was going? Good enough to say that we came from God. But in the woods there was this feeling that she'd come from wildness too, she and her race, her forbears, all from God, yes, the driving force of all that was, but more immediately and tangibly from inarticulate grunting flesh and bone mucking about in the wet dirt and forest as she was now, fearful of lurking dangers, huddled together for protection and warmth, the odds stacked steeply against them, dogged, almost uncanny in their ability to survive. Was it just dumb substance with an indomitable instinct to continue or was it something grander than that? And she, the product of this ancient, copulating mud bath with its bloody struggles, its fears, superstitions and unimaginable tragedies, groping her way through woods as ancient as the history of her race, no more understanding or intelligent than her pre-verbal uncles and aunts, in fact, less so, less understanding, less purposeful, indecently corrupted by a tawdry culture, self-deceptions, her alcoholism. How hard they worked, these extraordinary, hirsute, muscular creatures— to arrive at this! Well, at least she was paying them and their wildness—their mad God-glory—the tribute they deserved. She thought she might worship them if they suddenly returned in some sort of time machine. Maybe it was the extraterrestrials she imagined that were the true descendants, and on earth merely the discards, the mentally defective, the dangerous, kept safely in quarantine lest they infect the rest of the universe. The earth as a kind of lazaretto.

Ah, God, the Earth. Mostly water. Dumb beauty spinning in space. Dragged ourselves out of the water to blow it up with atomic bombs. Simply an innocent act of trying to recapitulate the divine, unattainable light. Didn't they wear goggles at Alamagordo? You couldn't look at it directly. And yet it was but a feeble spark. She drank and stumbled through life because she was but a feeble spark herself and knew it. Here in the woods though was the tragic, obvious truth. Tragic because the truth was lost as well as obvious. Fashion! Money! Fame! And fear. These people in their houses would be afraid even to wander into this gentle grove at night. Why? What were they afraid of? Wilderness. Afraid of the wildness. The very thing that might save them. Why did The Savior go into the wilderness and then return to do His good work? Why didn't He just stay there and hook up His loudspeaker and tell all and sundry to join Him? Get the hell out of your houses that will go up like tinder when the big flame arrives! Come into the wilderness with Me so that Ye might truly be alive!

Now the rain came a bit harder, or the sound of it at least, as Carol was still protected by the trees. If it were warmer she might take off her clothes. Would Jesus have bid his followers to remove their clothes after having made their way into the wilderness to him? Most certainly. Remove their clothes and entwine themselves in his presence, roots growing from their feet into the soil, his crown of laurel and hyacinth rather than thorns, the clear rain dripping from his brow instead of blood, a smile and not the grimace of agony. This Jesus of Paul's was not her Jesus. This Jesus was the symbolic removal of the race from the soil, a slaying of the natural spirit and its replacement with something thwarted, mean and sterile, the dubious triumph of civilization over the wild. Paul had discovered his faith in the midst of the overwhelming, horrific suffering of the war, a different kind of wildness. Faith was his anchor. He survived. But to what end? So that he might "defeat" a fearful chaos and bloodletting with surrender and slavery? Onward Christian soldiers, marching back and forth from home to job as mumbling, genuflecting robots on the well-trod path, known and comfortable, while just beyond, the dark and threatening wilderness, spooks, devils, the wild beasts, the unknown. To market! To market! Better to surrender in slavery than face the darkness and attempt to navigate by one's own lights. Let Jesus do it for you, Paul. It was all a mad conspiracy, perhaps Lucifer himself responsible, leading humanity around by the nose, the crown of thorns pulled over its pierced, purulent eyeballs. One had to go into the darkness, as she was now, to hope for a flicker of light. The blind leading the blind, indeed. One must reject the hand that guided, for it was a fool's errand. Deeper into the woods she had to go, a forest, Carol hoped, almost without end. And yet, dismayingly—all the more so because she recognized that part of herself that yearned for "safety" and "civilization," the houses, the manicured lawns and paved driveways—she knew that this little forest would come to an end much sooner than later and that she would be back into the place where she was unquestionably lost.

Carol moved forward into the increasingly dark thicket. Surely, it was no larger than a thicket—not really a "woods," or a "forest." One was safe if "out of the woods." Yet maybe indeed this was a forest, one that she hadn't been aware of. If it was, they'd certainly be looking for her. A regular posse fanning out into the forest. Were there bloodhounds up North? More likely she'd get to the edge and, peering out, see Phil and a couple of police cars waiting. The trees and foliage grew denser, her progress a wet slog, slacks soaked to the thighs, hair dripping with water sloughed from leaves and branches. There was no telling if she still felt the drinks.

The trees cleared and Carol found herself walking into a large ditch or gully where the brush grew more densely, almost halting her completely. As best as she could determine she seemed to be in the middle of a concavity about the size of a tennis court. Carol moved forward cautiously, instinctively hunched forward, feeling exposed in what in effect was a small clearing. It was lighter here owing to the absence of trees, which circled her like a somber convocation of druids. Roughly in the middle of the depression—perhaps it was an old pond—her progress came to a virtual standstill, the thick-growing bushes chest-high, vines clutching her ankles and legs, her sweater snagged on branches and thorns. Surely, she stood out like a billboard in the middle of this woman-trap. They were watching her from behind the trees and ready, once she was immobilized, to move in, throw the net and drag her away, Phil observing of course, resolute, having exhausted all possibilities. She heard a noise and ducked into the brush, scratching her temple. Carol raised a finger to the scratch and licked it, tasting the blood. She hunched down farther, the heavy growth grudgingly admitting her, gouging and scratching, a stubborn feline adversary. Deeper she went, almost sitting on the small bit of damp earth down among the bushes so that she was fairly certain her head would not be visible to any searching gaze, and she stayed that way for several long minutes, her hearing alert for any of the telltale noises that might be made by the stalkers, for now they would be practicing their own stealth to capture the fleeing animal. Here the steady drizzle came down directly, unblocked by the trees. Carol heard a twig snap, and what sounded like footsteps, and then whispering. She could feel her heart's pounding through her sweater. More whispering came from the surrounding woods. She'd sunk as deeply into the brush as she could, almost completely immobilized by the sharp branches, unable to move her head without being scratched or pierced. She wondered about the wound on her temple, if it was bleeding. The wind increased and with it the murmuring in the trees. Occasionally she heard distinct voices and once, she thought, her name, and then laughter. They were all there, watching her, pinioned in the brush like a helpless animal, waiting for her to tire and give herself up, submit to the inevitable, be carried back to the sanatorium and locked in her room. It was an alternative. What was the point of this ridiculous struggle? How far would she get with this childish game, and where the hell was she going, anyway? Give up, she thought, give in. Back to the known, the security of having one's life in the competent, pedestrian hands of others. Of course, it was death, a death of the spirit, but there was always hope, after some dark dormancy, that what spark remained might eventually kindle something. Perhaps there would be a miracle. Her children were still young and would eagerly, greedily, respond to the nurturing she could give them. She was still young. thirty-thre. The body ached so from this awkward position. How long could one stay thus? And then an awareness of thirst that became for a moment almost desperate, so that she licked the moisture from her upper lip and turning her head slightly was able to extend her tongue like a giraffe and with its very tip reach a drop of rainwater from the underside of a branch. Then, as suddenly as she'd become aware of her thirst, Carol forgot it, the pain of her rigid, contorted body returning to consciousness with something close to agony. She was crouched in a kind of squat, with no space to rest a knee. Slowly Carol moved her right hand so that she was able to grasp one of the thicker branches with her fingertips, which afforded some bit of relief, an ever-so-slight shifting of weight. Within moments however, the pain returned and grew more intense. The bastards are all watching and know my suffering. Waiting in amusement for me to give up. She heard the whispering voices all around. They'd followed her and she was surrounded. Carol wondered if it might be possible somehow to burrow through the bushes and, unseen, escape from one of the ends of the hollow. But the growth was too thick. Trapped. They had her. The devil and the deep blue sea. She hated them, this faceless company of pursuers who knew nothing about her and cared less, tracking her for sport, *un divertissement*. They stood behind the trees and whispered, watching and waiting. Why didn't they call out? Were they afraid of spooking the mental patient? She imagined the bit of extra excitement they felt at tracking some-one who was unpredictable, under duress, perhaps dangerous. Yet now they had her at complete disadvantage, pinned down, exposed, her body aching from the contorted posture she'd been forced to assume. They'd simply wait until she could stand it no longer, rising not without drama into the spattering rain and wan light, alone like an actor illuminated on an empty stage with the audience poised in delicious anticipation. Carol pictured the scene, what she would do. Rise slowly like a ghost, stand straight and still for several minutes, drawing it out, increasing the tension. It would be her turn to force a move. How long could they bear silently to watch behind the trees as the strange creature of their search stood brazenly in heraldic mystery before them? She imagined their smug excitement of a few moments before turning to unease, perhaps even fear and awe. Then she would walk calmly straight into them, her gaze level and unmoving, Joan of Arc once again, into the dark woods as they parted before her, their dull eyes staring. Ah, they were all children, weren't they, when you got down to it. Full of self-importance in their participatory, dutiful moments, but let the situation go beyond the accustomed boundaries and they were all-too-easily struck dumb. They knew only so much, and it was enough to make her accepting of their essential pathos and innocence, even to feel sorry for them.

She stood up—not slowly as she had envisioned, but abruptly, feeling the redemptive strength of her isolation and vulnerability. After all, I am one of you, she thought, no different, just a few trees and bushes between us, a bit of understanding, not much. You have fathers and sisters and brothers like me, all of us part of the same fabric, turning our faces to the flickering lamp. From behind the trees came no movement or response, only wind and pattering rain. "Come out, come out, wherever you are," said Carol, spreading her arms and turning slowly in a circle. "Yes, the world does revolve around me. Don't be afraid, I won't hurt you. I give up. You've won." Her voice seemed small and inconsequential, swallowed up by the trees. Or had it not even reached them? Had they not heard her? She yelled. "Hey! You out there! I give up! Come get me!" Again, only rain, wind and gathering darkness, dark enough now so that it was not so easy to tell where the trees actually began. "Hey there!" She touched the scratch on her temple, which, while still raw, seemed no longer to be bleeding. Why did they wait in silence? "Okay, here I come." Carol moved forward, plowing as strongly and as rapidly as she could through the brush, which grasped and made little tears in her slacks and larger ones in her sweater. In the darkness she had a sense of herself as a large animal moving through the thickness, a stirring, intrepid force trampling the foliage, heedless of the noise it made, confident in its power. She resisted the temptation to make growling noises—it might really scare them (what a comical bunch of nonsense—and wouldn't Phil be delighted!) and, who knew, maybe they would jump out from behind the trees with their crossbows and riddle her with arrows like St. Sebastian. Not an agreeable thought. Instead, she decided on obvious surrender, mollification, the reassuringly verbal. She slowed her pace a bit as to make less of a crashing spectacle and began talking in a soothing, matter-of-fact tone. "I'm sorry for all the trouble I've caused, really I am. I don't know what came over me. Perhaps an archeological impulse. Botanical, meteorological. I don't really know, but very inconsiderate of me to drag you out here at this hour and under these conditions. Phil, please don't be too upset with me for leaving you in the restaurant. I don't suppose you ordered dessert. That cherry pie looked awfully good. Maybe we'll go back and get some. What do you say? I'm quite serious. A piece of cherry pie would do me wonderfully before going back to dear old East Hill. Then again, I'd understand if you weren't in the mood for dessert. I really managed to bollix up a perfectly good dinner. I'm sorry."

Carol stopped and looked into the trees, now right before her, silent and noncommittal. She might as well have been in the northern wilderness for the vastness and lack of human presence she felt. "Well then," she said, addressing the trees, "don't mind if I do." Carol walked up the slope and entered the dark woods. No spooks or devils or humans jumped out from behind the trees to grab her and it was dead soundless except for a sudden rush and flapping up ahead, the harsh, irritated croak of a raven once, twice, three times, receding. Then enveloping silence, the encroaching night's opacity over her like a cloak, the wind quietly encouraging, the rain a steady smattering of applause acknowledging the renewal of her audacious flight.

Albuquerque, June, 2022

Richard Ward's work has appeared in the Apple Valley Review, Bosque, the Concho River Review, the Gettysburg Review, and the Southern Humanities Review. His two previous books, *Maninthemiddle, A year's Travels and Adventures at or Near the Equator,* and *Over and Under,* were published by RolyPoly Press. His short story, *A Persistence of Memory,* was nominated for a Pushcart Prize, and "Best of the Net" for 2020. He divides his time between New Mexico and Ecuador. He can be reached at: r.ward47@gmail.com.

Cover photos by the author